THE CHRONICLES OF BANAIN

NORTHLINGS

BOOK TWO

PAUL SVENDSEN

About The Author

Paul lives in the west of Ireland with his wife Stephanie and an assortment of mostly rescued animals.

He enjoys trying to be self-sufficient, looking after the animals, writing novels, poetry, and writing and playing music.

Printed in the United Kingdom

First Printing, 2016

ISBN-13:978-1540488626
ISBN-10:1540488624

Email paul.svendsen@wtfaw.org
Book cover design by BespokeBookCovers.com

My thanks to Dad, Matt and Ross for providing
feedback on the drafts.

A special thanks to Audrey, who sadly passed away.
She always encouraged me to keep writing.

Prologue

Izotz shielded his eyes and scanned the stark white horizon. A sixth sense that had aided him well in the past, was telling him that they were not alone in this desolate icy wilderness. He was a large man, with an almost square head set atop massive shoulders, his size augmented by the hide of a black plains bull he wore to keep out the biting arctic cold. A large white wolf glided easily across the deep snowdrifts a few hundred paces in front, its huge paws hardly seeming to break through the crusted frozen surface that was causing him so many problems. Seeing nothing, he forced his tired limbs back into action, every push sinking him deeper into the frozen snow, every pull sapping a little more of his considerable strength.

The cold was so intense it felt like the exposed parts of his face had shrunk, squeezing his head in an icy vice like grip. A shaggy beard had sprouted over the past few weeks. It was abhorrent to his soldier's sense of order and discipline and had become a solid mass of ice frozen to his face. He had to be careful not to get his tongue stuck to it, should he attempt to lick his severely chapped lips. However, he was a warrior and he would die before showing any weakness. So he kept following the white wolf, his face literally frozen with determination. In the stark pure white arctic landscape, his dark profile stood out like a beacon to any who may be watching.

He replayed the events in his mind that had led him to this harsh frozen land, in the company of the oversized arctic wolf. A few weeks earlier, he had been in charge of an army of nearly a thousand men. Then, events that had shaken the foundation of his world, had forced him to re-evaluate everything he thought he knew about the intelligence of other species. After losing a major battle to a well-disciplined animal army, hundreds of massive plains bulls attacked his night camp, followed by wave after wave of ferocious wolves. The sight and sounds of his men screaming as they died under the merciless bovine's hooves and the wolves' jaws, would stay with him forever.

He had only escaped with his life by leaping on the back of one of the charging bulls and riding a roller coaster from hell out of the camp and into the plains beyond. He had hung on with every ounce of his considerable strength, until his unwilling mount had thrown him as it leaped across the bank of a river, the following beasts nearly crushing him as they trampled past. As he fell, he had gashed his left arm on the wickedly sharp horn of the bull and dislocated his shoulder on landing. Knocked unconscious, luck had been with him and he had rolled under the lee of the riverbank, safe from further killer hooves.

Many hours later as he had regained consciousness, his eyes had met with those of the large white wolf he was now following. It's almost orange orbs had locked onto his, its tongue lolling out of the side of its mouth. He had watched mesmerised, as the massive wolf padded up to him, and had mentally prepared for the grip of the monsters teeth on his throat.

Instead, the wolf, called Arkta, had spoken directly into his mind. Izotz knew that mind-to-mind communication with animals was possible; his former master, Lord Erador, had spoken to this very wolf, but he had never experienced it first-hand. To his amazement, the voice of the wolf in his head made him an offer, to come with him to the frozen north and raise an army.

It had been a simple choice, a matter of survival in fact. If he had stayed where he was, Banain's animal army would have hunted him down. So he had agreed to the wolf's terms, figuring it would give him time to mend his wounds and build his strength. He did not believe the wolf's claim that it could raise a new army in the frozen north, and although the creature had spared his life, he did not trust it. However, his options had been limited. So he had reset his shoulder, dressed his wound as best he could, and followed the beast.

The journey had started well enough, with the pair covering around twenty miles a day through the mountainous region of old Spain. With the wolf's keen sense of smell, they had skirted settlements, avoiding people. Every evening Arkta would leave Izotz trundling north and hunt for small game, which he brought back to Izotz at the night camp. They could not risk fires, so they ate the animals caught by Arkta raw. When the temperature dropped under zero each night as the pair moved further north, they had reluctantly taken to curling up together behind any available shelter to share bodily heat, rising with the sun to continue their journey.

On the fifteenth day of traveling, there had been imperceptible changes in the landscape, signifying that they had reached the edge of the icecap that covered almost half the planet. After a few hours of further walking, the shrubs and grass started to disappear under a growing layer of snow covered ice. The level slowly climbed up the tree trunks, until by the time they stopped for the night, there were only a few tips from the tallest trees poking through, bereft of any growth, just dry brittle remnants of their former selves. For Arkta, sleeping in those conditions was no problem, as wolves can sleep soundly at temperatures under twenty degrees, but even with the warmth from the wolf's body, Izotz had been desperately cold and had slept little.

After five days of freezing conditions and little food, Izotz was struggling. However, he was not going to show any weakness to the wolf, which was naturally adapted to deal with these conditions and could go without food for many weeks.

Although still uncomfortable with mind-to-mind communication, Izotz had recovered from the initial shock of talking this way. He concentrated his tired mind on sending a message to the wolf, which had stopped and was intently studying the area around them.

"Are we still being followed wolf?" he sent falteringly.

"I am sure our presence is noted human. Without you, I would be like a flake of snow blending with the drifts. But you can be seen by any hunter with eyes or a nose, it can only be a matter of time before we are discovered," Arkta snarled.

Why had he not just left him to his fate? When he had found him, bleeding and unconscious, his primal desire had been to rip the heart from his body and feast on it. However, the power of humans fascinated him and he knew that to raise an army, he would not only need the wolves and polar bears of the frozen north, but the thousands of small hardy humans that lived there as well.

His father Bodolf, had spoken of the small men that they used to hunt, or were hunted by. It was before they had travelled south, pursuing the human baby. Before the madness had taken over his father and turned him from hunter, to servant of that human, Banain. It was before Lord Banain had ravaged his mind and turned the love for his father, to an all-consuming hate. As a wolf, he might never convince the arctic humans to fight with him, but having this one with him could make a difference, although now his slow speed was frustrating and potentially life threatening.

When the attack came, it was so swift and deadly that neither Arkta nor Izotz had time to react. The snow around them exploded upwards and twenty massive polar bears erupted from their places of concealment, blocking out the weak arctic sun with a bear powered blizzard. In deadly accord, they used the temporary white out to surround the startled duo.

Izotz tried to raise his sword, but a large paw swiped it away, as if it were a toy. Arkta fared no better, thrown easily to the floor beside the human when he tried to attack one of the beasts. The bears were massive, each weighing over one thousand kilograms, and measuring nearly twelve foot from head to tail. As one, they dropped to all fours and with a military precision that impressed even the ex-general, formed two lines either side of the subdued pair. The bear closest to Izotz, moved to within inches of him, its hot fetid breath, visible as it mixed with the frozen arctic air, assailed his nostrils. Then the bear turned and lowered itself in front of him and a single word, "CLIMB," ripped into his mind. Izotz looked towards Arkta, who was now facing off three of the beasts, his hackles raised.

"What do we do wolf?" He sent.

"We do as they say, or we are both dead. If they had wanted to kill us, they would have by now." Arkta replied.

Seeing no other course of action, Izotz reluctantly approached the recumbent bear and climbed gingerly onto his massive shoulders. As soon as he was in place, the bear rose quickly to his feet and moved into line with the others. Arkta heard the command "MOVE" in his mind, as the polar bears on either side moved off at a measured gait. He knew that to hesitate would not be a good idea, so he matched pace with them, as they headed further north into the frozen wasteland.

For four days they kept up the same routine, marching from the first light of morning, to well after the last light from the sun had expired. On the rare occasions when the wind died down and the snow stopped falling from the sky, they could see the mountain peaks pushing through the top of the ice cap. However, these glimpses of a land that used to bask in the warm Mediterranean sun were very rare. They were able to continue traveling after the sun had dipped below the horizon, due to an auroral curtain of red light that danced on the horizon in front of them. It was like a beacon to the bears and they marched towards it with relentless pace, and a seemingly endless supply of energy.

Arkta had struggled to keep up with the pace for the first few days, although he was an Arctic wolf, he had not been born in that frozen land. Estranged son of Bodolf, he had been pupped from Honi, on the plains to the east of old Seville. Captured by Lord Erador and submitted to terrible mind torture, Arkta had learned to survive, using the only emotion that he could count on...hate. He hated weakness in any form and he focused his hate on his father, Bodolf, who had dragged his pack thousands of miles to the warm south, to kill a child, but had instead befriended him. In Arkta's mind, Banain was the cause of his father's weakness. Without his interference, things would have been as they should be.

As the days of marching in the frozen landscape passed, Arkta became stronger. He was now able to keep pace with the bears with ease; Izotz on the other hand was not faring so well. Even though carried on the back of one of the huge bears, there had been no hunting and he had finished his meagre supplies days ago. Arkta and the bears could go for weeks without eating if necessary, and the wolf enjoyed watching the human growing visibly weaker from lack of food. It was fitting really, Arkta thought, as Izotz had been Lord Erador's General and had watched his suffering, as the lord had ripped every ounce of compassion from his tortured mind.

Communication with the bears had been limited to basic commands to do with the journey, but the days of travel had given Arkta time to learn a little about his captors. The bear patrol leader, Nashik, said they were part of a large army, which was poised to invade the South.

Nashik knew he was at the right place; his internal compass and sense of smell had guided him around his allotted patrol route as unerringly as it there had been a line drawn in the ice, guiding him and the others along their route. The familiar peak of a nearly buried mountain came into view through the snow, and Nashik headed for a small trail that led up towards it. Around two hundred meters up the trail, he entered a large cave. Inside, the floor descended steeply and he led the group down a long winding tunnel. Izotz could see nothing in the almost total dark, but Nashik navigated unerringly, using his sense of smell and familiarity with their surroundings. After several hours of decent, Izotz detected a faint glow ahead, which quickly built to and eye jarring glare. A few moments later as they emerged from the tunnel, a spectacular view presented itself.

Around five thousand years ago, when nature had unleashed all her fury upon the earth, massive storms changed the face of the planet. Devoid of the warm waters of the Gulf Stream, the arctic ice increased quickly, moving south to devour over half of the planet. Preceding the ice were savage storms that lashed seas into frenzied monsters, pounding shorelines wherever they made contact and flooding large areas, which then froze in the constant minus fifty-degree temperatures. The ice that now covered over half the planet was over half a kilometre deep in places, enough to cover the tallest mountains.

In this location however, the geography had created an oasis in the otherwise ice-covered landscape. The long sloping fronts of a series of mountain ranges, which marched inland like huge granite waves, had deflected the wind snow and ice up and over their peaks. In this place, the elevated land between two of the mountain waves was too high for the invading sea to reach. The wind, screaming at over two hundred miles an hour over the peaks of the first set of mountains, piled snow deep on both sides of its sheltered back. The same wind created a vortex that swirled like a large permanent twister, sucking up any snow and ice deposited in its centre, and sending it hundreds of miles further inland.

The result of this unique set of circumstances was an almost perfect circular area of exposed land between two mountain ranges, with walls of ice scoured smooth by the vortex that created them. They rose vertically, leaving a nearly perfectly round opening to the heavens which was over a kilometre in diameter and some eight hundred meters in height. The floor mirrored the opening in both shape and size. Now, five thousand years later, it boasted the only trees, vegetation and fresh unfrozen water, within hundreds of miles.

Izotz was convinced that his eyes were playing tricks on him. After so many days traveling through the stark whiteness of the icecap, the colour of this oasis punished and overloaded his senses. As he grew accustomed to registering colours again, he took in the strange circular landscape arrayed before him.

Directly below the entrance to the tunnel, was a mini forest of fir trees, which clung to the side of the mountain almost down to its base. The trees were sustained by constant watering from the melting icecap above. The whole area was like a huge natural glasshouse, the sun's rays trapped and reflected around the ice walls, nourishing the flora and fauna.

Nashik led the group down a well-trodden trail through the firs, until they came to the base of the oasis. As the trees gave way to open ground, Izotz and Arkta saw a mass of bears standing completely silent, watching their approach. Their attention focused on a bear that was much larger than the others... He was also as black as the darkest night.

"I am Isbjorn, leader of the Northlings. What are you doing in our lands with this weak human, wolf?"

"I am Arkta, this human may be weak, but he also holds the key to raising an army that could conquer the planet, if that is your wish."

"I have many wishes wolf, but I doubt you or this human could fulfil any of them. Still, his type is new to me and wolves have been too elusive to act as hosts, until now." As Isbjorn spoke, two of the bears escorting him turned and pinned Arkta to the floor, leaving only his head and neck visible, try as he might, he could not break free from their combined weight. He watched helpless as the same thing happened to Izotz.

"There is no need for this, we came to help. You do not need to harm us!" Arkta sent in desperation to the large black bear that stood rock still watching the proceedings.

"You will become host to our elders and they will learn everything you know," Isbjorn said. Then dropping to all fours, he ambled up to Arkta, opened his huge jaws, and bit into his neck.

Chapter One (Five Years Later)

Banain was tiring. Sitting bareback on a large black horse on the bank of the Guadalquivir river far to the south of old Seville, he was holding a quivering wall of river water nearly thirty foot high in place, with the power of his mind. The wall was stopping the latest wave of sixteen ships full of raiders, from sailing further towards the city. The men in the ships were shouting and pointing in fear at the suspended watery barrier. Even the most war-hardened veterans stared open mouthed, fearing they would drown at any second.

With wide shoulders and a deep chest, Banain was an impressive figure. He had a thick mop of blond shoulder length hair, held in place with a black died flax headband and a classically chiselled face that belied its few years of existence. He was wearing the powdered light blue flax leggings and tunic, decorated with the motif of the Freedom Army, a green flying bird. However, it was Banain's eyes that were his most striking and powerful feature. At first glance, they were cobalt blue, but on closer inspection, they shifted in hue to almost black. Once looked into, they could change the viewer's life forever. The effort he was exerting to keep the water in place was channelling through those orbs, making them almost pulsate with power.

"Krask, are they ready?" He sent to his father, a very large golden eagle circling above.

Krask was not of course his biological father, but had raised Banain from three months old, after his mate, Krys, had died rescuing the child from a pack of Arctic wolves. Ironically, Bodolf, the leader of those wolves, was now a very close friend and ally.

In real years, Banain was not yet ten, but contact with the Immortals, an ancient race of jellyfish who lived in a different time phase, had accelerated his metabolic rate. The year he had spent training with them had aged his body ten years, but in return had allowed him to develop special powers, like the one he was using now to keep the huge water barrier in place.

"They are in position," Krask replied. From his lofty vantage point, the eagle could see the sixteen ships stopped in front of the wall of water and the lone figure of Banain, mounted on his horse, Star. Hidden from the ships by the high banks on both sides, was an army, a very strange army indeed!

Banain released the water from its suspended state, allowing gravity to rule once more. Freed from the constraint of Banain's will, it plummeted downward to find equilibrium. The surge caused by its return, sent two further waves just under half the original size charging like mini tsunamis up and down the river. The wave heading down was not large enough to sink the ships and it was not Banain's intention to do so. However, it was large enough to turn them about, all except one.

Concentrating on a section of the still disturbed waters, Banain focused his mind again on its surface, imagining it smooth and strong. The water molecules bonded together and on either side of the ships the river flattened and hardened into a glassy solid surface.

"NOW!" Banain sent, as he concentrated on keeping the water hardened and in place.

Chapter Two

Carlos Torre, captain of one of the raider ships could not believe what had happened. He had been a captain in King Iguru's navy for over six years. Before that, he had worked his way through the ranks, right from the day they pressed him from his island home of El Hierro after killing his parents for not paying their taxes. He was only seven years old at the time and from what he could remember of that harsh existence, his parents could hardly live on what they could scrape from the land, let alone pay tax.

For Carlos, life in the Kings Navy was better than anything he had experienced before. Slaving with his parents to grow enough food to survive from the barren island soil had been miserable and although life in the Kings Navy had been harsh, he had excelled.

He had always been a hard worker and possessed a keen intelligence, more than that he loved the sea and anything to do with boats. He was a natural sailor, always in tune with the wind, tides, and waves. He was able to anticipate Neptune's moods, which resulted in his ship surviving where many others may perish.

He also possessed a deep understanding of what drove the men under his command, as he had experienced and witnessed floggings and other methods of naval punishment and noted the resentment it built against authority. He preferred a reward based system on his ship with his men sharing in the bounties of all raids. This was unknown throughout the rest of the navy who payed all crew a flat rate. It was also illegal, as spoils of war were supposed to go to the captain who would pay part of his spoils to the King. He had received a summons to the fleet commander where he had tried to argue the effectiveness of his methods, pointing out that they took the king's bounty from the spoils before they were distributed, but it fell on death ears. They would bring him in front of the King on return to port.

He was immensely proud of his thirty meter, two-masted, eighteen oar Tyreme and the fifty-four rowers and forty marines that made up his crew. When the massive wall of water welled up in front of the fleet, his ship had been in the middle. With no time for commands from the admiral's galley to be made or obeyed, many ships ploughed into the crafts in front of them before they managed to stop. It took some time for the fleet to gain some type of order again. Luckily, none of the well-built galleys received seriously damaged. As soon as Carlos saw the water wall disintegrate and start to fall, his seamanship instincts had taken over.

He knew, from the direction and the size of the wave rushing towards the fleet, that it would turn them if it hit at their current angle, so he had ordered his stroke drummer to beat emergency speed on the port oars only. Most of the rowers could not see outside the ship, so had not witnessed the water wall, or the new events unfolding on the banks of the river and bent to the task with efficient enthusiasm. By this time, the wave had hit the front of the fleet and was turning ship after ship, sweeping them back down river. With no speed to steer by, the ships had been at the mercy of the wave and were smashing into each other as its force pushed them down the river like driftwood. As soon as he had the bows pointed directly at the wall of water, Carlos had ordered full ahead on all oars. Again, the discipline of his crew paid off and the ship surged forward, building vital speed. However, between them and the wave were two ships, locked together in a deadly embrace and they were turning towards them, driven by the wall of water. For Carlos, those few seconds had been the worst of his life. He had watched in morbid fascination, as the bows of his galley armed with a deadly ramming spike raced towards the vulnerable side of his own admiral's ship. Inch by agonising inch, his bow had swung along the line of the admiral's galley. He had seen the helmsman standing at the stern, staring open-mouthed and the admiral himself screaming for him to turn away.

With just inches to spare, the tip of the spike had missed the back of the vessel and Carlos had immediately given the order to raise the port oars, but he had been just a fraction of a second too late. At the back of each galley was a very tall stern carving, on the admiral's ship it was the trident of Neptune. The oarsmen on a galley sit three abreast to each oar, facing the stern of the craft and can, if given enough time; raise the oars to a vertical position. To do this, they have to move the oar outwards and then push the inboard end down. On hearing the order from Carlos, all the rowers on the port side had stopped rowing and started to move the oars out before lifting, but they ran out of time. The front oar hit the trident on the stern of the admiral's ship, momentum pushing its outboard end backwards and its inboard end forward. The unfortunate rowers trapped between it and the hard, unyielding bulkhead in front of them.

With nearly forty tons of weight fuelling its momentum, the ship had ploughed on and the oar had bent, until with a crack like thunder the tortured wood snapped. Men, who had just a few seconds before been its master, were its mangled and broken victims.

The second, third and fourth sets of oarsmen fared little better, as their bodies were thrown like rag dolls against the unyielding side of the ship; but from the fifth now vertical oar onwards the admirals ship slipped past and pushed by the immense wave, was left behind. Holding on to the mast for support, Carlos had prayed that they had enough speed, as his ship climbed up the face of the wave. He had sighed in relief as it crested the top and plunged down the other side. Then he had run from the command station, headed for the dead and dying men just in front of him. From his position, he had witnessed the whole scene, but had been powerless to do anything about it. It had sickened him to see men that he had known for years killed in such a way. He had grabbed the inboard end of the nearest shattered oar and pulled it away from the bodies, his second in command, Fermin, also running up to help.

He had left Fermin to deal with the dead and wounded and had run back down the fighting deck to the stern of the ship. Looking back, he had realised that the wave had turned the whole fleet with many of the ships still locked together in deadly embrace. The wave had taken them a distance downstream already and his ship was still moving with its retained momentum upstream, the gap increasing every second.

He had realised that he must turn and help them and had ordered his remaining left side oarsmen to back stroke, the right to row at full speed and for the helm to be put over hard to port, hoping it would be enough to turn the craft in the confines of the narrowing river. Then he saw the water on either side of the fleet seem to freeze as if all life had left it, leaving only a narrow ally of escape back towards the sea for the fleet.

Now on either side of the river, from behind high banks, came an army unlike any he had seen before. There were humans on horses and on foot, as you would find in armies all over the planet. However, there were also horses with what looked like apes riding them and groups of wolves and horned sheep! There were so many animals Carlos could not identify them all.

This army was marching in perfect synchronization, each group of animals, humans, or mix of both, wheeling and turning together. Carlos watched in disbelief, as with synchronized efficiency, the army entered the water of the river on both sides, moving towards the trapped fleet, but they did not sink!

Held up by the solid river, they moved across its surface, towards the stricken crafts. Carlos watched as the army stopped just out of arrow range of the fleet and waited. Then, from the direction of the sea, the sky darkened, as what appeared to be a dark storm cloud moved towards the fleet. However, this was like no cloud Carlos had seen before. It pulsed and gyrated, moving against the prevailing wind, carrying with it a terrible raucous noise. As it came closer, he realised it was a cloud of birds, of seagulls!

They flew above the fleet and then descended like a black and white mass through the rigging and around the deeply shocked raiders. Men tried to swipe them with swords and fire bows at them, but the birds were too fast. There were so many that they formed an almost impenetrable visual barrier, which allowed soldiers from the massed Freedom Army on either side to run in with lighted firebrands, which they threw on board the ships.

There was no chance of shooting the soldiers when the crews did get a chance to see them through the swirling wings and bodies of the gulls, as the quick-witted and agile birds plucked the arrows in flight from the sky.

Realising that he was about to lose his whole squadron, Admiral Ungula ordered the retreat along the only open stretch of water available to him. Fighting fires and trying to disengage from other entangled ships caused by the mini tsunami, the fleet managed one by one to disengage from the chaos and head with all speed to the safety of the open ocean.

Carlos had now managed to turn his craft, but it was reacting sluggishly.

"We are holed at the waterline on the port bow captain, it must have happened when we made contact with the admiral's ship. We are taking on water, fast!" Fermin reported as he ran back to the command station.

Carlos realised he would not be able to pass through the frozen water, or the army massed upon it, and his ship would not stay afloat for long without repair. Looking to his right, he could see the figure of the blond man sat upon a massive black horse. This man seemed to be responsible for the routing of his fleet, if he could not escape, he would at least go down fighting. His Tyreme was now at its current maximum speed of around seven knots, several below its potential because of the loss of four of its oars. Making his decision, Carlos ordered the rudder full to starboard and the bows swung towards the bank and the blond magical warrior.

Chapter Three

Banain watched with satisfaction as the enemy fleet turned tail and retreated in great haste and disorder. The sailors would greatly exaggerate the tales on their return to port, hopefully putting off another attempt to invade for some time.

"Bring the army from the water please Krask, I do not wish to hold them for ever!" Banain quipped.

"All this power is turning you into a tyrant Banain; they will be off shortly, but what of the last ship?"

Banain looked up the river to the galley that had managed to avoid the wave and navigate through the stricken fleet without major damage. He was no sailor, but he recognised that it was not blind luck behind these actions, but rather by good seamanship, leadership, and obedience from the crew, something he had not seen in the enemy... Until now.

"It looks like they intend to come ashore near me. Withdraw the army on this side to a safe distance from their arrows and let's see what they do."

"OK, but why don't you let me finish here? Teague and Bodolf are due to return from the east soon, I am sure Teague would appreciate it if you were there to welcome her back," Krask asked, noting Banain's frown the moment the words were out of his mind.

"Teague decided to go on that dangerous mission against my advice and I am amazed that Bodolf supported her! She will not want to see me, besides I need to talk to the captain of this ship and see if we face a new threat from the South," Banain replied. Krask could sense so many conflicting emotions in that reply. He did not answer, as he knew it would be futile, the rift between Banain and Teague was as wide, deep, and painful to watch as ever. Anyone could see that they were in love with each other, but both were obstinate and in denial of their feelings. Krask had tried to talk to his son on several occasions about the relationship, but Banain would not compromise on the matter. The eagle had to remind himself often, that Banain was still a child in an adult body. Although the training given by the Immortals had aged his body in years and his mind in intelligence, in terms of understanding women, he was woefully lacking in experience. Raised on a mountain ledge by Krask, Teague was the first female human he had ever seen. It was clear to Krask that the boy's feelings for Teague were something he could not control and Banain was not used to that sensation.

As the last of the Freedom Army left the surface of the water, Banain released it from his mental grip. As always, the effect of wielding his powers left him drained and light-headed.

"Are you ok Banain?" the big horse inquired, twisting his huge head to one side so he could view his rider. From the first time he shared the breath of friendship with this human and allowed him to leap nimbly on his back, they were attuned to each other. Since the great battle against his former master Lord Erador, life had been completely different for all horses, in fact all animals within the dominion of the Freedom Army. No longer could a human enslave an animal against his will. If a man, woman or ape wanted to ride into battle and not walk; they had to convince a suitable mount to accept them.

"I am OK thank you Star; I should keep up my exercise regimen better," Banain answered, sliding down from the black and reaching up to scratch him behind his ear after he landed.

"Hey Banan, how come you scratch that big ugly horse and not best friend Lepe?" The inquiry came from the squat dark black shape of a mountain sheep with one horn, which moved close to Banain and jabbed his single horn, non-too gently into Banain's stomach. Lepe was the first animal Banain had ever communicated with and had always pronounced his name Banan.

"I don't know why you are not banished to the wild lands forever Lepe, what use is a one horned sheep to anyone?" Star snickered, pleased with his comment.

"Pah, you very clever Star, but I have more use in my one horn then in all your overweight body; you need to go on diet fat horse," Lepe countered.

"Behave you two," I have enough trouble fighting our enemy. One day you will go too far and really upset each other. Now, can we concentrate on the galley please?"

"No problems Banan, me and fat horse never fall out, he respect me too much and no problem with floating people, Freedom Army already in place, see."

"OK, make sure no one attacks them unless I say so, or am harmed," Banain replied quickly, cutting off any further reply from Star to the sheep's last comment.

With that, he jumped back on Star and rode down towards the river and the fast approaching galley.

Chapter Four

Krask need not have worried about the expedition team arriving home without a welcome. They were still five days travel to the east in the heart of the great forest, and were just about to enter their final village before heading for home. The main purpose of the trip had been to convince the villages to become part of the protectorate, a task made much easier with the recent reduction in raider attacks, due mainly to the efforts of the Freedom Army. However, Teague had another reason for visiting the villages in this area. She was looking for the birth parents of Banain.

Since Bodolf had recounted the stories surrounding Banain's rescue over ten years ago, she was convinced that his parents must still be alive.

The reason why the expedition was already running behind schedule was partly due to the time it took to comply with the different customs of the villages, but also to do with Teague's questioning every member of the village regarding any past knowledge of the abduction of a child by an eagle.

Teague rode near the front of the expedition force. She was a tall slim twenty three year old female and had dark brown, almost black hair and dark brown oval eyes. She was dressed in a hooded robe tied in the middle with a flax cord. Currently her hood was hiding most of her face, protecting it from the biting spring breeze. On her back, a quiver held twelve arrows, their ends held above her left shoulder within easy reach of her right hand. She was mounted on Daze, a snow-white mare who had shared life air with Teague as soon as Banain freed her from Lord Erador's cavalry. Daze was carrying the scabbard holding Teague's bow, a further supply of arrows and Teague's medicines and stores in hemp panniers secured with a flax cinch. Loping around ten meters in front was Bodolf, a mighty arctic wolf who stood over a meter tall to the shoulder and weighed over one hundred and twenty kilograms. He was also white but with a small black mark over his left eye, both of which were a rich gold colour and flecked with swirling patterns. Beside him was Honi, Bodolf' s mate, also an arctic white wolf, smaller in stature but not spirit than her mate was. Riding alongside Teague was Garfled, an ex-soldier prisoner, rescued from the dungeons of Lord Erador's castle by Banain and now a mounted warrior in The Freedom Army. He was wearing the standard Freedom Army uniform of blue trousers and tunic with a green flying bird motif on his chest. The motif was also on his wooden shield strapped to the side of Torrent, a one thousand kilo, pitch-black plains bull; one of only a handful who had left the wild lands and accepted the rules and governance of the protectorate. It was said that whilst Garfled was hunting in the wild lands, he had rescued the bull from a pack of Jelks, a larger and more ferocious type of jackal, but no one so far had managed to get the full story from him; In fact, nobody managed to get much in the way of conversation at all from him. He had returned from the wild lands barely alive, carried unconscious by also injured mighty creature. Since then they had formed an unbreakable bond and were a formidable fighting force, intimidating to behold. Like Teague, Garfled used no bit to guide Torrent, sitting comfortably just behind the withers, with his legs between the large panniers that carried most of the expeditions supplies. Loping behind, came a further twenty arctic, grey and mixed race wolves from the ranks of The Freedom Army.

The expedition had heard a horn blowing several minutes earlier announcing their arrival. They moved at a slow walk, so as not to trigger a premature defensive attack from the villagers they could now see massing by the gates. Calling the group to a stop, Teague unfurled her white parley flag and moved past Bodolf to a point half way between her group and the village gates, holding it high above her head. This was always the worst time, and she could not help imagining herself and Daze falling to the ground, their lifeblood spilling on floor as a hail of arrows struck them. Shaking those negative thoughts from her mind, she called out to the villagers, who were staring with disbelief and fear at the collection of animals and humans standing outside the gate to their village.

"My name is Teague; I am here to speak to your elders about joining the Protectorate. My companions are part of The Freedom Army. They have been protecting these regions for the last year. We wish you no harm, will you let us enter?" Teague shouted, using the language of old Spain, which was the common human language in these parts before the great freeze. It was a language she had learnt as a child, having been raised in a similar village to the south.

"We have heard of you and your beasts, come no closer," the speaker, a young woman armed with a wooden bow shouted back, as she stepped onto a platform to the side of the gate, her bow pointed squarely at Teague's chest. The village was of similar design to many found in the great forest. It was laid out in a wide circle of cleared land with a large circular communal building in the middle and smaller dwellings set around its circumference at regular intervals. A perimeter wall made of earth and sharpened stakes pointing outwards had wooden platforms spaced evenly all the way around, these were currently occupied by more archers.

"We mean you no harm, we are here to help. Please lower your weapon and hear what we have to say before turning us away," Teague answered, sliding down from Daze and walking towards the gates holding both hands above her head, one holding the white flag and the other with the palm facing the woman in a gesture of peace and to show she was not armed.

"Teague... Do not do this again!" Bodolf almost shouted in her mind, she could clearly feel the anger and fear for her life in the message.

"I will be ok Bodolf, you know we have to gain there trust and this is the best way to achieve that."

"I know that you are risking your life again, we should wait and negotiate further with them," Bodolf implored.

"Please Bodolf, trust me, I know this woman will not harm me."

Bodolf did not reply, but mentally ordered his reserve force high above to move as close as possible, without drawing the attention of the villagers. Krask had insisted that two eagles accompany the group for navigation and communication purposes. Only Yrik was still with them, as Skara his mate had left to inform Krask of the delay. Receiving Bodolf's message he transformed into dive mode, partially folding his wings against his sides, and moving his legs and talons behind him. Traveling at nearly two hundred miles an hour, Yrik ate up the distance between himself and Teague.

The woman with the bow was Mariana Salvia. Both her father and Mother, members of the village council had been killed a few days earlier in a, so called, hunting accident. The other elders, led by a man called Judd Lark, were in a meeting about reports of recent attacks from massive beasts, and had told Mariana that they should not be disturbed. Seeing the ferocious creatures in front of the gates she was torn with indecision and fear, then the woman with the white flag moved towards her. What happened next was not what Mariana had intended, but fear played its debilitating part in her actions. Meaning to lower her bow, she let go of the bowstring whilst still fully drawn. Before she could correct her mistake, the arrow sprang forward with deadly intent and started its swift journey towards Teague.

Chapter Five

"Prepare to beach, defend, and repair," Carlos roared above the noise of the stroke drum, which was beating out the rate for the rowers to follow. He had practiced this manoeuvre many times with his men and they knew the routine well. The galley was moving as fast as her remaining fourteen oars would take her. All crew not manning the oars had moved aft to raise the bows as far as possible out of the water to slow the flooding, so that the craft would travel some way up the beach.

"Brace now!" Carlos shouted again, as the shore was reached. The next moment there was a grating sound from the keel of the ship, which quickly built to a screaming crescendo, as she drove almost ten meters up the beach. Before she stopped moving, he led the marines charging up the fighting deck and along the catwalk, picking up weapons and shields from the racks as they went. With the precision born of much practice, they split, jumping from both port and starboard front quarters of the galley and quickly formed a semi-circular defence perimeter. Some of the rowers grabbed bows and spears, forming up behind the wall of shields, the others grabbed materials and tools to repair the damage done to the bows. Carlos had deployed his forces in less than one minute from the time the bows of his craft had made contact with the riverbank. Standing slightly in front of his marines and the already labouring repair team, he surveyed the scene unfolding in front of him.

Just out of bow range, the mixed human and animal army was standing quietly in neat formation. He calculated that the opposition he faced must be at least two thousand strong, a definite challenge for his eighty, he thought wryly. Looking up he also noted that the army of gulls was circling in a strange silent way. The whole scenario made him feel most uncomfortable and he could tell from reactions of his men that they were scared.

"Do not worry men, we can hold against a few animals. We will soon have our craft repaired and be away from these strange lands," he encouraged, hoping his words carried more conviction then he felt.

The blond man on his black horse moved in front of his army and walked towards the stranded vessel, Carlos signalled for Fermin to come beside him.

"If he gets within bow range kill him, there is no flag of truce," Carlos instructed.

"Yes Captain," Fermin replied and moved back to the ten archers positioned behind the marines. Banain did not slow down when he came within range of the bows, or even note their existence. It was as if he was out for an afternoon stroll. The first thing Carlos noticed was Banain's smile; the second were his eyes, which were a very, very, deep blue.

"Loose," Fermin shouted and the ten archers let fly at the target, now only twenty meters in front of them. To the credit of the archers and the training, Carlos had put them through, every arrow was fired true and on target; they just did not reach Banain. To the men watching the approach of this young smiling man, it seemed as if the arrows bounced of the air in front of him, then fell, all energy spent to the floor.

"My name is Banain and behind me is a division of The Freedom Army. Please instruct your men not to attack; if I had wanted to harm you, I think you realise that I could have done so by now. The reason I am talking to you is because I am intrigued. All the raiders we have encountered so far have shown little in the way of intelligence, attacking wildly and then retreating in haste. But you are different Carlos," Banain said in perfect Spanish, stopping in front of the startled captain and jumping nimbly down from Star.

Carlos could not believe what he was seeing. How could this blond youth walk his horse through a hail of arrows and stand unarmed in front of nearly sixty armed men, seemingly without a care?

"Fermin, hold for a moment." Carlos instructed his subordinate. He found it hard to tear his gaze away from the blond youngster in front of him to confirm his orders. Although still in shock from the barrage of events that challenged his perception of the world and the rules of war, he realised that attacking again would be futile and possibly suicidal.

"How do you know my name?" Carlos inquired, his voice betraying the emotions welling within.

"Your name is carried on the thoughts of every person in your crew, they respect you, which is another reason I wished to talk with you," Banain replied.

"You can read our thoughts?" Carlos was dismayed, if his every move could be anticipated, how could he possibly gain the upper hand in this situation?

"I can, if the subject does not know how to shield them, but it is against my teaching to do so uninvited. In this instance, your men shout your name for anyone with the ability to hear. Now, about what I plan for you. The Freedom Army does not have a Navy, so I would like you to build one for me; you will have all the resources you need and I offer you and all your men citizenship in the protectorate."

Carlos was speechless, was this boy mad, he did not even know anything about him and yet here he was offering him everything he wanted in life. It was bound to be a trick.

"And if I refuse?" he asked.

"Then you are free to go, of course you will need to fix your ship first and we can help with that if you want. Take some time to talk to your crew and then we can talk again. In the meantime, we will bring you and your men food." With that, Banain leapt on the back of the great black horse, which without any visible input from its rider, turned, and galloped back through the ranks of The Freedom Army, who turned and melted into the landscape.

One minute there was an army standing in front of Carlos and his crew, the next the shores of the river were empty!

"Fermin, send lookouts to those high points, then find out how long it will take to make repairs. I need some time to think!" Carlos said to his second in command and walked back through his silent men, jumping on to the ship and moving to his small cabin. He needed time to try to make sense of what had just happened.

Chapter Six

Yrik was already diving at almost two hundred miles an hour, his powerful vision locked on the scene playing out below. He saw the woman who was directly below him release the arrow and instantly went nearly vertical, calculating the exact spot the arrow would be when he intercepted it, about three meters away from Teague. Bodolf had also seen the danger, his super-fast wolf reactions sending adrenalin coursing through every muscle, allowing him to leap towards Teague, his intention, to knock her out of the path of the arrow. However, even his lightning fast reactions were too slow this time. Yrik's outstretched talons closed around the shaft of the arrow and his wings started to spread to give him lifesaving lift, but he ran out of sky. Bodolf watched in horror as the great eagle first glanced of Teague and then hit the ground with a sickening thump.

"Garfled, go and stop those villagers from doing any more damage," Bodolf snarled as he ran up to the pair lying deathly still on the floor.

Garfled immediately instructed the rest of the expedition force to take up position between Teague, Bodolf, and the prostate body of Yrik. Then he moved towards the group of villagers at the gate.

"Now listen, if any of you make another aggressive move, we will retaliate, and you do not want that to happen. You have already attacked an envoy of the protectorate under a white flag; do not make this situation any worse than it is." The words were not shouted, as he was now close enough for them to hear every word and the deadly menace behind each.

Yrik had struck Teague on the side of the jaw, a blow similar in power to a boxers punch. With no memory of Yrik hitting her, she re-gained consciousness with a blinding headache. Bringing herself gingerly to a sitting position, she realised Bodolf was standing over the limp body of Yrik.

"What has happened Bodolf," She sent to the wolf, moving as quickly as she could manage through waves of pain and nausea to the pair.

"I am sorry Teague, I fear it is too late for your healing skills," he said, turning to look at Teague, deep sadness in his eyes.

"Move aside please Bodolf," Teague said, dropping to her knees beside the fallen eagle and holding her hands in front of her, fingertips together, with the thumbs pointing towards her and the little fingers pointing away. Teague was a gifted healer; her skills enhanced by the Immortals, but not to their maximum potential. She was not prepared to make the sacrifices of youth required through spending time in their company, as Banain had. Although she was not able to resurrect life if it still resided in the host, she had the ability to persuade it to stay a little longer and heal many ailments. In Yrik's badly broken body, she found the spark of life still glowed, although very faintly.

"Honi, please stand next to me, I need help to preserve his spirit whilst I mend his body. Bodolf, please go and make sure we are not attacked again" Teague sent. She needed to get Bodolf away, as his karma was almost palpably negative and would not help Yrik at this moment. Reluctantly, Bodolf left, as Honi padded up to take his place.

"Honi, look at Yrik and focus your mind on him. Imagine he is alive and flying above us all, see his power and majesty as he soars free in the sky. Do not let any negative thoughts enter your head." Whilst communicating her instructions to Honi, Teague channelled her energy into Krys, her vision changing from the scene in front of her, to what she referred to as the grey rainbow of life. The Immortals had called it Griseous Animus, but for her it was a rainbow and at its end the pot of pure white gold, was life itself. In Yrik's case, the rainbow was almost black, but there was still a pinpoint of bright white light in the centre of his chest. Teague called this the spark of life, for when it left the body, it took life with it.

Looking to where Honi was standing, Teague could see the wolf's bright white rainbow swirling around her. A few tendrils of almost pure white light were snaking out towards Yrik, momentarily connecting with his one remaining spark and in those moments fortifying its brilliance.

"That is good Honi, block everything from your mind other than Yrik, and let no negative thoughts enter. Let your positive energy feed and nourish him. As she whispered her thoughts into Honi's mind, the tendrils of white light increased in number and intensified, connecting more and more often with Yrik's spark, until with a flash, there was constant connection. Honi was now a life support system for Yrik.

Happy that Yrik was safe for the moment, Teague concentrated on repairing the terrible damage done to the eagle's body. First, she concentrated on his heart, sending tendrils of white healing power down to its stilled muscles. As the tendrils entered, small sparks of energy leapt from them like tiny electric shocks, healing small ruptures and tears. Then in unison, the tendrils let out a single pulse of power, constricting the heart and then releasing it. This happened several times, until the heart woke to pump life-giving blood around his body again, its black shards turning to white, streaking out to add light to Yrik's rainbow. For the next hour, Teague worked on Yrik, until she was satisfied she had done all she could and that he was out of danger. Then she released Honi from her life support role and gently withdrew from his resting body.

Chapter Seven

Banain stood before a crystalline clear cylindrical column of water. It rose from an ornate pool in the centre of a circular domed cellar, deep below the castle of the protectorate in old Seville. The inhabitants of the city had built this room, the massive chamber underneath and the tunnel connecting it to the Guadalquivir River. Its construction allowed better communication between the Immortals and Banain. Although he could speak to the Immortals by being close to any water mass that they occupied, this place would allow Banain to continue his training. Now one of their numbers, Turr, was floating in front of Banain.

Due to the magnifying effects of the water, Turr looked to be around one metre high and the same wide, but in reality, his species grew to no more than half an inch in any direction. His outer body was a translucent blue, revealing his inner organs, which were a darker blue, except for a centre organ, which was a vibrant red. He had ninety-seven blue tentacles, which undulated mesmerizingly in front of Banain. Light came from the column of water and from the walls, which the Immortals had imbued with a subtle multi-hued radiance that gently bathed the cave in a shifting spectrum of colour.

The Immortals were the most ancient species on the planet; they could not die of natural causes. When they reached maturity, they had the ability to regenerate, retaining the memories and experiences of their previous existence. They also had the ability to communicate with other species and to unlock the dormant potential within them.

It was a long and complicated story, but Banain was not able to complete his training, only managing one year before he had to stop and fight a powerful army and establish a base for the newly emerging Protectorate. Now five years later, the Immortals hoped they could complete the training they believed Banain still required.

"Are the facilities to your satisfaction?" Banain enquired. For a few moments, nothing happened and then Banain felt the familiar gentle drop in temperature, the change in wall colour to a bright white and the chanting almost singing voices in his head.

"We are very pleased Banain, not all the number required have gathered yet, but we have enough to work with you for several hours. When all are here we can continue your training," Turr sang in Banain's head.

"I am not happy about that Turr; I do not want to become old before my time. I have already sacrificed my childhood for the cause, besides; I have mastered my powers, what more do I need to learn?" Banain said.

One of the side effects of being in contact with the Immortals was that his body's metabolic rate was increased. Every hour he spent training with them aged him at a greatly increased speed, but it also allowed him to master new skills incredibly quickly. The time he had already spent training had aged him physically and mentally by ten years, giving him the appearance of a sixteen year old. However, in terms of emotion and life experience, he was still only ten.

"Banain, you have learnt a great deal, but there is much more we can teach you. You yield your powers with great zeal, but you need to learn the nuances behind your gifts to realise fully your potential. We know you are worried about aging Banain, but remember, when the time comes we can regenerate you and unlike the ex-lord Erador, we can return all your memories when you are reborn," Turr sang gently.

"How is baby Erador?" Banain enquired, remembering his battles with the ex-lord, before the Immortals had regenerated him without his old memories.

"Although he is not as gifted as you Banain, he has come on considerably under our tutelage. Grindor has him on a gruelling routine, an experience I am sure you will remember."

"Yes I do Turr, are you sure there are no signs of his old ways? I would hate to have to face him after being trained by the Immortals."

"We have been careful to monitor him at every stage and we are sure that he was turned by the negative side of his power. There is no guarantee that any creature is immune from the dark side of their own psyche, including you Banain, which is why you must continue your training."

"Ok Turr, but I cannot spend every day at it; there is so much to do and I am worried that I have not heard back from Bodolf and the expedition party."

"I am sure you will soon Banain. We were pleased to see how you handled the latest invasion attempt from the south. This captain from the stranded ship seems to be an interesting species," Turr said, steering the conversation away from the expedition. Turr was very aware of Banain's feelings for Teague and could sense the maelstrom of emotions in the youngster. However, it was the one area the Immortals would not become involved with, for they knew very well the power of love and the effect it could have on any creature.

"Yes, I have not seen any raider exhibit such skills and have the ability to command respect rather than fear in his men. Which reminds me, he has asked to talk to me and is waiting, so with your permission, I will go and see what decision he has come to."

"Of course Banain, but we must agree a training schedule for you soon."

"Agreed Turr," Banain said, as he turned and walked from the chamber, the chanting in his head dissipating and the light returning to is soft multihued quality. He knew as he walked away, that he would find any reason not to spend more time than necessary with the Immortals, although he did not fully understand why.

Chapter Eight

"We apologise for our actions again, the whole of our village has been in a state of fear since reports of the beasts have reached us. When your party approached our gates, I'm afraid that fear took over."

The speaker stood in front of Bodolf and Garfled, just outside the makeshift gates to the village, flanked by two large men. He was visibly shaking under the feral stare of the large white wolf, echoed in the eyes of the massive wolves ranged behind him, and amplified in those of Torrent and his rider.

"Your apologies are accepted, you need not fear us, although some of our members do indeed look fearsome. Garfled, I think we are safe now, is that not so, uh... who am I addressing please?" Teague said aloud, pushing through the bristling line of wolves to stand in front of a plump man who was constantly wiping his profusely sweating head and neck with a soiled rag. Teague guessed he was in his late middle years, but lack of exercise and a rich diet had taken its toll on his body and it was hard to be sure.

"My name is Judd Lark; I am the leader of this village. I told that stupid woman to report any events to me, not fire on anyone who approaches our gates. Her family are known for their stupidity, however do not worry, she will be punished, or killed if you desire it. You are welcome to enter and enjoy the hospitality of the village as recompense for our actions towards you."

Lark said, looking between the woman standing in front of him and the man riding on the massive bull, not sure to which he should be ingratiating. In his experience, woman were good for little more than pleasure and menial work, but there was something about the one stood in front of him now that was telling him to be careful... very careful. Although Judd Lark was fat and unfit, he had an intelligent ruthless streak, bordering on cruelty that he had used to work his way to being village elder. A journey assisted by bullying, threats, bribery, blackmail, and any other methods that precluded hard work or direct danger to himself. He had a team of henchmen that enjoyed privileges for doing his dirty work for him. Like most bullies, he was a coward, and was only standing in front of this frightening group now, because he could see no other way of dealing with this situation, without losing face and his perceived fearsome reputation.

"Teague, do not enter the village, I have bad feelings about this man and this place; please do not ignore me this time," Bodolf said in Teague's mind, his wolf instincts raising the hackles on his back. Something was wrong here, he could not place what it was, but he knew it was a threat to all of them.

Teague was already thinking along the same lines as Bodolf and recognised in this fat leader, a dangerous and narrow-minded intelligence. As the man was clearly uncomfortable talking to a woman, she made her decision, turned and walked back through the wolves, communicating with Garfled as she went.

"Give the woman to us now, so that we may punish her as we see fit; we will take you up on your offer of hospitality later," Garfled said to Judd moving closer on Torrent as he spoke, every word reinforced by the warrior's icy stare.

"Send the woman forward and let this be a lesson to you all, not to attack gracious guests at our gates," Judd shouted back to the mass of villagers standing behind the gates, glad that he had not been forced to take instructions from a woman. From within their midst Mariana was pushed forwards and through the gates. One of the men standing beside Judd walked back and pulled her roughly forward, throwing her to the ground between Judd and Garfled. Boiling with rage inside, but mindful of Teague's instructions, he slid down from Torrent and went quickly to her; not losing eye contact with Judd for a second, he helped her to her feet.

"I hope we meet again, soon," Garfled said in a deadly quiet voice to Judd, then sent an instruction to Torrent, who moved up alongside the pair and lowered his huge body to the floor. In one swift movement, Garfled hoisted Mariana effortlessly onto torrents back and leapt up in front of her.

"Hold tight girl," he instructed, as Torrent lurched forward and upwards in one mighty movement, nearly bowling Judd and his men over as he turned and charged back through the wolves, which also turned to follow his massive form. Teague had already left and was some way down the forest path before he caught up with her and fell into step alongside. Yrik was secured in a sling over

Daze's withers where she could keep an eye on her patient. Bodolf passed both of them, scouting ahead for a suitable spot to camp for the night.

From the moment Torrent started to move, Mariana had thrown her arms around Garfled. Although terrified of the man, for she knew how bad men were, she was more terrified of this huge beast. She had never in her life experienced anything like it and expected to die at any second. Despite her fear, she could feel the solid muscle of this man, and something else. The only other man she had been in physical contact with was Judd, an experience she tried to forget. Although this man did not say a word to her as they moved, she sensed something from him that told her he would not harm her and she relaxed her grip, just a little.

Teague looked up to where Mariana was clinging to the back of Garfled, realising that his silent approach was helping to calm the girl, not that he knew any other way.

"Please do not bore our guest with your inane chatter Garfled," she sent to him, attempting a joke to lighten the mood. His stony stare in reply cut short any further attempts at humour and the party rode on for another hour, until Bodolf appeared in front and directed them to a clearing just off the path.

"We will eat travel rations tonight Teague, I have a bad feeling about this area and want everyone close," Bodolf said, looking around the temporary campsite for defence points and deciding where he could best place his lookouts. Normally the Daze, Torrent and the wolves would wonder off to feed, returning in the early hours of the morning; but Bodolf wanted everyone close by tonight.

Some hours later, with no fire burning as per Bodolf's instructions, the campsite was bathed in moonlight filtering through the trees and ringed with vigilant wolves. Teague sat opposite Garfled and Mariana, resting against the warm body of Daze, who lay behind her providing a warm equine shield against the night's cold. Similarly, Garfled leant against Torrent, the girl a few feet away. She had not moved far from his side since she had been taken from the village.

"What is your name?" Teague asked. However, the frightened girl did not reply.

"Can she speak Garfled?" Teague asked, via mind-talk.

"I will try… Speak girl," he instructed in his normal curt style, the instruction spoken aloud and with authority.

The words from Garfled instantly changed her demeanour and she looked first at him and then Teague.

"My name is Mariana," she said.

For the next hour, Teague questioned the girl, gently peeling back the layers of fear to find out her story. What she learned sickened and alarmed her greatly. According to Mariana, Judd Lark had changed what was once a pleasant village, into a place of fear and unrest. She was sure he had her parents killed, because they tried to stand against his abuse of power. He had abused her and many of the young women in the village. However, what alarmed her most urgently, was Marianas description of a small strange looking man, riding a great white bear, who had met with Judd in the woods outside the village just the day before. She had been hunting and had witnessed the clandestine meeting and overheard Judd saying that he would make sure that they met with no opposition from the villagers, in exchange for his safety.

"Thank you Mariana, you have been most helpful. What do you wish to do now? You can stay with us or go your own way, but before you go, I just have one further question for you. Do you recall any stories of a baby being abducted from the village around ten years ago by and eagle?" Teague asked, as she always did when she spoke to someone new.

"I cannot go back to the village, Judd will kill me and I cannot survive on my own. I will stay with this one. I owe him a life debt and am his to command," Mariana said, looking at Garfled.

"Uh... Garfled was just doing his job Mariana, you do not owe any of us; but you are welcome to stay if you wish," Teague said, looking at Garfled. A slight narrowing of the eyes was his only reaction to the girl's statement.

"Of course everybody knows the story of Judoc and Nimean. They were driven from the village because of their wild stories. They claimed their baby had been taken by an eagle. It is believed Judoc was attacked and wounded by raiders and the baby was taken for the slave market. Although, why they were not taken as well is not known. They live not far from here," Mariana said. As she talked, she noticed Garfled reaching with difficulty towards a pack on the floor to retrieve some more travel rations. Moving swiftly, she grabbed the pack and passed it to him.

"I think you have found an admirer Garfled, please take care of her whilst I talk to Bodolf about the news she gave us," Teague sent, standing up, she noticed the marked drop in temperature away from Daze's warm body.

"Look after her....how?" Garfled sent back, frowning at Teague, who just smiled at him and walked off into the gloom. He did not know how to deal with this woman; in fact, he was not sure how to deal with most people, especially women. He had left the city of old Seville and gone into the wild lands, as he had not been able to adapt to the new ways under Banain initially. He was a warrior and was not interested in the nuances of polite conversation and endless discussion. The whole system of change since Lord Erador had been defeated, had left him without purpose, which was why he had decided to find a new life, away from well-meaning people and complicated females. It was during his travels on the wild plains, a vast area where any animal or human could live without rule or restriction that he had come across Torrent.

The bull was in a life and death battle with a pack of Jelks and his warriors mind had already calculated that the bull was seriously outmatched. He was standing with his back protected by a small bluff, his mighty head swinging from side to side and his horns sweeping a deadly no go area in front of him. However, Garfled could see he was weakening from blood loss and every now and then, a Jelk would find its way through his defences and make another wound. Then the bull must have sensed him hiding and looked directly at him, in that moment, his life changed forever. Of course he had been aware that Banain and most of the others in the city could mind-speak with the animals, but it was not something he had wanted anything to do with. Life had been complicated enough with humans, never mind adding animals to the list of beings he had to inanely communicate with. Until then, he had resisted using Banain's gift, but as the bull had looked at him, a message invaded had his brain, unbidden and un-ignorable.

"Behind you..." The thought had been like hot gravel in his mind, tearing through years of denial with savage force. Without thinking, he had spun around just in time to see three more Jelks stalking him, their jaws open and salivating at the prospect of human flesh. Years of training took over and instead of retreating, he had leapt at them, charging the short distance to the startled beasts and drawing his sword as he went. In a short, but brutal display of skill, he had dispatched two of the Jelks: their teeth and flesh no match for his honed steel blade. The third Jelk managed to avoid his sword and ran to join the rest of the pack attacking the bull.

Being a warrior, he lived by the code that you protect those who protect you. Therefore, he had chased the Jelk and helped the bull in his desperate fight for survival. The Jelks had decided that he was an easier target then the bull and had turned from it to attack him. He had managed to kill many of them, but their sheer numbers had driven him to the ground and their teeth had found him. Then, just as he thought his time was up, a pair of horns, powered by a mighty head had ploughed in, throwing damaged yelping bodies left and right and another message had invaded his brain: "Hold onto my horns!" and as they came within range, he had. The bull had lifted his mighty head, dragging him up through the bodies of the Jelks and tossed the badly wounded warrior onto his back. There had been just four Jelks left and one of those had been badly wounded. Realising their meal was lost to them they had skulked away. The last thing he had remembered was thinking how much he needed Teague's healing skills. Then he had fallen unconscious on the bulls back. When he had woken, he was in a hospital bed in Old Seville, later to learn that the bull had carried him back there, before collapsing himself outside the gates.

Since then, he and Torrent (a name Garfled had chosen, although the bull did not see the point of such things) had become almost inseparable, both being against any type of superfluous conversations and both being mighty warriors, they soon became an unbeatable combination, if not a bit unapproachable. They were certainly not a pair with whom you could have a long conversation!

The last thing he or Torrent needed was a woman. Strangely, Torrent, who normally sent waves of negative emotions to Garfled when anyone got to close to him, seemed not to mind Mariana. In fact during the ride and since being in camp, he had sensed something different about his large bovine friend. He could not decide what it was and was considering this when Torrent said in his mind, "Woman cold."

It was true; she was shivering in the early evening chill. Sighing inwardly and feeling under pressure from two women and now Torrent, he said to the girl, "Sit here," indicating a spot next to him, just behind Torrents front legs. Mariana looked at Garfled and then the huge bull, who was staring at her, but she did not move, torn between the orders of the man who had saved her and the fear of this huge animal.

"Sit here, Torrent will not harm you." It was a very long sentence for Garfled and he did not like repeating himself. Mariana stood up and walked slowly to the spot indicated. She sat down slowly, leaning back until she encountered Torrents warm chest. She could not believe how warm it was and she could feel his massive heart beating beneath. Despite her fear, she felt safe somehow. Then his massive head moved to within inches of hers and she could feel his warm breath on her face. She reached out a shaking hand and instinctively scratched him behind one of his massive ears. Torrents eyes half closed in pleasure and he lowered his head to the floor, so she could reach both. Garfled could not believe what he was seeing and got up to relieve himself, leaving the two lovebirds together. By the time he returned, the girl was fast asleep. He found a blanket in his pack and placed it over her, not that she really needed it, as she was almost enclosed in Torrents warm embrace. Then he went to find Bodolf and Teague.

"Where is the girl?" Bodolf asked.

"With Torrent," Garfled replied.

Bodolf and Teague exchanged glances, but said no more.

"This is worrying news the girl has brought, I know the beasts she talks of, and they are indeed mighty. Just one of them could beat five wolves, such is there strength and ferocity; and for them to be ridden by a human is unheard of. We must try to find out more about their strength, so we can assess the level of danger. I have sent a Wolfe back to old Seville, but it will take him several days to get there. First thing in the morning, you must go back with Garfled and the girl," Bodolf said to Teague.

"I am going nowhere, until I have followed up this report about Banain's parents. We are so close Bodolf, we must try and find them first, they can only be a short distance away," Teague said, imploringly. Bodolf was about to argue, but stopped himself. He knew that tone very well.

"Ok, but if we do not find them by mid-day, we go back to Old Seville, agreed?" Bodolf sent, with as much conviction as he could muster.

"Agreed," Teague said.

"Understood," Garfled said and then returned to find a warm spot to lie against Torrent, close to the sleeping form of Mariana. A strange day, he thought to himself as he lay back and listened to the reassuring gurgling sounds coming from inside his friend, a strange day indeed.

Chapter Nine

Just outside Mariana's village, Judd Lark moved as quietly through the forest as a man could with a fully laden mule, until he came to a clearing. Sitting in the middle, was a massive man dressed in white skins and next to him a white wolf.

"You are late Lark, we have no patience for those who do not please us," the man said.

"I am sorry, but we had unexpected visitors from the Freedom Army, in fact they had a couple of wolves with them, very similar to your friend there. Do not worry though, I sent them away. I have made sure there are no sentries posted as you asked and that most of the able-bodied men have been drugged or incapacitated. Now give me my payment and I will be on my way," Judd said, squirming under the feral stare of the wolf, which had not broken eye contact with him since he had lumbered into the clearing.

"What was the Freedom Army doing at the village and where are they now?" The man asked.

"They wanted us to join the protectorate and were looking for the birth parents of their jumped up leader, Banain. As I said, I sent them away, now give me my payment or I will go back to the village and make sure you are not able to raid it for easy pickings. There are men woman and children there, who will make you much money on the slave market, all unprotected, thanks to me."

For the first time since coming into the clearing, the man and wolf broke eye contact with Judd to look at each other. For several moments they said nothing, but it felt to Judd like they were communicating with each other in some way.

"Look, I want to get away from here and you have a village to raid; so for the last time, give me the rest of the gold you promised and we can all get what we want," Judd said, not happy at all about the way things were developing. When the large man had shown up at the village a few days before and offered a reward in return for uncontested access to the village, Judd had been going to call the guards and have him thrown in the single village cell. However, when the big man produced a gold nugget almost as large as his fist, with the promise of another to come, his civic duties were forgotten and a deal agreed quickly.

"Do you know where the birth parents of this Banain live?" the man asked again. As he spoke, the wolf raised itself from its sitting position and moved closer to Judd, spooking his pack animal, who reared up, its eyes rolling.

"Yes yes, keep your cursed dog under control," Judd said, turning to pull savagely on the mule's reigns, in a futile attempt to calm it down. By the time he turned back, the wolf had leapt the distance between them, catching him squarely in the chest, the momentum and weight of the beast sending Judd crashing to the ground. With the beast pinning him to the ground, the spooked mule charged from the clearing, leaving a trail of belongings behind him.

Before Judd had time to move, the wolf's massive jaws were around his neck, its fetid breath hot on his face.

"You really shouldn't insult Arkta, he is such a sensitive soul," the large man, who was now standing over him said."

"You kill me and you will not get the information you need about Banain's parents," Judd gasped, struggling to get the words past the constricting jaws of the wolf.

"Oh, I think we will find out everything you know, wont we Arkta." In response, the wolf bit down and Judd's world went black.

Chapter Ten

Banain was sitting on a couch in one of the smaller rooms of the castle built by the slaves of Lord Erador and his for-fathers. Not that any of the rooms were small by most people standards, this one could accommodate at least twenty people comfortably. It was furnished with wood carved furniture, made by citizens of Old Seville, in return for accommodation and the shelter of the protectorate. Sitting alongside him, was the imposing figure of Wayland, dressed like Banain, in the powder blue trousers and tunic of the Freedom Army. Captured with Banain by slavers, and had helped him to overthrow Lord Erador's troops and capture the town and castle of Old Seville. Although promoted by Banain to leader of the free species council, a job that would sap the energy of most beings, Wayland had also set up a forge and provided blacksmith services to the denizens of Old Seville. A trade he learnt loved and excelled at, almost from birth. The highly physical work involved in his craft, meant that his already large frame, was further enhanced with coiled muscle, which threatened to rip free from his tunic at any time.

"Captain Torre, this is Wayland, who apart from running the free species council, is the best blacksmith you will find anywhere. Should you agree to stay with us, you will be working closely with the captain to build a freedom navy. Have you come to a decision yet?" Banain asked the pirate captain.

"Yes, but I and my men are still not sure of the rules of this place and the relationship with animals," the captain said, sitting stiffly opposite Banain in an upright chair, his hands gripping each other on his lap.

"I know it is difficult, but let me try and explain how our system works. Within the Protectorate, we have established protected and wild zones. The protected zones are very small compared to the wild and are managed by mixed species committees. They are policed by creatures indigenous to the region. For instance, in the plains to the east of Seville, there are a high number of horses and their natural foe, Jelks and Wolves. The horses have the choice to live in the protected zone, but in return must do something for the protectorate, such as be cavalry mounts or help with labour tasks. In the protected zone, no species may prey on each other. It is the job of the Freedom Army to inform all species about the protected areas and enforce the rules. It is also their job to deal with raiders and other dangers to the Protectorate."

"I am sorry to interrupt, but what benefit is there for the species living in the wild that do not want to interact with other creatures by being part of the Protectorate, are they forced to comply?" Captain Torre asked.

He and his men had been used to living in a dictatorship, where any breach of rules was dealt with harshly. The use of the word enforce by this strange boy, was the first concept that was familiar to him.

"Perhaps I can help, it took me some time to come to terms with the ways of The Protectorate," Wayland interceded.

"Many creatures choose not to have anything to do with, or are ignorant of the protectorate and that is fine. Even though every wild creature is protected against invaders and commercialised exploitation, many species like wolves and horses choose to serve, simply because they want to, or because they understand that by working together, we are all protected," Wayland continued. Over the next few hours, with Wayland's help, Banain continued explaining about the workings of The Protectorate. He also explained how he could communicate with other species and trigger the same ability in them; about how the Immortals were one of the first species to exist on this planet, and how stored in their collective memories, they retain the history and development of most of the species on the planet.

He did not explain the Immortals belief, that during the millions of years that they had been recording events, there has never been a more destructive influence on the planet, then that of man. He did not explain this, as although he understood the teachings, he was not sure how the captain, being a human, would react to claims that it was his species alone, that was responsible for the ruination of the planet. Additionally, he was not sure that he believed that humans were solely responsible, having been in contact with other species that in his opinion had the potential to be just as destructive.

"I think you have enough to think about for now Captain. As I stated before, you and your men are welcome to stay or go. If you stay, I would like you to build a navy for the protectorate and train crews. Go and talk with your men and let me know what you decide,"

Banain said, but was not surprised when the Captain replied:

"As I said, we have come to a decision already. My men have made it clear they do not want to go back home, although many are leaving behind family. If we go back, we will be chained to the oars of slave ships or killed. I imagine much of the rest of the fleet will not go back and will become independent pirates. So you see we have little choice," Captain Torre said, looking at Banain and trying to work out if he should be happy or worried by the events of the last few days.

For the next few hours and over dinner, Banain and Wayland listened to Captain Torres ideas for a Freedom Navy. The man was a mine of information and knew his subject very well. Wayland was also able to add some unique and novel ideas, regarding the building of the ships. Banain had to leave the Captain with Wayland, when a messenger arrived to inform him that one of the two eagle scouts had returned from the expedition and that Krask said he should come and listen to the report.

Standing on the balcony outside his quarters, Banain listened intently to Skara, then said: "So when you left all was well with the expedition Skara," Turning to Krask he said": So why are you concerned Krask?" Banain was not sure why he had been disturbed to hear this report; it seemed that everything to do with Teague caused trouble these days.

"The problem is, that on her flight here, Skara lost contact with Yrik's miles before she expected to. As she was already well over half way, she decided to continue on and let us know of the delay with the expedition; she thought you may be worried!" Krask answered, frustrated by Banain's lack of concern.

"I am sure they are very capable of taking care of themselves, perhaps Yrik's had to fly in the opposite direction from Skara on the instruction of Bodolf or Teague. There could be any number of explanations," Banain said. Whenever he had to do anything involving Teague, he felt an uncontrollable frustration, which boiled deep inside him. It angered him that he felt this way and it affected his decision making.

"I will fly back with Skara Banain; I should be able to contact Yrik's at a longer range," Krask said, barely concealing his annoyance at Banain's lack of concern.

"Ok," was all Banain said, as he turned and walked from the balcony to his quarters. He knew Krask was not happy with him, but he was at a loss about what to do. He was concerned, but he did not want to show it for reasons that even he did not understand. With all his power and knowledge, he could not understand why Teague had this effect on him.

Chapter Eleven

As the first rays of the morning sun filtered through the canopy of trees, the expedition was ready to move. Taking the lead, Garfled set Torrent through the forest paths that widened with his passing. Mariana sat behind him, providing directions to the possible home of Banain's birth parents.

"It is not far now, we should come to a large clearing soon, the house of Judoc and Nimean is on the far side," Marian said.

Receiving this news, Bodolf ran forward to check for danger. All his senses were telling him that things were not right, and then his main sense, smell, confirmed his suspicions.

The stink of smoke assailed his nostrils; taking cover just on the edge of the large clearing Marian described, he identified the source of the smell and a lot more besides. A small log cabin was burning fiercely, and a short distance from it, a group of small humans, dressed in strange furs and carrying long spears and shields, were forcing two humans into a caged trailer, pulled by a massive polar bear. Bodolf counted ten humans and relayed the information back to Garfled and Teague, instructing them to wait until he joined them.

"We have the element of surprise Bodolf; we cannot let Banain's birth parents be taken now!" Teague whispered urgently in the wolf's mind,

"I know this Teague, but what if more of them wait concealed; we have not scouted the area. But I agree, I think we have to do this, or we may never see them again," Bodolf replied, not happy about the situation at all, but realising if he did not act now, Judoc and Nimean would be taken.

The rescue plan was a simple one. Bodolf and the wolves would burst from cover and charge the humans, frightening them from the bear and trailer. Then, Garfled would ride in with Marian on the back of Torrent and rescue Judoc and Nimean. They would need Marian, as the pair knew her. Teague would stay where she was with the wounded Yrik.

Against a raiding party, it would have been a good plan. However, these were soldiers and as Bodolf and his wolves charged across the open space, they did not run as expected. With cool efficiency, they organised into two lines, facing the charging wolves and crouched behind their white shields, pointing the wickedly sharp points of their whalebone spears towards the oncoming wolves. Realising the danger from those spears, Bodolf ordered the wolves to split and attack from behind. However, the small warriors anticipated the move and their small formation changed to keep facing the wolves. Although not able to scare off the soldiers as intended, Bodolf at least had them pinned down and gave the instruction for Garfled to carry on with the rescue.

Bursting from the edge of the woods, Torrent charged towards the polar bear and its trailer, which was a little way from wolves, now in a deadly dart and retreat battle with the soldiers. Some of them had already received nasty wounds from the honed blades of the small soldier's spears. The soldiers had lost none of their number. As he rode closer, with Marian holding on tight behind, Garfled studied the large white bear; he sensed that it was not a willing beast of burden. The idea was to either force the bear to pull the trailer, or kill it and free Judoc and Nimean. As they approach the bear, it looked directly at Garfled and spoke in his mind: "You make big mistake human, many more come now."

Looking past the bear, Garfled saw what looked like an avalanche of white, coming from the other side of the clearing. It was in fact, hundreds of white fur clad humans, charging towards the small rescue group.

"BODOLF...TROUBLE..." Garfled mind shouted to the wolf, who had not yet seen the bigger threat approaching.

"See if you can free Judoc and Nimean before they get to you, then get Teague and get out of here. We will try and hold them as long as we can," Bodolf replied, relaying the message to the rest of the wolves, as he tried to pass the small group of humans and head towards the main group, who were now half way across the clearing.

"Free me human, I will help you," The polar bear spoke again in Garfled's mind, and for some reason, he trusted the bear. Sliding down from Torrent, he slashed the leather straps fettering the bear to the trailer. Finding its freedom, it turned towards the group of humans and charged at them, uttering a feral roar. Still concentrating on the wolves, the men were completely surprised by the lighting attack from behind, in a few seconds the razor sharp claws of the bear had ripped through the ranks of men, leaving them all dead or dying on the ground. Taking in the situation, Bodolf bounded past the bloodied bear and headed towards the first of the main group.

"Do not charge them wolf!" Bodolf heard in his head from the bear, but he was already committed. As he and his group of wolves drew close, the white army split in the middle passing them on both sides and then re-joined surrounding the startled wolves. The move was expertly executed and within seconds, Bodolf found himself surrounded by a circle of shields and spears. Then a large net made from animal gut was pulled over the wolves from both sides. There was no way of stopping it happening and as hard as Bodolf tried he could not escape through the shields and spears, or chew through the tough material of the net, which was pulling him and the other wolves closer together, immobilising them under its sinewy strength.

Garfled watched as the army swallowed up Bodolf and the other wolves. He was desperately trying to open the door to the cage to free Judoc and Nimean, but could not work out the strange lock holding the gate firmly closed. The army was just a short distance away and he knew time was running out for him.

"Torrent, get Teague out of here now." Garfled sent. He knew he would not have enough time to get back and drawing his sword, turned to face the approaching wave of white clad soldiers. Starting to follow Garfled's instructions, Torrents mind was assaulted by a primal thought from his passenger, he was already torn between leaving to save the girl or save his friend but he knew the girl would jump from his back and run to Garfled if he tried to leave. As he lowered his head to charge at the advancing army, he knew he could not reach Garfled in time. However, before he reached the lone soldier, a white shape flashed in front of him and the next second Garfled was mounted on the back of the polar bear and heading at a run towards him... Torrent immediately started to turn to follow, but was dangerously close to the front line of soldiers, who started throwing spears at the massive bull and its female rider. Torrent felt several of the projectiles hitting him, but he kept running after Garfled on the bear. Any pain was masked by the adrenalin coursing through his body. On his back he felt Marian slump forward and knew she had been injured, he adjusted his gait to keep her balanced on his back with her weakened grip.

As they charged into the spot where they had left Teague, they saw the mangled dead body of Yrik on the floor, but no sign of Teague or Blaze. With the soldier's close behind, the group had no choice but to plough on through the forest, headed towards the west and the safety of Old Seville.

As they ran from view, a large white wolf stalked out of the forest and barked a command. The soldiers that had been pursuing the remnants of the expedition party stopped and formed up in front of him. Further soldiers emerged from the forest, dragging Teague and Daze with them, along with twenty wolves.

"Please let me tend to the eagle," Teague shouted to her captors, as she spotted his still form lying in a pool of blood and feathers on the floor. When their small party had been ambushed, Yrik had been torn from the saddle in the ensuing struggle and she had seen him trampled under the feet of the soldiers.

"The bird is dead, you cannot help it. The horse will help feed the army. Your healing powers will be useful to us, so you will be honoured to receive an ancient Northling," A gravelly strange yet familiar voice said in her head.

"RUN FOR HELP... NOW..." Teague shouted in Daze's mind. Knowing that her friend would not want to leave her in danger, she hoped that the plea for help would convince her to escape.

"I cannot leave you," Daze replied, her head shaking from side-to-side as the two soldiers holding the rope around her neck started to pull her away from her friend.

"You cannot help me now; they are going to kill you, but not me. NOW RUN! Daze hesitated a few more seconds, not sure what to do. The large wolf barked an order to the others and four immediately turned, moving towards the captive horse. Recognising the stare of hunters, Daze's flight instincts took over and she reared upwards, dragging both of her captors off their feet. As she landed, she exploded forward, dragging them on either side of her. She veered to the right and swiped one against a tree, forcing him to let go and then did the same on the left. She looked back to see the wolves only a few feet behind her, and gaining. On this narrow winding trail, with logs and branches in her way, her progress was slowed, but the wolves had no opportunity to attack in unison. The leading wolf sprang for Daze, but she lashed out with a back hoof and caught him in mid-flight, sending him barrelling back into the others. This slowed them for a moment, but they were soon back snapping at her heels. They did not try to leap at her again, but nor did they show any signs of giving up their pursuit. As the deadly chase continued, the adrenalin that had released into her system initially to help her flee could no longer mask the terrible strain on her system. She could feel every pump of her laboured heart, as she galloped along the winding trail. Then she entered a large clearing and could see with her large peripheral vision the wolves spread out and move either side of her. Wolves were very fast runners, but these were running much faster than they should.

Using every ounce of her flagging energy, she kicked out at one that leapt from her left, hitting it squarely and sending it flying; but the action slowed her, giving the two wolves on her right the opportunity to leap together, one biting into her back leg and the other managing to secure a hold on her neck. The combined weight was too much for Daze, she felt her legs buckling under her, and she crashed to the ground. From her prone position, she could see the wolf she had kicked get up and move towards her now exposed neck. She could smell the fetid breath of the animals, as they moved in to finish her off. She tried to bring her legs under her to rise again, but now one of them had her by the throat and Daze felt her world turning black. As she started to slip into unconsciousness, the pain of the bites left her. She could see her attackers savaging her, but was somehow inured from it. It was as if the attack was happening to someone else. Then, in her semi-conscious state, she saw a massive white paw swing past her eyes and hit the wolf at her throat, sending it flying, and a pair of booted feet standing firmly beside her. Realising this was not a dream; Daze summoned her energy to stand. Pain flooded into her body from several locations, providing the stimulant she needed to force her torn weary body to its feet. One of the wolves was still attached to her left leg and she turned her head and bit the creature in the back of the neck, feeling the bone crunching under her teeth. Then she tore the beast from her leg and hurled it onto the ground, where it lay still. Beside her, Garfled and the massive white bear were battling the other three wolves. One was already lying still on the floor, blood smearing its white coat; the other two were trying to find a way through the pairs defences. However, between Garfled's flashing sword and the bear's lethal claws, they soon lay bloodied on the floor as well.

"Are you ok Daze?" Garfled sent, as he ran up and around her, checking her wounds as he went.

"I will live Garfled, but where did you come from, and what is that creature?" Daze sent back. Now that the immediate threat from the wolves was gone, she eyed the white bear with suspicion.

"Well like you we were running from the enemy. When we reached this clearing, we stopped to gather ourselves and check Marian's wounds. Then we heard you and your pursuers coming down the trail. We thought they were still chasing us, so we concealed ourselves, hoping they would charge on by. When we realised what was happening, we left Torrent with Mariana, and well, you know the rest. The white beast is called Inuka; he claims to have defected from what he calls the Northlings army. We would be captured or dead without his help, so I guess he does not mean us any harm; he wants to come back with us. We will let Banain decide what to do with him. Now if you feel able, we need to keep moving, in case they have sent more forces after us," Garfled replied, satisfied that Stars wounds, whilst nasty, were not life threatening.

Chapter Twelve

Ten days later, Banain stood again on his balcony looking to the East; he was gripping the balustrade so tightly, that his knuckles had turned white. Krask was perched further down the ornate balustrade, having just informed his adopted son and leader of the Freedom Army, of the expedition teams encounter.

"I am sorry Banain, Garfled and the remnants of the expedition are a few hours away, they have had to travel slowly because of Mariana's wounds. I have sent our best medic to meet them. After losing the pursuing soldiers, he thought the best course of action was to return, so that reinforcements could be sent out to rescue them," Krask said, noting the deep lines of anguish on Banain's face.

"I can't believe that Bodolf has been taken! He is always so cautious," Banain said, the enormity of the situation still not registering fully in his mind.

"Garfled said that Teague had found your birth parents Banain, and that she had persuaded Bodolf to try and rescue them. That was when the expedition was ambushed," Krask explained.

"You are my parent Krask. Why is she so keen to find something I do not want found; her actions have caused all of this." Banain almost shouted, gripping the balustrade even more tightly, as if it held the lives of his enemies.

"I raised you Banain, but your birth parents lost you through no fault of their own. From what Bodolf has told me, your father was badly wounded trying to protect you, and your mother must have gone through hell when you were carried away from her by Krys, even though she was saving your life. I will call the animal council together to discuss our options, perhaps you should seek council from the Immortals Banain," Krask said, not sure how to help the distraught child, trapped in a man's body; but hoping the Immortals would.

"No, go and tell Garfled to get here as soon as possible and to bring this white bear with him. I will come to the council meeting after I have talked with them, then I will go and see the Immortals," Banain said, turning and walking away as he spoke.

A short while later Banain was sat opposite the burly warrior, who was still covered in the dust of travel and looked totally crestfallen.

"How is Torrent Garfled? I hear he was injured," Banain said, not sure how to start the conversation with the clearly distressed warrior.

"He will mend... I apologise Banain, I failed you," Garfled said, sitting stiffly and looking into Banain's troubled eyes.

"From what I gather from Krask, it was Teague that failed everyone; if she had not persuaded Bodolf to try and rescue my so called birth parents, the whole team would have been safe now," Banain said.

"That is untrue Banain. Yrik sustained his injury before we knew of your blood parent's location, and it was

Bodolf's decision to try and rescue them," Garfled replied, surprised at Banain's animosity towards Teague.

"Bodolf will do anything Teague asks of him, so she is to blame. But I expected more from you, Garfled; you know better than to charge in without scouting first," Banain retorted, instantly regretting lashing out at the distraught warrior.

"Bodolf's plan was the right one, but we were not expecting to face a trained army," Garfled replied, not backing down from Banain's cold stare.

"Well the damage is done now; but we need to know more of the army that is invading our territory and how to rescue the expedition party," Banain said, trying to replace his sense of loss with practical solutions.

"And your birth parents?" Garfled asked, risking that stare again, but Banain's countenance softened.

"Did you see them Garfled, were they killed? Banain asked, not wanting to hear the answer either way, but knowing he had to ask. He could not explain why he had shied away from searching for his birth parents himself. He could have done so years ago, but something deep inside had always stopped him. Teague had quizzed him many times about them, always ending up annoyed by his apparent indifference to their existence. Turr had told him that deep down he blamed his parents for abandoning him, for not keeping him safe; but Banain did not think that was true. He did not want to find his parents, because he was frightened that they would not want him. In addition, because he was raised by animals and had these strange abilities, they would not love him. So rather than risk realising these fears, he had not looked for them. He also believed that he would have the same emotional problems with his parents that he had with Teague. With Krask and other animals, the rules were clear and simple. However, with humans, an undercurrent could slip past his carefully built mental walls and play havoc with his emotions.

"I saw them, and I do not think they or Bodolf were killed. It seems that the objective of this invading army is to capture, rather than kill. I spoke with Inuka, the bear that defected from the ranks of the Northlings Army, and he told me some of its purpose; I think you should speak with him Banain.

Much later that night, Banan was once again standing in front of the gently undulating form of Turr.

"The threat from the north is serious Banain, you must not underestimate the power of its orchestrator," Turr sang.

"It sounds like you know something about who is behind these attacks Turr?" Banain said, surprised that his mentor had not mentioned this before.

"There is a force that dwells under the deepest ice, far to the north. It seeks to leave its frozen domain, and spread its evil across the world, using other creatures to help it achieve its goals. If it seeks and finds you Banain, you may not be able to resist it. This is why we have tried so hard to prepare you; we fear that you are not ready to face this threat."

"I talked to the bear, Inuka. He told me that many creatures of the north are enslaved by a force that controls their minds. Those who are able to fight it, have to hide the fact from all around them. Inuka was one of those able to do so; when he had the opportunity to escape, he took it. It was strange talking to Inuka, although I could understand his mind talk, it was as if the rest of his mind was closed. I could sense none of the emotions that normally accompany mind-to-mind communication... Have I done something to anger you?" Banain said, noting that Turr, who normally swayed gently, was pulsating; it was something he had only witnessed once before, when the Immortals were angry with him for going against their wishes.

"We were not told that a Northling had been captured Banain, or that you have been in communication with it," Turr replied, an edge to his normal calm tone.

"He was not captured, he helped some of the expedition force to escape and we have offered him the safety of the Protectorate, as we would any species in need. He has been most helpful in providing information regarding the invading army's strength and location; he also knows the location of their base in the north. Why do you call him a Northling?" Banain asked. He was beginning to think that Turr and the Immortals knew a lot more about this threat from the North then they were telling him.

"It is just a term we use for some of those who come from the far north. You must not try to read his mind again Banain; even communicating with him could be dangerous. You need to bring him to us right away. There is more to tell you Banain, but now is not the time."

"Early the next morning, a very tired Banain, stood in front of the senior members of the ruling council and his trusted lieutenants, in the Animalis meeting hall. The hall had been constructed, so that any animals that walked, flew, crawled, or swam could attend. There was a large pool in the centre of the hall, which joined the tunnel linking the Guadalquivir River, to Banain's training room, providing access for aquatics. There were also entrances and perches for Aves, and massive gates, allowing entrance to the largest of creatures. Today the largest of these was Torrent; who despite not having fully recovered from his wounds was determined to attend. To Banain's right, was Krask and on his left, Lepe. Bodolf would normally have been beside him and all noted his absence. Banain had organised for Inuka to be taken to see the Immortals, he had to admit, that since mind talking to the bear, he had felt very strange, but he shrugged the feeling aside and tried to continue with the task at hand.

He was almost overwhelmed by the cacophony of noise being mentally transmitted by the members of the council. Recent events had given everyone something to think about and he was now receiving all those thoughts, which in his current tired state, were close to overwhelming. Then Krask cut through the mental chatter.

"Members of the council, I am sure you have all heard much about recent events. Please now give Banain your attention, so that he can update you on the situation." As Krask spoke, the mental hubbub subdued to a whisper, and Banain could feel the minds of the assembled variety of species, tuning to his.

"My friends, a few days ago the expedition team led by Bodolf, was attacked by a large force from an unknown army in the great forest east of the plains. Bodolf and all the expedition wolves were taken, along with Teague." Speaking the words brought the realisation that his best friends, Bodolf and Teague, were captured and could be dead. It took all his self-control to keep his composure and carry on his address to the now fully attentive audience.

Banain addressed the council for as long as he could, describing events leading to the attack and other relevant information; but then he excused himself, leaving Krask to continue with the proposed plan of action. As he walked through the long corridors, he felt anger building and spreading through his body with every step. Why had Teague done this...? Why could she not have just let things alone...? He had told her that he did not want to find his birth parents, but she had insisted on looking anyway, and this was the result. As Banain walked, every beat of his heart felt like it was fuelling a rage that until now had remained trapped deep inside him. As the door to his chambers came into view, he threw a bolt of pure anger fuelled energy at it. The door exploded into a million tiny fragments, which instead of falling to the floor, swirled around in a vortex, rising to pass over his head as he swept into the room. As he entered, every piece of furniture and every loose object also disintegrated and joined a growing maelstrom of particles rotating at a dizzying speed above his head.

Sinking to his knees, Banain raised his hands and sparks of yellow flew from them to ignite the mass swirling above his head. Slowly from the now flaming vortex, a shape started to materialise, indistinct at first but slowly morphing into the shape of an Immortal, almost black in appearance. The figure hovered over Banain, pulsating with power supplied by his mental energy, feeding from it and expanding in size and intensity every second.

"Banain, we know you, we see you; your energy is our energy; your body is our body; your life is our life," a silky smooth voice spoke in Banain's mind.

As the entity above Banain's head spoke, from each of its many tendrils, wisps of dark energy snaked down to enter Banain's mouth, ears and nose; growing thicker every second, as it started to take over his mind.

Realising he was in terrible danger, Banain tried to control his raging emotions, to block the alien force he could feel invading every part of his being. However, his anger had opened up the deepest recesses of his mind, letting this dark force in with little opposition. He focused every ounce of his reserves on fighting whatever this was, but try as he might, he could not find a way to stop it from invading more and more of his mind. As the tendrils grew, resistance crumbled, and the being started to transfer itself into its new home... Banain.

Chapter Thirteen

"Everything went according to plan?" The question came from the massive black bear, Isbjorn, who was standing with Izotz and Arkta in front of the cages holding Bodolf and the other wolves from the ill-fated expedition team. He had just arrived from his base in the north, to check on the progress of his army, which was under the control of Izotz's and Arkta. To say they were Izotz's and Arkta was not strictly true, as both were infested with ancient Northling entities and had no control over their own actions.

"Yes Isba, Rekk should have reached Banain by now. Our plan was devised and executed perfectly," Arkta's Northling, called Nezz replied.

The response from Isbjorn was so fast, that Nezz never had a chance to defend himself. One of Isbjorn's huge paws swiped at the wolf, sending him flying across the floor to crash into the cage behind him. Isbjorn moved with incredible speed to stand over the wolf, placing a massive front paw on his neck.

"I have warned you before Nezz; my name is Isbjorn. You will call me by that name and treat me with respect, or I will rip the throat from this mangy cur and let you fester and die in its body." As he spoke, Isbjorn pushed down on Arkta's neck, watching with satisfaction as the wolf struggled to breath. Beside him, the largest of the captured white wolves threw himself at the bars of the cage, driven it seemed by his treatment of this wolf. He was surprised to find resistance when he probed its mind and had to rip through quite sophisticated defences before he could access its memories and thoughts.

"You know the cur you occupy is the son of the big white in the cage?" he sent to Nezz, releasing the pressure on his neck.

"Yes, Leader Isbjorn, I think he would make a very good host for an ancient. We have also captured a human with healing powers," Nezz replied, with as much respect as he could muster, whilst keeping some dignity. He was fighting the wolf's natural response to cower in front of a pack leader.

"Very good, I will send for Sarr and Kirr, they will be able to make the most of these two. See that the rest are converted with clones. Now, how is your plan for the conversion of the local population going, Koll? You said you could manage it without resistance, yet I see only half the trailers full," The black bear asked Izotz, who was Koll's host. He was moving away from the cage containing the growling figure of Bodolf and the other wolves as he spoke, towards further trailers parked in a large circle around the army's camp. Some of the trailers were full of humans, but many still stood empty.

"We are only a little behind schedule, Leader Isbjorn. Bribing the senior villagers has not always worked and in those cases, we have had to take the villages by force. Unfortunately, word of our presence is traveling before us and some manage to put up quite a strong resistance," Koll answered, deciding to show the correct amount of deference in view of the treatment of Nezz.

"More excuses? You need to move faster and build forces so that we can take the protectorates base. How long before you are ready?" Isbjorn said, turning to face Koll's host. Although Izotz was a huge man by human standards, he was dwarfed by the black bear and Koll was surprised that he showed no fear. If he let go control of the human, he had no doubt that it would attack the bear in an instant. Part of him would like to see that happen, but now was not the time.

"It will take at least three months to convert enough villagers and build the necessary siege weapons required," Koll replied, forcing the human to downcast his eyes and show deference to the leader.

"Make sure it is no longer. I will send Kirr down to claim this wolf and help you convert the locals. Do not disappoint me again!" Isbjorn sent to both of them, before turning to continue his tour of the camp.

Chapter Fourteen

Lepe was worried, he had seen Banain angry before and he had seen him tired; but this was the first time he had seen him looking so drained, so... almost haunted. He had known Banain longer than anyone, except Krask. They first met, when Banain was just a baby who could hardly walk, and Lepe was a very young mountain sheep living near to Krask's nest, in a small mountain range to the south of Old Seville. He remembered his first contact with the child. Banain had enticed him with mental images of food and once he had looked into Banain's eyes, he had been able to communicate with him. They shared great adventures in those mountains, and had saved each other's lives on several occasions.

Lepe could sense something was wrong with his lifetime friend and slipped out of the hall to find him. As he approached the smashed doors of Banain's quarters, he saw a sight that would live with him for the rest of his life. His friend was on his knees, bent over backwards, with the back of his head on the floor. Above and connected to his head, was a large black swirling figure shaped like an Immortal. As it hovered, its long tendrils, which connected to Banain, seemed to be literally sucking the life out of his friend. Blood was pouring from Banain's nose, pooling on the polished floor beneath his head. Taking only a second to decide, Lepe charged. The entity had no time to react, as the barrelling sheep with one horn leapt and connected with Banain, the momentum sent them both crashing into the wall, severing its connection with him. With its link to Banain lost, the entity had only seconds to find a new host. Unlike Banain, Lepe had no mental powers to protect him and was and easy target for the desperate being. In a flash it changed its focus to Lepe, but denied the usual preparation time to enter another being, it caused considerable damage, as it insinuated itself in his brain, instead of Banain's. The shock to Lepe's mind was too much to bear and the only way it could protect itself, was to shut down, sending Lepe into a deep coma.

Several hours later Banain tried to open his eyes, but the blinding pain that accompanied the attempt, quickly persuaded him to keep them closed.

"Please keep still Banain, we are trying to repair the damage," the familiar voice of Turr, sang in his head.

"What damage Turr? I remember being so angry and then I was fighting against something terrible; it looked like you Turr!" Banain sent, unwelcome memories of the entity forcing their way into his brain.

"Had you not possessed your powers, it would have taken you over completely. The only way it could lower your defences, was to get you angry and use your anger to feed its own power. Had Lepe not turned up when he did, you would have been infested. We have…

"Lepe…is he ok" Banain interrupted Turr.

"I am afraid not Banain, in managing to disrupt the entities attempts to take you over, Lepe became it's only available host," Turr said.

Banain forced his eyes open again, ignoring the terrible pain that accompanied the action and looked for his friend.

He was in the underground room designed for communicating with the Immortals. In the middle, encased in the column of water, was the gently floating figure of Turr, but there was no sign of Lepe.

"Where is he Turr...? Is he dead?" As he spoke the words, a terrible weight seemed to crush his chest from within. He could not imagine life without his best friend and just thinking that his actions had caused his death, was too much to bear.

"No, he is not dead Banain; he is in a very deep coma. If he does wake, he will not be the Lepe that you know. The entity is within him and we do not have the power to remove it; he will be a danger to anybody he comes into contact with," Turr sang.

"I do not understand. What does Inuka have to do with this?" Banain asked, the blinding pain in his head making it hard to think.

"You should be resting and healing now Banain, but we know you will not, so I will try to explain. Our species has been in existence for over three hundred and fifty million years, we first gained sentiency in what was called the Palaeozoic period of earth's development. At that time, the planet was much warmer than it is today and our species was spread across the globe. Later, much of the world was plunged into the life-destroying grip of several severe ice ages. The majority of our species were killed, except for those living far to the south; or so we believed. Recently, we have become aware of entities, like the one who tried to possess you and who now resides in Lepe. We believe they are our very ancient ancestors, separated from us millions of years ago. Not able to survive in their original form, a few of them found a way to take over other species. They have become parasitic, feeding off the life of others and bending both mind and body to their will. One of these, Northlings, as we call them, was in Inuka and it was this entity that tried to take over your mind."

"So what of Inuka, is he still under the control of these Northlings?" Banain asked. He was worried about what they could do with the bear if he was a threat to the protectorate.

"We believe that Inuka no longer carries a Northling, at least we cannot sense such a presence in him. We think that in normal circumstances the process for invading a host, takes several hours, if not days. As only one Northling can occupy a host at a time, to procreate, they need to revert to their polyp state and create a genetic copy of themselves, which they then transmit via the blood into a new host. In this case, we believe that it was the Northlings intention to allow Inuka to be captured, in the hope that he would be brought to you. When you met with Inuka, the Northling parasite, who must be a very old and powerful member of his species, managed to transfer via some type of telepathy from Inuka's mind to yours. Your innate abilities would have detected the invasion and blocked the entity from taking over, but you were not trained sufficiently to recognise what was happening. If not for the actions of Lepe, a very powerful Northling would have been in control of your powers, making you a formidable foe in the midst of the protectorate."

"Not trained, I was not aware that a threat like this even existed!" Banain countered, the effort of raising his mental voice causing further waves of pain to crash about the inside of his skull. Why did you not tell me about the threat from the Northlings before, Turr?

There are many possible threats on the planet, as I said, we only became aware of the Northlings a few thousand years ago, and understood that they could only control the minds of creatures of the sea. It would appear that their powers have grown far beyond our realisation. Now that we know more, we can resume your training and equip you to resist them. You can start..."

"Before I do anything else, we need to get this thing out of Lepe; why have you not done so already?" Banain interrupted for the second time.

"There is nothing we can do for Lepe, his mind has shut down, if he awakens, he will be under the control of the Northling that now resides within. If that happens, the entity will be able to move to any human or creature it is in contact with; we cannot allow that," Turr intoned, and for the first time, Banain felt that he detected a small tremor in the normally calm voice.

"Lepe is my best friend and has sacrificed much for the protectorate, what do you suggest we do?"

"We have a plan Banain, but it involves great risk. The only way to be completely safe is to let Lepe pass away in an area far from any other sentient beings. That way, the Northling will have no new host to move to and will....

"LET LEPE DIE!" Banain shouted." That is not going to happen. I will not..."

"Please Banain, let us finish," Turr sent strongly, interrupting Banain this time. "We knew that letting Lepe die would not be acceptable to you, so, as we said, we have devised a plan. For this to work, you have to agree to train with us here; so that we can teach you how to resist invasion of your mind better and how to make more use of your latent skills. It will also allow time to make the necessary preparations to take Lepe to the only place where he may be parted from his parasitic host, without losing his life.

Chapter Fifteen (Four Months Later)

Banain, Wayland and Garfled, stood beside Captain Carlos Torre, on the deck of Freedom. In her former life, the ship only had a navy serial number, but it was a matter of great pride to Carlos, that she now bore her name in gold lettering on her stern. Behind her, a further three ships about half the size of freedom moved gently on the waters of the river. It had been a testament to the knowledge and skills of the captain and his crew and the resourcefulness of Wayland that they had been built at all. With the need to protect Old Seville from the advancing Northlings army, Wayland had been hard pressed to find the resources to get both jobs done. However, get it done he had, the proof floating behind him and all around the now strongly defended and provisioned city. He, Krask and Garfled, had debated deep into many nights, as to how best to fight the Northlings, for to kill one of them meant killing their host, who were mostly unwilling participants in a war not of their choosing. A crucial point working in the Freedom Army's favour was the fact that the Northlings wanted to take over their enemy and not kill them, so they had also been keen to wage a non-lethal war, thus far.

The only plan the three could come up with, was to buy as much time as possible and hope that the Immortals would work out a way of defeating the Northlings without killing their hosts. Messengers were sent to all parts of the protectorate and beyond, informing all creatures of the threat; encouraging those who were agile enough to keep out of harm's way and those who were not, to move to the relative safety of Old Seville. They had waged a harrying war on the enemy, slowing their advance by placing obstacles that ranged from large trenches, dug along the route of the advancing army, to aerial bombardments with non-lethal sized sticks and stones. But now all Freedom forces were packed behind the walls of Old Seville, their roles changed from harrier to peacekeeper; and the Northlings army had taken up position around a mile from the city, cutting off all routes except for the river, which for the moment was the only way in and out.. Old Seville was under siege.

Carlos was quite relieved to be leaving the city, which was packed to bursting point with every species under the sun. Even with the nonviolence agreement, keeping the peace between so many natural enemies was hard to enforce. He was keen to be heading for the familiar territory of the open seas, as were he suspected, his crew. He could still not believe the changes in the young man he now saw before him talking to Wayland and Garfled. Few had seen Banain except for Krask in the last four months. However, instructions on revision to this galley, the building of more ships and on defending the capital from invaders, had come on a daily basis via the eagle. The rumour was that Banain had spent every day below the castle, training his mind with the aid of the Immortals, and most of the nights training his body with a strange looking ape called Grindor. Carlos believed the rumour regarding the physical training, judging by Banain's appearance. In four months, his already impressive stature had become even more muscular and agile. However, it was his eyes that had changed the most; they had lost most of their blue colouring, and were as dark as the depths of space. Carlos felt as though those eyes could suck the soul right out of him, should he look into them for too long. He just hoped that the boy's magic was as strong as everyone said it was, and that he had not thrown himself and his crew from the sharks to the whales, by deciding to stay with the protectorate.

"The ship looks good and I see you have included the modifications I asked for, are the others ready?" Banain enquired, as he cast his eyes over the newly installed post in front of the main mast and the rope and hemp appendages attached to it.

"Well they are seaworthy Lord Banain, and yes, the modifications you requested are incorporated in Freedom and the new vessels. But with most of the rowing ports gone, we can only move by sail; which is no good in confined areas, or when the wind is blowing from where we want to go," Carlos replied. Although he had continually tried to tell Krask that the ships needed oars as well as sails, the eagle had just told him that Banain had a solution that would negate the need for oars. In truth, Carlos was quite annoyed that as the admiral of the Freedom Navy, such as it was, his expertise on this matter had been ignored. He was afraid that the error of the decision not to install oars was going to become apparent in a short while, when the fleet tried to leave harbour.

"Do not worry about moving the ship's Captain," Banain said, then turned towards Wayland and gripped his shoulder.

"It is time for us to leave. Krask will be our communication channel; he will find me wherever I am. I know it is an almost impossible task, but try and keep the inhabitants of Old Seville safe until the Immortals can find a way to defeat the Northlings," Banain said, feeling terrible about leaving like this.

"I have never fought a war where you were not allowed to kill the enemy; it is like trying to fight with both your legs and arms tied together. I hope they can find the solution Banain and soon, as we cannot last more than a month without supplies. I am not sure what will happen when the inhabitants of Seville run out of food, but I suspect that their old ways will return and it may be safer outside the city, then in!" Wayland replied, a frown of worry creasing his brow, as he turned and walked down the gangplank of Freedom.

"Ok Captain, let's see how your ships perform. I will go and organise the help I promised," Banain said, smiling at the captain as he turned and strode to the front of the ship.

As Banain turned away from him, Carlos noted for the first time a strange pack, strapped to his commanders back. It was semi-circular in shape, with the flat area uppermost. Two flaxen thongs secured a strange implement in place, which looked similar to half a starfish in shape. The weapon, if that is what it was, was as black as Banain's eyes, but seemed to be almost translucent. It looked to Carlos, like its legs were slowly undulating. Shaking his head, he forced himself to look away from the strange looking device, reluctantly giving orders to Marcio, his newly promoted second in command, to cast off as instructed.

Carlos had requested that Fermin and the remainder of his original crew, help with the building of the freedom Navy; and then for their number to be split equally amongst the fleet as captains and senior crewmembers. He had devised competitions and challenges to determine who would captain the new ships, and then allowed them to pick their own crews. The process had thrown up some unexpected results. Fermin, his second in command had as expected, sailed through the tests, securing his place as the captain of one of the ships. He had named it, Funchal, after the Island in the Atlantic where he was born. The other two captaincies both went to previous rowers, who had remained under Carlos's radar, but who had showed amazing aptitude and intelligence in the challenges. They named their ships Oldore and Neptune, showing that as well as intelligence, one of his captains, Hasis, had a sense of humour and the other, Jacob, knowledge of the old sea gods. Both attributes would become necessary before this journey was over. As good as he perceived his captains to be, Carlos was still worried about what was going to happen to his ships in the strong currents, with no oars to control them.

Reluctantly, Captain Torre gave the order for all ships to cast off and waited for the mayhem that was bound to follow. He was sure that released into the currents, they would be swept into each other. To his amazement and that of the other seafaring folk on board, the ships turned as one and started moving in line, towards the open river.

Carlos ran to the side of the ship and looking down he saw that the water seemed to be boiling with silver shapes. As he watched, he realised that there were thousands of fish pushing the galley! He stared mesmerised, as they propelled Freedom and the other vessels, albeit slowly out of the harbour, towards the river.

"How did you get them to do that?" Carlos asked, moving to the front of the ship, to stand with Banain.

"Although I asked our friends of the rivers to help, it was nothing to do with me really. The Immortals have agreements with denizens of the rivers and oceans that go back millions of years. It is at their request that we are aided thus. They will take us down the river as far as the ocean. Once we reach the sea, please call me."

Banain left Carlos to tend his ship and moved back through some of the varied collection of species that had volunteered to come on this dangerous mission. By far the largest of these was Torrent, who had refused to go below, saying that he did not want to be trapped in this floating coffin, should it sink once leaving the safety of land, as he suspected it would. Beside him, trying to reassure the dubious plains bull was Garfled, and beside him, the ever present figure of Mariana. Since being rescued from her village by the expedition force, she had formed an extremely strong bond with both the silent warrior and his massive friend and mount. Everybody could see that she was besotted by Garfled, except of course, Garfled himself.

Nodding to the warrior as he passed, Banain moved towards his cabin, at the stern of the ship. He needed some time alone, so that he could put his thoughts in order and go over the plans for the coming mission again. He had to keep himself busy; as whenever he had time to think, he was flooded with the guilt of leaving his friends to suffer, or worse. Waiting all this time to act was alien to his nature and every fibre of his body had wanted to leap on

Star, charge up to the frozen north, and rescue his friends. However, it was clear by what had almost happened to him, that he had not been equipped to deal with the Northlings. It would only have aided them, if he faced them unprepared. He had welcomed the hard physical and mental training he had received during the last four months; it had allowed him to concentrate his mind on something other than the terrible thoughts of what might be happening to his friends and family.

The arrival of Grindor, from the Rock had also been of great help. The steely-minded ape had given Banain no time to think of anything, other than the rigorous training schedule he had devised for him. Grindor had also brought Nust, a weapon, imbued with special powers. It was believed to have been the body of an ancient starfish, which were comparable in abilities to the Immortals. It was said that they did not survive the ravages of the planets reshaping, and that as the last of them died, the knowledge and power of their species was locked forever into this relic. At first, Banain wanted to keep his sword, preferring its familiarity to this strange weapon. However, with help from the Immortals, he managed to master the rudiments of its powers. They were in essence, the ability to magnify and extend his existing powers, whilst also being a physical deterrent. Every time Banain had practiced with the weapon, a feeling of euphoria had washed pleasantly over him. The Immortals had warned him that he should only use Nust as a last resort, as its actions could be unpredictable if not given clear and concise instructions.

The worst of his guilt was reserved for Lepe. The little sheep had again literally leapt to his defence, this time sacrificing almost all for his lifelong friend.

He stopped at a newly constructed hatch amidships, which was nearly concealed by bundles of dried grass. Inside was a long ladder, which went all the way down to a specially constructed cabin in the bowels of the ship. Part of Freedom's conversion program, had been to replace a section of the bilges with a chamber filled with seawater, and thousands of Immortals. A special hatch connecting to the sea, allowed the Immortals access to the chamber. A cabin was constructed directly on top, and in its centre was a smaller version of the pool used to communicate with the Immortals in the bowels of the castle. Housed in this specially constructed cabin, was Lepe. He had been lowered by rope into the cabin, where he was close enough for the Immortals to keep the Northling in his mind, from using most of its powers. The hatch was only to be opened when they reached their destination, except to lower down food.

Banain shook himself from his thoughts, and on reaching his cabin, lay down to sleep whilst he had the chance.

Chapter Sixteen

It should have taken most of the day to reach the sea; but only a couple of hours later, he was woken by the noise of a loud bell, accompanied by the sounds of running feet on the deck above his head. Rising and strapping on Nust, he left his cabin and made his way up to the fighting deck, above the cabins at the stern of the ship. Banain quickly realised the reason for all the commotion. There were two huge constructions on either side of the river, about a mile distant. Banain could not yet guess their purpose, but he knew whatever it was, it would not be good for them.

Joining Carlos, the two watched the constructions take shape as they closed the distance. The other ships had been instructed to drop back and follow in line behind Freedom.

"What do you wish me to do Banain?" The captain asked, not taking his eyes of the constructions.

"They are obviously some type of weapon, but from this distance I cannot make out their purpose. We have to get passed, so let's keep going until we find out," Banain replied.

As the ships closed the distance, more details could be discerned about the structures. They resembled large windmills, but instead of the sails being vertical, they were mounted horizontally. In fact, they did not have sails; the mills had massive outstretched arms of wood, which started to turn as the small fleet closed. At the end of each of the four arms, were large rocks, held by ropes that were led through eyes to the centre of the structures. As the arms built up speed, the ropes were gradually released, allowing the rocks to move further and further out from the centre structures on either side of the river. As this happened, they emitted a strange and frightening humming sound, that became louder with every rotation. In a short while, they had both almost reached the centre of the river, leaving no place for any vessel to pass. The noise of their rotation was now deafening.

Banain sensed powerful minds at work driving these machines, but every time he tried to locate the sources of the power, he was forcefully rebuffed. Concentrating on the machines themselves, he tried to affect them, using his telepathic skills; but again his attempts were blocked. Then, from the banks of either side of the river, hundreds of white bears emerged from concealment, entered the water, and swam towards the trapped fleet. As they reached Neptune, the bears used their superior power to wrestle control from the fish and started to push her towards the shore. Banain realised that if he did not act soon, he was in danger of losing his force, before the expedition had started. He concentrated his mind, focusing on the training rituals he had learnt from the Immortals. Being in close proximity, meant that they could help by providing energy. As he went through the rituals, his view of the world changed. It was as if he had leapt from his body, to a viewpoint some one hundred feet above his head. From here, he had a bird's eye view of the events unfolding in front of him.

Apart from his high vantage point, Banain could also see so much more in this enhanced state. The Immortals had taught him how to discern the life aura of every creature and the influences upon it. Looking down at his own body, he could see a strong white aura surrounding him, with small tendrils of energy snaking out and connecting to those he was in telepathic communication with. A larger tendril connected him with the Immortals, in the centre of the ship. Turning his attention towards the towers, he could see similar swirling auras, powering and protecting their operation. Thinner tendrils also snaked out to the bears, which had already moved the first of the ships, half way towards the bank. Focusing his mind back on the bears, Banain sent tendrils of confusion out, which on contact, caused them to forget their purpose and swim in circles. Then he sent a burst of severance to each of the tendrils controlling the towers. The jolt he received on contact with the entities, felt as if a thousand shards of glass had travelled back along the tendrils, to shred his brain. Looking down, he could see and hear that the whirling stone windmills were slowing, the rocks dropping closer to the floor every second. However, Banain was not sure how long he could hold on. As well as terrible pain, Banain could also feel the powerful entities attempting to break down his defences. Even with the support of the Immortals, he was hard pressed to hold off the powerful aggressors and as he watched, a black veil started to descend over his vision.

He was being driven back into his own mind and he could hear the thrum of the towers picking up again. Banain realised that he could not defeat the powers he faced. He attempted to pull back the tendrils of severance, but now the creatures were using them to connect to him, and the assault on his tortured mind continued.

"Use Nust now Banain," the voice of the Immortals sang deep inside his embattled psyche.

With his right hand, Banain felt over his shoulder for the exposed tip of the ancient weapon. As he made contact, power shot through his arm and into his body. Instantly, the pain that had been eating into his brain stopped and his vision returned. The two tendrils of severance connecting him to the Northlings either side of the tower, shrivelled and faded. Holding the weapon high above his head, Banain envisaged the rocks stopping their deadly rotation.

The consequences of this one thought were mind shattering to every member of the expedition that witnessed what happened next. Four of Nust's arms detached themselves from the body of the Starfish, two speeding towards the tower on the left bank and two towards the one on the right. As they encountered the swirling aura surrounding the towers, it writhed, as if stung by a million bees. In less time than it takes to blink, the arms cut through the ropes holding the circling rocks. Then they dived into the main structures, turning wood into dust. Freed of their circular constraint the rocks continued in a straight line on the path of least resistance. For two of the rocks, this was directly towards the expedition ships.

For Banain, the change in circumstance was more than a relief; the power of Nust was euphoric. Restricted by the walls of the Immortals training hall, his experience with the weapon had been limited. However, with each new destructive action, waves of euphoria washed over him. As he looked down, he could see writhing coiled tendrils of energy, connecting the body of Nust to its destructive free ranging arms. Banain discovered that he could move his view to any of the four arms, experiencing the whirlwind path of their destructive journeys.

Somewhere in the far recesses of his mind, Banain heard the voice of Turr, warning him of something. Dragging his concentration from the devastations of Nust's appendages, he realised too late, the cost of his lack of attention. One of the two rocks released by Nust, passed without harm between the stern of Freedom and the bow of Funchal, bouncing like a skipping stone; until spent of energy, it disappeared beneath the disturbed surface of the water. The other bounced once, before hitting Oldore amidships at the waterline. The rock tore into the vessel and almost out of the other side, smashing human and animal flesh apart, as it careened around inside the hull. The gaping hole left by its passage let thousands of gallons of water into the ship, further adding to the mayhem on board.

Banain focused his mind again, imagining the damage to the ship repaired and the bears gone. One of Nust's arms went to the sinking Neptune and restored in seconds, the damage done to the hull. The other three moved to the swimming bears and with horrific efficiency, removed their threat forever. In a few short seconds, the swirling arms of Nust, cleaved through the bodies of the bears. The only evidence left of their existence, was the bright red waters of the river, which flowed with the fleet towards the sea. Through his critically tired mind, Banain witnessed the events unfold in front of him, powerless to stop what he had instigated. With their grizzly tasks completed, all four arms returned to the main body of Nust. As the ancient weapons power left him, Banain's world turned dark, and he collapsed to the floor.

Chapter Seventeen

Bodolf watched the world through eyes that were not his to move, and with a body that was not his to command. As host to Kirr, an elder Northling, his job was to enable his occupant to convert more hosts. The process was abhorrent to his every remaining sense. He only had access to his sight fleetingly and almost always when something terrible was happening. He suspected that Kirr was letting him see these events, just to help break down his mental barriers. Along with a large mixed group of wolves and humans, including Honi and Teague, they had just raided a human cave settlement, not far south of the ice cap limit.

There were eight men, twelve women, three children and a baby, trussed up so that they were completely immobilised on the floor of a cave. Bodolf stood over the Mother, who was trying to calm her child that was laying on the floor close by, screaming in fear. He was powerless to stop his head lowering towards the woman, or his jaws opening and his teeth closing around her neck. As his teeth broke through her skin, Kirr shut down all his senses leaving him wretched and alone; trapped in the recesses of his own mind. Unknown to Bodolf, microscopic planula, mutated from his own DNA by Kirr, which was swimming in his saliva, moved towards the scent of her blood. Once in her blood stream, the planula would be carried to the brain, where within a few days they would develop into polyps. The first of the polyps to evolve would consume the rest of the planula and take over the host's body, evolving into a Northling clone.

After about an hour, Kirr let him see again, as he moved on to the next victim and continued the abhorrent process. From the corner of his eye, he saw that Teague was also busy, healing any friend or foe wounded during the brief battle to capture the villagers. The Northlings wanted their soldiers in good condition and Teague's skills were in constant use. Honi was sitting on guard with the rest of the wolves, just outside the entrance to the cave.

The infestation process had not been the same for Bodolf or Teague. Recognising their existing powers, the Northlings had selected them as hosts to ancients, who had the ability to move from mind to mind telepathically. The relationship between both Bodolf and Teague with their Northling parasites was akin to a constant and literal battle of wills. When clone Northlings infest most animals or humans, they control the host by influencing their emotions and making the host subservient. If the host is not complying with their wishes, they can use pain or fear to bend them to their wills. Because of Bodolf's inherent gifts and training with Banain, who had shown him how to block parts of his mind with mental shields, he still fought against the creature inside him; forcing his Northling to take control of his body completely to carry out its grizzly tasks. This gift was both a blessing and a curse; and part of him just wanted to give in to the demands of the creature in his head and welcome the darkness.

"Why do you fight me Bodolf, what can you gain from it? You know that you cannot hide from me; you know that if I wanted, I could take the rest of your mind anyway. It intrigues me the way you fight for the small and insignificant thing your mind is," Kirr sang in the tortured wolves mind.

"If you could you would, worm." Bodolf growled in reply, fortifying his mental defences for the pain that normally came along with conversation with Kirr.

"Your son does not fight us; he came to us with the human Izotz. Your son and Izotz have helped us; helped us to rid the world of chaos and are helping us to ensure this planet survives. Why can you not be more like your son? He understands that the species on this planet are too dangerous to be left to their own devices. He understands that the only solution is for every intelligent lifeform, is to be controlled by one magnanimous species. We Northlings have seen everything Bodolf. Left to your own devices, it is inevitable that you will repeat events that nearly rendered this planet barren to any life form. Our species would be extinct had we not taken action and yet you fight us. All of those you were supposed to protect are now part of the Northling collective Bodolf. Teague, your brother wolves, your son, all are ours now Bodolf. By now, your leader and best friend, Banain is one of us Bodolf; with his power, we will move quickly through the protectorate.

All you need to do is join us Bodolf. Look how happy Honi is. I think she will need to find a new mate if you continue to resist me," Kirr continued. The topic of conversation was always the same. One by one, everything Bodolf cared about was ripped apart by the maggot in his brain. And, one by one, he infected the innocent.

Chapter Eighteen

Thousands of miles to the South, in the Gulf of Cadiz, Banain sat in his cabin, still battling the demons in his head. Unlike Bodolf, his were mostly of his own making, created through guilt and regret. The Immortals had warned him about the power of Nust, but when it mattered most, he had lost control and others had been killed. They had tried to allay his fears, telling him that with time he would master his gifts, but Banain did not believe them and would gladly give them up if there were a way to do so. The small fleet had been at anchor in the mouth of the river Guadalquivir for the past two days, the fish had disappeared after moving the ships there. Captain Carlos would have set sail, but he did not know where they were going and all attempts to gain instruction from Banain had been met with a stony silence.

Now, relegating the demons to the back of his mind, where they still nagged, but did not control him, Banain rose and left the cabin to continue the task in hand. Striding down the fighting deck, he noticed that none of the crewmembers would make eye contact with him, and he could sense a heady aura of respect tinged with fear from almost every person on board except Garfled, who walked up beside him and putting a muscle bound arm over Banain's shoulder, accompanied him.

"It's good you are better Banain, we have much to do and have been here too long," The warrior said.

"Indeed we have Garfled; please forgive my absence. Captain Torre, signal the fleet to weigh anchor and throw the hoops," Banain instructed the Captain, who had joined them at the bows of Freedom. Acting on the signal from Freedom, all ships raised anchor and threw the ten hemp hoops attached to different lengths of rope to either side of the vessels. Looking towards the nearest hemp circle of rope floating on the surface, Carlos saw the water darken, and the head of a massive killer whale emerge. Then the sea around the ships erupted as more of these lethal creatures surfaced, swimming around the small fleet.

In the last five thousand years, like most creatures, killer whales had evolved and were now stronger and much larger. Carlos had nearly died when a ship he had been rowing was attacked by a pod of these creatures, the largest measuring over fifteen meters long and weighing over eighteen tons. He still heard the screams of his shipmates in his dreams, as their bodies were tossed around like toys between the creatures, before being devoured in front of his eyes. How he had escaped, he did not know; clinging to a part of the broken ship, he had held one of his crewmates above the water as the largest of the whales slowly moved towards him. The creature had, almost gently, locked his massive jaws around his crewmates arm and pulled him away from Carlos, then it opened his huge mouth and the man disappeared with a scream and sickening crunch inside the beast. Carlos had grasped the knife he always kept strapped to his leg and waited for his turn, determined not to die without inflicting some pain on his tormenter. However, the whale gave him one last baleful stare, slipped under the waves and left with the rest of the pod. Many hours later, another ship had picked Carlos up, the only survivor.

Acting from fear and instinct, Carlos rushed to the weapons store by the foot of the main mast and grabbed a spear, shouting for his crew to do the same. However, before he could return to the rail and attack the killers before they sunk his ship, he found himself and the whole world around him frozen in place, and then Banain spoke in his mind.

"Carlos, do not fear the whales, they are here to help us. I can feel your fear of these creatures, but believe me, they will not harm us."

Carlos felt like he was trapped in time, which in actuality was true. This close to the sea, home to millions of Immortals and with his newly trained powers, Banain had the power to shift himself and those around him into an alternate time zone. To Carlos it seemed like the world was playing in front of his eyes at ultra-slow speed. He could see the shapes of the killer whales suspended in slow motion, some clear of the water almost frozen in mid leap. He could see the individual droplets of water catching the rays of the sun and moving in slow motion to dance in front of him. However, strangest of all, Banain was walking towards him unaffected by the event and Carlos realised he was also unaffected.

"What is this Banain? What is happening?" Carlos managed to gasp. He was in shock from all that had happened in just the last few moments.

"I am sorry Carlos, but I could not allow you to attack Kia and his pod, they are here to help us," Banain said calmly in Carlos's distraught mind.

"Help us! They are killers and they will sink this ship and kill everyone on it; release me from this trick and let me defend my ship!" Carlos shouted, not thinking to use his recently learnt telepathic skills.

"You need to calm down Carlos; the whales are here at the request of the Immortals. I will only release you from this state when you assure me you will tell your men not to attack them. I can sense that you have suffered some terrible ordeal with the Orka's, but again I assure you, they are not here to harm us." Banain's gentle assurances were slowly replacing the numbing fear in Carlos's mind with a palpable, but manageable anxiety.

"I will tell them Banain, I am sorry, but I believed the whales to be a danger and I have good reason to do so. But if you say it is ok... then I will accept your assurance," Carlos sent, remembering to use mind communication this time.

Banain shifted time back to normal, leaving Carlos reeling from the sensations that had assailed him in shifted time.

Seeing his men running towards the side of the ship with weapons in reaction to his last order, Carlos belayed it, and joined a group of nervous sailors at the side of the ship watching the massive Orca's, fear showing openly on their faces.

"They will surely kill all of us captain," one of the sailors said, gripping the spear he still held ready to throw in his hand ever more tightly.

"I have Lord Banain's assurance that we have nothing to fear from these beasts Miguel. So far everything this man has told us has been true, so we must trust him again now," Carlos said, reaching out to grab the man's spear and push it firmly to the deck.

As the frightened group watched, the Orka's disappeared under the water for a brief moment and then re-appeared, each pushing up through the rings of the floating hemp harnesses. Then they dove with the loop under the water pulling the slack from the hemp rope as they went.

"STAND CLEAR OF THE ROPES," Banain shouted, pushing fear struck sailors away from the coils of hemp lying on the deck. His actions were just in time, as within seconds the coils starting quickly unwinding, until with no more slack, they sprang taught. With a loud groan, the whole ship lurched over to starboard, as it tried to adjust to the immense pressure now being excerpted by the twelve Orca powered hemp ropes.

"Captain, tell the helm to keep the ropes directly on the bow at all times, otherwise the sideward force could have us over. And send the same instructions to the other ships," Banain said, as he strode up to Carlos, who along with his men and Garfled were still standing at the side, trying to work out what in Hades was going on.

Carlos looked at Banain for a moment, not registering what he was saying, then his experience and training took over. Feeling the ship under his feet listing to starboard and the immense pressure from the bar taught ropes, he ordered the helm over and had the signal relayed to the other ships. Under killer whale power, they turned in unison and quickly gathered speed. After checking his orders were being carried out on the other ships, Carlos joined Banain and the rest of the crew on the foredeck to watch the incredible scene playing out a little way in front of Freedom.

At the end of the twelve hemp lines was a team of Orca's, working in perfect harmony. At any one time, six of the giant killers would be below the waves pulling strongly, whilst the other six were above taking air. Carlos and his men stood mesmerised as they witnessed these powerful creatures pulling his craft unerringly, at a speed he could only have dreamed of prior to today. To either side of the pulling team further whales cruised along, there massive grey and white torsos moving easily through the choppy waters. After some time of watching, Carlos noted that every now and then a fresh whale would move in and relive one of his brethren.

"So what do you think Captain?" Banain said.

"What do I think," Carlos replied, still not able to take his gaze from the whales.

"I think this is a dream and that soon I will awaken to find that you cannot defy the Gods and be aided by the sworn enemy of every sailor since time began. I think that had I not witnessed this with my own eyes, I would have had any sailor foolish enough to tell this story, sent to the oars for life," Carlos said, turning to look at Banain."

"You talk about the beginning of time and sworn enemies, but you do not understand where time begins or ends, or what has passed and will come to pass again," Banain said, his deep blue eyes drilling into those of Carlos. For the few seconds that Carlos looked into those eyes, he realised; that apart from incredible power, Banain also possessed an inner turmoil that could, if provoked, be very dangerous. Carlos decided that he would not want to be the one to set Banain's demons free. He was relieved when the young leader moved his gaze towards the following ships.

"Tell me Captain, how is Oldore and her crew?" Banain asked. He had not spoken about the ship since she was nearly sunk by the massive rock flung from the tower and even now, days later; found it hard to deal with the feelings of helplessness as he watched her crew suffer because of his actions.

"You're… weapon or whatever you call it, repaired her hull so perfectly that you would not know it had been damaged. Once the hull was sealed the crew managed to remove the water, but the rock was so large it had to be left within her. We lost twelve wolves that had their ship den where the rock breached the hull, a further seven were injured but are making good recoveries. We also lost three crewmembers that were down below. Without your swift actions, we would have lost her and all the crew," The Captain replied, noting the lines of grief deepening on Banain's face.

"If I had paid attention, she would not have been hit in the first place. I will be in my cabin if you need me," Banain said, turning to leave as he spoke.

Chapter Nineteen

Garfled, who had listened to the whole exchange, watched Banain stride away with mixed emotions. As a warrior, he respected the power and the ability to defeat ones enemies; but Banain acted as if these powers were a curse. To his mind, Banain had no other option but to destroy the towers and kill the bears. The fact that there were some casualties was to be expected. Should he not have taken the action he did, they would all have been taken by those foul mind-devouring Northlings. He turned to look at the Okra's, effortlessly pulling the ship through the waves of the Atlantic and enjoyed the salty spray against his skin. There was a power and majesty to these creatures, which any warrior could respect. They had no compulsion about killing to survive; they were supremely adapted to excel in their environment. I would love to be like those whales, Garfled thought to himself; free of the trappings of the emotions of man, free to just hunt, eat, and mate.

The last freedom was one that Garfled found the most difficult. Since rescuing Marian, his simple world had changed beyond recognition. He had trained himself to live life in a simple straightforward manner, dependant on no one and responsible for no one; and for most of his life he had managed to keep the influence of any species that interfered with his way of life at arm's length. His interaction with women had been on a purely physical level. The closest he had come to a relationship before Mariana, was with Nadia, one of the women that lived above the drinking house. Then in the time, before Banain freed Old Seville, during a raid of a village in the great woods, he had been ordered to take a woman against her will, but had made the mistake of refusing to carry out the order from a senior officer. Well it was not a mistake; no man could force him to commit acts of violence against a woman. However, his refusal had landed him in jail, awaiting the judgment of Lord Erador. He had no misconceptions about what would have happened if Banain had not turned up when he did. It was well known that if you were unlucky enough to enter Lord Erador's cells, you were never seen again, so he owed Banain his life. Since then, he had visited the establishment that still operated under the protectorate and paid for his pleasure as before. Life had been simple, right up to the moment they had rescued Mariana.

When they returned from the ill-fated expedition, he made sure she received the medical attention she required and expected that to be the last contact with her, but Torrent had other ideas. For some reason this woman had a great effect on him, and he spent most of the six weeks it took her to recover from her wound with his head through the window next to her bed, despite the protestations of her nurse.

He had tried to get his life back to normal and ignore both of them. Nevertheless, gradually, he found himself at Mariana's bedside more and more often. He had told himself that it was for the sake of his friendship with Torrent, but he was drawn to her. Once she had recovered, he had invited her to stay in his quarters and she had accepted. He had stopped visiting Nadia at the drinking house, as he'd felt it might upset Mariana, although she was not sharing his bed. She had looked after him and

Torrent, cleaning, washing, cooking and grooming, but not shared his bed! It wasn't that he thought she would refuse him, if he asked her to lay with him, he just knew that if he did, things would be a lot more complicated. And Garfled did not like complicated...

It had been over four months now and the large warrior thought this expedition would be a chance for him and Torrent to get back to normal, away from the problems women seemed to bring to every decision, no matter how small. But no... She had volunteered to come as well and Banain had agreed, even though he had indicated to his leader and supposed friend that it might be too dangerous for her. Banain had just laughed and said he was sure that he and Torrent could look after her, and that was that. Now they were confined together on a small floating twig, being towed through the Atlantic by these powerful but simple warriors of the sea.

At that moment, he was shocked out of his contemplations by a deep and gravelly voice in his mind

"Simple...SIMPLE... Ok that is enough Mr we are the only species with emotions and problems. I think I am speaking for most denizens of the water when I say, not only do you not have a clue about the opposite sex of your own species, you also don't know anything about others either, which is surprising considering your relationship with the overgrown land creature you are attached to."

Whilst Garfled was used to mind speaking, from very early on he had learnt how to block his thoughts from others. This was the first time another creature had pushed itself into his mind uninvited and he was not happy about it.

"I am the Orca leader Kia; do not waste your energy trying to block your thoughts from me. As many have found before, it is impossible. We have the dubious honour of being able to hear the thoughts of every human, apart from one; and that one is not you Garfled. I would not normally mention this, as it has the habit of upsetting most humans and we do not tend to be in contact with your kind for long. But as we are forced into proximity by circumstance and considering your ignorance regarding my species, I thought it best to let you know." Garfled focused his attention on the whales pulling the vessels and cruising alongside the fleet, trying to identify which of them was speaking in his head. Then, a few feet in front of the bows, the water heaved upwards and the massive head of an Orca was powered towards the blue sky above, by fifteen meters of muscle packed black and white torso. The whale had a dazzling white back and round patch above and behind its eyes, one of which was looking, it seemed to Garfled, directly into his soul. The whale seemed to climb an impossible distance into the air, before reluctantly submitting to the laws of gravity and returning with a salty explosion, to its watery home. The wave it created broke as it lifted Freedoms bows and along with the spray of its re-entry, soaked Garfled and most creatures near the bows of the ship. The deep voice continued; "I travel with my mate Kaska and four generations of my family in our pod. We also travel with our clan members, none of whom is simple. We share our kills, feed and educate our young and like you have difficult relationships with members of the opposite gender. As I have heard the thoughts of all humans on your vessel Garfled, let me help you to resolve the situation with your mate and stop you casting aspersions on me and my family, by telling you that she is totally frustrated by your unwillingness to mate with her and believes that her looks do not please you. I think the feelings you have for her are called, "love," in human language and it will not go away, until you face it. Now I have to take my turn pulling these sea sows you call ships, or my mate will be giving me, a hard time. A word of advice Garfled, if you are to continue with these thoughts about my species, I wouldn't go swimming alone!"

With those final words, the voice left him, to be replaced by the gentler but worried tone of Mariana who was running towards the bow of the ship along with several other members of the crew, concerned by the actions of the Orca.

"Garfled are you ok? Did the whale try to attack you? I do not trust those creatures," she fired off, visually checking for any injuries and on satisfying her worries on that matter, scanning the water for any further threats.

"I am fine Mariana and the whale did not mean me harm…He, well I cannot explain what he did, but you should be careful what you think about them my love." Garfled said, his eyes also glued to the water.

"My love… Did you just say my love Garfled? Or was it just the shock of the water, or a slip of your normally silent tongue?" Mariana said, turning her full attention back to the usually stoic warrior.

"It was neither of those things Mariana. I have feelings for you is all," The large warrior said, feeling quite uncomfortable under her glare.

"So all this time you have led me to believe that I was unattractive to you, do you know how hurtful that was? If not for Torrent, I would have left you months ago, but he persuaded me to stay. And when Nadia from the drinking house told me you stopped visiting when I moved to your house, I was sure I had somehow turned you away from women completely." As Mariana mentioned Nadia's name, Garfled flinched, as if struck in the face and his eyes locked onto those of the women standing in front of him. Neither of them had noticed the growing audience gathering around, drawn initially by the watery explosion, but now held by the interesting conversation. The group included Torrent, who had no problem pushing to the front so that he could hear the exchange more clearly.

"You talked to Nadia? About me?" Garfled exclaimed, utterly shocked to find that what he had believed to be a sacred confidence, had been broken. All soldiers believed that the women of the drinking houses never discussed their business with anyone. It was sacrosanct.

"Of course Garfled, I went to see her as soon Torrent told me of her. I thought that as you did not want me in your bed, you were still mating with her. However, she told me you stopped seeing her around the time I arrived; she was disappointed, as she said you were a very good lover. You are also held in high esteem there, as on more than one occasion you have helped the women from violent or non-paying customers. They miss your visits Garfled.

Garfled was near dumbstruck, in a matter of a few minutes; his well-organised existence had been turned on its head. Then he noticed the growing audience gathering around him and in particular Torrent, whose large body was almost shaking with mirth. Before he had time to tell the oversized plains cow what he thought of him, Mariana grabbed his hand and pulled him through the crowd towards their sleeping area.

"Let's get these wet things off you and see if Nadia was correct. I think I have waited long enough to find out... My love...."

As she pulled, Mariana looked back and gave him a smile so radiant, that it melted away any growing anger. For once Garfled let his emotions take over, swept Mariana into his arms and accompanied by the cheers and bellows of the assembled crew of Freedom, carried his love to their sleeping area.

Chapter Twenty

Six days later, Banain and many of the crew not involved in sailing the ship, stood at the bow of Freedom looking at the immense towering cliffs of ice that spanned the entire horizon. The whales aided by the wind, when in the right direction; had moved the ships nearly five hundred nautical miles to the north and the edge of the ice cap was just ahead. The journey would have been almost enjoyable; if it were not for the terrible worry that was with him every waking moment and which tormented him in his dreams. He had witnessed the highly public realisation of love between Garfled and Mariana and had helped Marcos to resolve his differences with the Orcas. As it transpired, the pod that attacked Marcos's ship, were retaliating for an earlier attack on one of their young, by members of Marcos's crew. After many hours of mentoring, both whale and human now understood, if not liked each other a little better.

Lost in his thoughts and almost mesmerised by the ethereal vista growing every minute in front of him, Banain hardly noticed Marcos moving alongside.

"What now Banain, we have a following wind, so we need to shorten sail soon, lest we be driven aground," Marcos said quietly, also mesmerised by the beauty of the ice.

"Lower the sails and let the whales take us as far as they can, then we will be taken into Artakra," Banain said, not taking his eyes from the scene in front of him.

Marcos did not ask what Artakra was; he knew by now that Banain only gave information on a need to know basis. As the sails came down, the whales moved the ships a short distance from the sheer ice face and with a final leap in formation, left the fleet rolling in the large Atlantic swell. The noise this close to the ice face was incredible. As each wave hit the unyielding ice, its energy converted to sound and boomed back out to sea, as loud as a thunderclap. On closer examination, Marcos could see large circular holes in the ice, where the waves had found and exploited weaknesses. Along with the booming of the waves hitting the ice, there was a more eerie sound, akin to the noise made when you breath in and out, but magnified a thousand times. Then in the midst of this cacophony of noise, gravelly trumpet like sounds could also be heard. Looking towards the source of the sound, Marcos could distinguish flashes of black against the stark backdrop of the ice cap. After a few moments the trumpeting grew louder and he saw the black and white shapes of hundreds, maybe thousands of sea creatures; smaller than the Orcas, moving towards the fleet. Like the Orca's, these creatures surrounded the ships and then splitting into groups of around ten, picked up the hemp towing ropes in their beaks and started moving the fleet again.

"They are moving us towards the ice face; we will be smashed upon it by these waves," Marcos shouted at Banain, he hated not being in control of his fleet. All his years of training were telling him that the ships were in peril so close to the ice, but he could do nothing about it.

"Have faith Captain, no harm will come to the ships, look ahead," Banain said quietly into Marcos's mind.

At first, Marcos could not see what Banain was talking about, then he realised that part of the wall of ice was a headland, its existence not discernible except at close quarters. As the fleet moved closer and turned to go between it and the main body of ice, both wind and waves stopped, leaving only the trumpeting of the strange creatures pulling the vessels and the breathing like sound. The contrast between conditions outside the ice sea wall and within was immense. One moment they were rolling sickeningly from side to side on the large Atlantic waves; the next they were cruising serenely inside a protected ice bay.

Whenever the conditions had been rough, Torrent had been forced to lie down. He was fed up with feeling sick, lying down, and the inactivity of life aboard a ship for a bovine. Now with freedom gliding through sheltered waters, he raised himself, moved carefully towards the starboard rail, and joined a growing number of crewmembers taking in the spectacular view.

A few days ago, everyone who did not have natural protection from the elements, had been issued with special warm uniforms to cope with the freezing temperatures. They consisted of hemp salopettes with braces and long coats, all stuffed with donated wool. They had high collars attached to hoods that could cover the face completely, just leaving eye slits. There were also similarly padded hemp gloves and boots. Each uniform was a bleached white instead of the customary blue, but retained the green bird emblazoned on the breast.

The ships were pulled into a crevice in the ice by their trumpeting pilots. It was just wide enough for a single ship to pass with a few meters to spare on either side. Torrent, who was not impressed by many things, stared in awe at the beauty of the ice towering above his head. At its base it was almost turquoise blue, changing to the purest of whites towards the top. Spanning the top were bridges of ice, beautifully carved and smoothed into elegant structures by the arctic wind. The whole panorama was set into mesmerising action by the sun. The colours and brightness of its rays shifting in the melt waters that cascaded down from the structures above, to produce an almost hypnotic display of beauty that changed in colour and intensity every second. After some time, the crevice opened into a large lagoon; at the far end, an ice trail rose almost towards the top of the ice cap. At the top of the trail was a huge ice wall, which surrounded a city of ice, which glittered with every colour of the rainbow.

The small fleet was propelled towards several fingers of ice that projected from one side of the lagoon, and made fast with iron grappling hooks. Standing on the shore was a welcoming party of around twenty of the strange creatures that had brought them here. There number swelling as some of the ones in the towing party rocketed out of the water and waddled to join them. Banain noticed that more of them seemed to be emerging from the face of the ice itself in one place and disappearing into it in another. Most of the ones going in waddled from the water's edge with wiggling fish and other sea creatures in their beaks. The ones going out used their momentum to slide in a well-worn channel to the sea and enter with a splash.

With the crews from all ships looking on in amazement, Banain, Marcos, and Garfled left Freedom and approached the strange reception party, who were standing in perfect formation. Each of the creatures was just over a meter tall. They had two very short legs and large dark grey webbed feet. There torsos were long and stark white in front and dark grey behind, with large flippers on either side. To Banain it looked like they had a grey cloak, which went around their necks and clasped under their chins with a bright orange clasp. They had long slightly curved beaks, which were bright orange underneath and orange markings on the back of their heads. A single creature stood in front of the formation and watched Banain and his group approach with small eyes that shone with intelligence.

"Welcome First King Arka Banain friend Immortals Oka advisor to First King City Artakra." The tall creature sent to Banain, the words formed so fast that Banain could only catch some of their meaning. As it sent, it also made a loud trumpeting sound. The Immortals had told him that the King Penguins mostly talked by voice and had a very complicated and sophisticated communication method, and that only a few had the ability to mind speak. They had said that even his powers would not enable them to mind speak and that it was this resistance to telepathy, which had allowed them to resist infestation by the Northlings.

"I thank you Oka, for bringing our fleet here safely. The Immortals told me that your species goes by the name of Aptenodytes Patagonicus. It is an honour to meet with a new species," Banain sent.

"We Penguins where Northling?" Oka sent in a short staccato burst. As he sent and said the word, Northling, every penguin raised its head and trumpeted into the sky, the noise was deafening.

"Uh, you mean the Northling that has taken over Lepe?" Banain said, slightly taken aback by the turn of events. He had been expecting to be taken to see the First King and propose an agreement between the protectorate and the penguins. Although he wanted desperately for Lepe to be helped, he was worried about how the penguins were acting. There were hundreds now massed behind the slightly taller advisor to the king.

"Perhaps I should speak with the First King first?" Banain sent, trying to take back control of the situation.

"First Northling," Oka sent and trumpeted, the sound multiplied hundreds of times in the throats of the gathered penguins.

"What is happening Banain, they don't look very friendly and there sure are a lot of them," Garfled said, who was also not happy with the wall of creatures massing in front of the small fleet and their almost deafening cries. Banain quickly explained the situation to both Garfled and Marcos, whilst keeping a wary eye on Oka and the gathered penguins. Turr had told him to trust them, so making his decision he nodded once towards Oka.

"Marcos, please bring Lepe," he instructed. The captain looked as if he was going to object, but then turned and returned to Freedom to carry out Banain's instructions.

"Are you sure about this?" Garfled said, completely unsettled by the now silent ranks of penguins lined up in front of them.

"We have no choice Garfled. They outnumber us a thousand to one and I do not wish to kill another thousand creatures. They are the only ones who may be able to help Lepe. Let us hope the Immortals are right and that they will help and not kill us, or worse." Banain replied.

"Worse, what could be worse...? Ah yes of course," Garfled said. He and Banain had talked on the voyage and both agreed that death would be preferable to infestation by a Northling.

It took some time to bring Lepe from the hold of Freedom. For the whole journey the little sheep had been almost docile, subdued by the Immortals, but now he was in frenzy inside his cage. The four crewmembers left Lepe beside Banain and retreated quickly. Banain watched helplessly as his friend rammed the bars of the cage repeatedly. Then the penguins started chanting a strange sound in unison, "krakaka krakaka, krakaka," as they chanted, their heads rolled around on the top of their torso's, their beaks pointing towards the sky. The chanting was soft and subtle and had an immediate effect on Lepe. He stopped and stood completely still with his head resting against the bars, one horn poking through and the other stump bloodied from repeatedly striking the cage.

Banain and Garfled were also mesmerised by the sound of the penguins chanting and watched captivated by its potency, as a single bird separated from the gathered ranks and shuffled towards Lepe. With each webbed footstep, the chanting grew in intensity, until the bird was directly in front of Lepe's head. Then the chanting stopped, and its beak came down and buried itself deep between Lepe's eyes.

Chapter Twenty-One

Banain could not believe what he was seeing. As the chanting had stopped, both he and Garfled had been freed from its effects. The instant Lepe was stabbed he had reached for Nust. Now a few seconds later he felt powerless to do anything, He did not know if his friend was dead, and if he attacked the penguin whose beak was still inside the sheep's head, he could kill them both. Garfled also reached for his weapon, taking a couple of steps towards the macabre scene and stopping like Banain, unsure what to do next. Slowly a low trumpeting sound came from the single penguin imbedded in Lepe's head, which rose in intensity. As it rose, the other penguins joined in; creating a haunting melody that filled the arctic air, precluding all other sounds. Then like the chanting, the sound stopped abruptly and the penguin pulled its beak from Lepe's head and waddled back to stand beside Oka.

"Northling no Ket in," Oka said in Banain's mind.

"What... What, I do not understand. You have killed him; you stabbed him in the head. We came here for help and this is what you do?" Banain shouted, turning away from the still figure of his friend to face Oka and the penguins. He felt the power of Nust in his hand and raised it above his head beginning to imagine the penguins ripped apart by its power.

"He said, Northling no longer in me, is in Ket Banan. What the matter with you, did you grow stupid while Lepe away?" That voice could only belong to one creature. Turning, he was greeted with the sight of Lepe staring at him from the bars of the cage. Thrusting Nust back into its holster on his back, he ran toward Lepe, pushing his arms through the cage to hug the sheep.

"Hey Banan, you gonna keep hugging me all day, or let me out of this cage, this very unseemly."

"I… I, don't know, is it really you Lepe?" Banain replied, worried that the Northling may be using his friend to deceive him.

"Look Banan, the bad Northling who invade Lepe's head gone now; he in that penguin over there, it's me Lepe. Anyway if I not Lepe what I gonna do? Kill you all with my one horn and take over world...?" On hearing those words in Lepe's uncopiable style, Banain knew it was his friend talking and undid the front of the cage, letting the sheep trot out and jab his friend in the belly with his one good horn. Banain grabbed hold of Lepe, planted his head firmly against the sheep's, and fought to stave of tears of relief.

"I have missed you Lepe, I was so worried that we would not get the real you back. Mind you, it was nice and quiet for a while," The blond warrior sent, using humour to help with the tear fighting.

"Huh, it not quite for me, with that stupid Northling jabbering in my head and those noisy Immortals telling me resist, resist, resist, all time. Hey not so rough; I wounded you know!" The sheep sent back flinching from his wound.

"Oh of course, sorry let me fix that for you," Banain said reaching behind him for Nust again and placing one of the tips of the ancient artefact against the base of Lepe's broken horn. Making sure to control his thoughts, he envisioned the wound healing as he had been taught by the Immortals. Nust started to pulsate gently with a subtle white light, the tempo and brilliance increasing every second. Then a tendril leapt out from the tip and into Lepe's wound, causing the broken skin to knit back together.

Completely wrapped up with healing Lepe, Banain had not noticed a change in the penguins, which had started the moment he used Nust. Now he was aware of an increasing wave of noise emanating from the assembled birds, which sounded like a rhythmic chanting, similar to the one used when the Northling was being removed from Lepe. Turning to look at their gathered ranks, Banain noticed that they were all focused on Nust. Then Oka assailed his mind with a message that kept on repeating.

"ark ka ka rik...... ark ka ka rik...!"

"Sorry Lepe, but I have to try and deal with these penguins. For some reason I cannot understand them; I managed a few words before, but now none of it makes sense to me," Banain sent, trying to decipher what was being sent to him.

"I understand them, they chanting, the lost is returned, the lost is returned, over and over," Lepe sent back.

"How can you understand them? Never mind, see if you can find out what they want," Banain sent back, the chanting in his head and around him almost too much to endure.

"Ok," Lepe sent, then a couple of moments later the chanting stopped, but all penguin eyes remained fixed on Nust.

"I only able talk to Ket. He say something about we linked after he take Northling from me. Anyway, he translate for Oka, who say, you have lost relic of the sea, which is very dangerous. They say, you not able to control it and they want you to leave now." Lepe sent.

"They mean Nust?" Banain queried.

"Yes, they call relic of sea, they very frightened of it, and now you Banan," Lepe replied after a few moments.

"But what about rescuing the others? We need their help. There must be some way we can sort this out? Ask them Lepe. Banain replied, despair flooding through him at the prospect of not being able to continue with the rescue mission.

"They say, if you give Nust to them they help you with rescue, otherwise you leave now." Lepe eventually turned back to his friend and said.

"Tell them I need time to consider and talk to the Immortals Lepe," Banain said after a few moments, thinking that as Nust came from them, they would know what to do.

"They say no! They say you must give Nust now, or leave. They also say that they not trust Immortals, because they gave you Nust and that Nust must not go to the Northlings." Lepe replied. Banain did not know what to do. If he relinquished Nust to these strange creatures, he would be losing a very powerful weapon, which he may need to complete the rescue mission. He knew nothing about the penguins, except that they were supposed to be allies of the Immortals, and now that relationship seemed to be broken.

"What do you think Lepe?" He asked his friend. He had always trusted Lepe's advice and he badly needed guidance now.

"I don't know what is Nust Banain. But I sensed that the Northling who take me could feel it very strong and it wanted it. I also sense that something not right between you and Nust. I do not know why, but I trust penguins. You should give to them," Lepe said, joining the penguins in staring at the ancient artefact. Banain nodded at his friend, turned to Garfled, and asked him the same question.

"Nust is a mighty weapon Banain; I have already seen its power demonstrated, it could wipe out an army. I respect your skills Banain, but it seemed to me that the weapon might have greater powers than even you can control. Like you I have concerns about giving it to the penguins, we know nothing about them. It is a difficult decision and one only you can make.

Banain thought a little longer and then made his decision. Lifting his arm above his head, he concentrated his thoughts and threw Nust as hard as he could. Before the penguins, Lepe, or any one could do or say anything, the weapon flew above all of their heads and then streaked towards the edge of the ice cap. With an explosion that sent icy shards and meltwater down on everyone, Nust disappeared into the ice face freezing the water behind it, the only evidence of its entry, and a slight radiance around its entry point. Wiping the water from his eyes, Banain turned back towards the penguins and looked directly at Oka.

"Tell them that the found is lost again Lepe. Tell them that I instructed Nust to bury itself many miles inside the icecap and to return only if called by both the King of the penguins and the will of the Immortals. Tell them that I understood they could not trust me with its powers and they must understand that I have the same misgivings about them. And finally, tell them that Nust is no longer a threat to anyone and that they should honour their agreement to help us rescue our friends," Banain said, then listened to the strange exchange between Lepe and Ket, only understanding a word every now and then.

"Oka say Banan wise for child, penguins help, but not only rescue friends, need to defeat Northlings. Lepe translated.

"Tell Oka that it would have been easier to defeat the Northlings with Nust, but we have a plan that may achieve both objectives. We need to speak to King Aka. And find warmer clothes!" Banain said, starting to feel the chill of the ice through his thin foot ware.

"Oh you such cry-baby Banan; Oka say, no possible for you to travel to king, as special tunnels only big enough for penguins. The King come here tonight, meet you and Immortals." As Lepe talked, the penguins turned as one and shuffled off towards the ice face and into the round openings in the face of the ice wall. One by one, they disappeared into the opening, accompanied by a loud whooshing sound. Within a few moments, all the penguins had disappeared.

"It's ok for you, with your built in footwear and warm coat; us humans are fragile creatures and need our comforts. Let's get back to the ships, we have much to do," Banain said, realising how much he had missed the friendly banter with his lifelong friend.

Chapter Twenty-Two

Wayland stood on the highest balcony in the castle of old Seville, accompanied by Krask. They were surveying the forces facing them on all sides and trying again to think of a plan that might save the city from annihilation. The Northlings army had surrounded the city and were building massive structures made from wood transported from the great forest. Yesterday, he had shared breath with Sark, his horse, before watching him charge out to the relative safety of the open plains along with many other animals, through the last heavily defended rout in and out of the old city. The Northlings army were mainly interested in capturing humans so few were hurt during attacks, but any other species were killed without hesitation. It had been agreed that those animals that were fleet of foot and adapted to surviving in the wilderness, would have a better chance of survival outside of the city. Looking at the mass of forces surrounding the city, Wayland wondered if it would be the last breath he shared with his friend.

During the night, the Northlings army managed to defeat his depleted forces, who were trying to keep the last route in and out of the city open. They were effectively blockaded. Apart from the sheer number of infested soldiers, the Northlings also had several of their ancients present in the army, similar to the ones who fought Banain as he tried to leave Old Seville. These creatures had powerful telepathic skills. From what Wayland could gather, the army they faced comprised mostly of three species, humans, polar bears, and white wolves. The human army was divided into two distinct sections. One had around a thousand small slant eyed warriors, all dressed in white skins and furs and carrying hide shields and bone tipped spears. The second, consisting of an amalgamation of races from south of the ice cap. They wore a variety of clothes and sported a mix of weapons. Although they were not equipped or dressed like their brethren from the north, what they lacked in gear, they made up for in numbers. From his aerial reconnaissance, Krask reported that there were around three thousand of them. Then there were around three hundred polar bears and five hundred arctic wolves.

From what Wayland could observe, the polar bears seemed to be the most senior rank in the Northlings army, followed by the wolves, then the small humans. None of these was involved in the majority of the fighting, if that's what you would call it. That was left to the ranks of recently infested humans. Many of them were people that he knew. He was still shuddering inside after reading the contents of Krask's report on the activities of the Northlings. They had imprisoned all the recently captured human defenders of the route in and out of the city in cages. Then the wolves had gone in and pinned them by their necks for hours. At first Krask thought the humans had been killed, as the bodies just lay still for days without moving; but then he witnessed them reviving and joining the ranks of the other infested human soldiers.

"How do you defend against your own countrymen and friends Krask?" Wayland sent to the eagle, which was perched on the railing, preening his recently used flight feathers. It was something Krask did, not just when he needed to, but when he was worried; and he was very worried now.

"I do not know what to advise Wayland and I have more bad news... I cannot locate Banain, or the expedition force. I last saw them two days ago, but now I cannot see or sense them.

"How can that be Krask? I thought you could sense Banain's presence over a great distance," Wayland said, turning to look at the eagle. He noted that Krask's normally perfectly groomed feathers were looking dishevelled and the birds aggressive self-grooming was doing nothing to improve the situation.

"I do not know Wayland, it is as if there is an impenetrable barrier to my senses in that area and the glare of the ice makes it impossible to see very much from a distance. I would need to spend days at very close range just to search a small area. It is most upsetting. In addition, during my scouting of the Northlings army, I recognised Izotz and Arkta. They appear to be in charge of the army!" Krask replied, almost pulling out a flight feather.

"That is very bad Krask. With Izotz's training and knowledge of the castle, it will give them a great advantage. However, we need to deal with one disaster at a time. With most of the animals gone, we are not short of food, and water is not a problem with the tunnel from the river. The problem is what the Northlings are going to do next. There is no way I am going to kill my own countrymen, but I will not allow myself, or the remaining Freedom Army to be captured and infested by those things. I think the outer walls will hold them, but if not, we can withdraw to the castle itself," Wayland sent.

"I am going north again. I need to find Banain and let him know what is happening here. Good luck and may the animal spirits protect you," Krask sent, as he launched himself from the balcony and soared away towards the north.

"I am going to need both protection and luck, if we are all to survive this," Wayland thought, as he took one last look at the army camped outside the walls of Old Seville, turned and strode from the balcony. He navigated the spiralling stone staircase, that led from the tower down to the main hall and when he arrived there, he found Grindor waiting for him.

"What do the Immortals say we should do Grindor?" Wayland ask the ape, who looked markedly older then when he had seen him just a day ago. Grindor had been involved with the Immortals for hundreds, maybe thousands of years. No one really knew how long, as he spent so much time with the Immortals in their shifted time zone, and had been regenerated so many times, even he did not know his true age.

"I am sorry Wayland, but they cannot offer much advice; except that you should not harm the Northlings hosts," Grindor said, chattering his teeth as he sometimes did when nervous or excited.

"Oh well that will be easy, wont it! You are a warrior; you know that when you have a war people get hurt! Just tell me how to protect everyone here, without hurting someone? I do not understand why the Immortals were not able to find out what was going on from the Northling inside Lepe. Surely they had him here long enough to discover something?" Wayland almost shouted at the ape, instantly regretting his tone.

"The Immortals discovered much from the Northling. Unfortunately, not much of it was good news for our current situation. I should not tell you this, but I feel you have the right to know. The Northlings are Immortals, separated for thousands of years by miles of frozen ice. They were not aware of each other until quite recently. I think the discovery has shocked the Immortals and they do not know what to do."

"Well they need to work it out soon, or there will be no free people left! In the meantime, I will try and defend against the indefensible," Wayland said as he strode of, leaving the perplexed ape chattering.

The attack came just a few hours later at the main gate to the city. Wide enough to let two large wagons pass side-by-side and tall enough for the tallest animal or vehicle, the double gates were built of seasoned oak. A massive wooden bar, so large it had to be winched in and out, was currently in place to lock the gates shut against the invaders.

Around a thousand infested humans moved slowly towards the gates, some of them pushing a massive wooden tower that had long struts spreading out on either side. Others were clearing barricades, placed by the Freedom Army to hamper their approach to the city. Wayland had plenty of time to position around a hundred of his archers on top of the walls either side of the gate. They were equipped with stone tipped arrows, which he hoped would stun, rather than kill. As the force came within range of the archers, he gave the order to fire and watched the rise and fall of the bow driven projectiles towards their targets. Around fifty arrows found their marks, some glancing harmlessly away, some stunning or incapacitating, and a few killing the recipients. With an unseen or heard order, the advance stopped and soldiers from behind rushed forward to collect the fallen. Wayland ordered the archers to stop and watched, hoping that the Northlings did not want to risk losing more troops. Although he was saddened that troops had died, he felt it was a small price to pay, if it would save the last of the free people from enslavement. His hopes did not last long though, as in a frenzy of activity, the enemy troops swarmed over the construction and started pulling out large sections, which he could now see were attached to the struts above. In a short time, the construction had been transformed into something akin to a large winged creature, which started to move forward again, this time with the troops sheltering under its massive wings. Wayland had anticipated an attack of this type and ordered his archers to change to arrows tipped with flaming tar. Sending in the first volley, he smiled in relief, as the tower started to catch light in several places. Any troops trying to douse the flames were taken out quickly by the stunning arrows. Wayland's relief did not last long, as he watched an icy mist, conjured by an ancient Northling, rose up from the ground and around the tower. Any exposed wood it touched, was covered in a layer of ice that extinguished existing flames, and prevented any further from taking hold. Out of options, Wayland could only stand and watch, as the deadly and now strangely beautiful sparkling structure, moved ever closer to the gates. As it moved forward, it created a mist that hung suspended in place behind it, effectively hiding any activities in its midst.

Within an hour, the structure reached the gates. Rocks thrown from the battlements bounced harmlessly off its wooden wings, and fire could not get a hold through the thick layer of ice on its surface. Inside the structure and hidden from the view of the defenders, was a large rock, tied with rope to a point at the top of the tower. Driven by the will of the ancient Northlings, the rock started to swing backwards and forwards, with each swing bringing it closer to the gates. The first the defenders knew of its existence, was when it first gently kissed the hardened oak of the double gates, with barely more than a soft knock. Then, around six seconds later, the time it took for the rock to move backwards and return to the gate, a second harder knock was heard. As each swing of the rock took it higher and higher, the time it took to hit the gates increased, as did the intensity of the contact. Wayland rushed down from the wall and watched in dismay, as with each blow the bar locking the gates shut shuddered.

Chapter Twenty-Three

Deep in the bowels of Freedom, Banain stood in front of a crystalline pillar of water, where the amplified image of Turr waved gently in front of him. Locked into the Immortals time zone, he experienced the familiar mesmerising chanting, the warming of the air around him and the bristling of hairs on the nape of his neck, as if charged with tiny static shots of electricity.

"You should not have lost Nust Banain; it is the only weapon powerful enough to defeat the Northlings. Had we known you would have acted thus, we would not have entrusted it to you," Turr sang in Banain's head, an edge to his song that Banain knew from experience was anger mixed with disappointment.

"Nust is not lost Turr; it is in a place where it can only be retrieved when both you and the Penguins are in agreement on its use. Did you think I was going to stand by and see the only chance to free Lepe slip through my fingers?" Banain replied, angry that the Immortals could not see that he had no choice in the matter.

"You place the life of one against the freedom of the many Banain. Had you spent the time we required of you to train properly, you would have been strong enough to control Nust, and none of this would have happened," Turr replied, the disapproving tone moving up a notch.

"Lepe is more than a friend to me Turr; he has risked his life on more than one occasion to save me. However, had it been any other, I would have done the same thing. The penguins were right when they said I could not control

Nust. You should never have given it to me if you did not believe I was ready, now at least we have a chance to rescue the rest of the expedition team and find a solution to the Northlings threat," Banain countered, standing his ground against the will of millions of Immortals.

"We had a plan Banain, but central to that plan was Nust, with such a powerful weapon you could have defeated the Northlings army and they would have had to negotiate with us for peace. Now we have no way of forcing them to capitulate. With your rash actions, you have sealed the fate of the free people Banain."

You speak of my failures Turr, but what of your own species? Lepe told me that the Northlings are your long lost brothers, separated by a wall of time and ice and that there is no difference between you and them, other than they have mutated into evil corrupters of thousands of other species. That proves that given the wrong circumstances, you are also capable of acting for self-preservation regardless of the cost. That makes you just as fallible as the rest of us... I am surprised that you wanted to use Nust to kill thousands of your brethren, not to mention their hosts Turr. Surprised and disappointed," Banain retorted, his view of the perfection of the Immortals and their vision for a perfect world, marred by the revelations disclosed by Lepe.

"These are matters that you are not equipped to comprehend Banain. The Northlings are no longer our brethren; they are corrupted beyond recognition. There is no way to best the Northlings army without defeating their clones and this cannot be achieved without harming the hosts. Now thanks to your actions, we no longer have the means to defeat them. Isbjorn, the Northling leader, is an abomination; he has used his powers in a way that could threaten the existence of all. Your actions may help him to achieve his purpose," Turr sent, anger and frustration clear in every word.

"I will not be a part of a genocidal plan against your own kind and thousands of innocents. I am going to rescue Bodolf, Teague, my birth parents and as many victims as I can from the Northlings. You need to find a way of stopping your estranged family from doing whatever you think they are doing, without killing either them, or their innocent hosts Turr," With those words, Banain severed his connection with the Immortals and strode from the chamber.

Some hours later, Banain stood with Lepe, Ket, and King Aka, at the top of the long ice slope that led up from the bay to the gates of Artakra. The King had agreed to meet with Banain here, as the city was only suitable for penguins. Lepe had explained that they had designed an intricate system of tunnels, all powered by air generated by the force of the sea filling and leaving hundreds of ice caverns far below. The penguins utilised the blown or sucked air, to power travel to any part of the city. Lepe had further explained that there were many miles of tunnels, but they were uniquely suited to penguin travel only, hence the meeting outside the gates.

"Will the penguins help us Lepe?" Banain asked his friend.

"The King say he no give Banan army. He say if the Northlings attack Artakra, soon he need many penguins to defend city. He say you only want save your friends, not help win war. He also say that you not stand chance against Northling Army on ice. If you try free friends, they catch you." Lepe translated.

"Tell the King it is true I want to save my friends, but I need their help to find a way to stop this war without thousands being killed. If I can show him a way we can travel faster than the Northlings on the ice, would he give me enough penguins to save my friends?" Banain asked, realising he was almost out of options.

"The King say show him, then he decide."

Chapter Twenty-Four

A few hundred miles to the East, Bodolf, Honi, and an escort of two bears were just entering the ice cap, on their way back to the Northlings base. Kirr had been called back by Isbjorn, and Bodolf sensed that the worm in his head was not happy with the summons. He was not sure why Honi was traveling with them, but guessed that she was to be used as a lever against him, again.

"How do you do it wolf?" The voice of Kirr asked in Bodolf's mind. These were the first words he had uttered for quite some time.

"What do you mean maggot?" Bodolf snarled, taken aback by the sudden resumption of conversation and the question.

"How do you fight me? How do you stop me taking over your mind?" The voice continued. Bodolf was convinced that this was just another attempt by the maggot in his head to take him over completely; but he also sensed something new about his abductor, it seemed less sure…less, confident.

"I just do," Bodolf snapped back, sure now that this was a new type of attack and not wanting to give anything away.

"There is something that protects you. I sense a purpose in you that binds your resolve, an outside influence maybe?" Kirr probed.

"I have belief, perhaps that is what you lack; if my belief helps me, then I am glad of it. You will find out you are not so almighty when Banain catches up with you worm," Despite his resolve not to communicate with Kirr, Bodolf could not resist letting this creature know that its days in his head were numbered.

"Banain, this name is known to me, what significance is he?" Kirr asked.

"You will find out slug," Bodolf replied, realising he had divulged more than he had intended.

"He would have to be very powerful indeed to defeat Isbjorn," The entity said. Again, Bodolf sensed something different from the usual commanding tone of his tormentor. This was also the first time that Kirr had mentioned the name of any other Northling.

"Is Isbjorn your worm leader?" Bodolf asked, sensing an opportunity to learn something that might help him.

"Isbjorn is leader of all and has power such as you could not comprehend. He is the creator of the Northlings Empire and your beliefs mean little to him." Again, Bodolf sensed hesitation in the entity.

"A belief is a difficult thing to control; mine is shared with thousands of humans and animals who believe in the protectorate and its values. It is the pulse that beats in the hearts of all free beings."

"A pretty speech wolf, but if your own son ignores your beliefs, how strong can they be?"

At the mention of his son Arkta, Bodolf's heart sank. Normally he kept the terrible relationship between him and his firstborn hidden deep in the back of his mind, but now anguish washed over him and terrible memories came unbidden to the fore of his mind again.

"Arkta never had a chance to believe. He was taken at a young age and subjected to relentless physical and mental torture. His mind was shaped by evil, and the evil remains with him to this day. I was responsible for letting him be captured then, and now I am part of spreading your evil. The fact that I can hold a small part of me back from you is more of a punishment than a victory. It allows me to remember how useless I am, how I ruin the lives of all those who come near me." As the words poured out of Bodolf, he felt his defences slipping and realised that he wanted to stop fighting, to be inured from the persistent guilt that ate into his soul.

"Again a very nice speech wolf, but your timing is terrible. I have been more than a little impressed with your ability to block me; yours is one of the few minds closed to me. I only know of one other creature that could do this and he is much more powerful than I am. I have visited your sons mind and it is a dark place, full of fear, hate, and anger. However, like you he keeps his deepest feelings locked away, not from me of course. Deep down Arkta cares for you Bodolf. At the moment he is an easy target for Isbjorn, as he feeds off fear and hate," Kirr said.

His words shocked the wolf, causing him to push his feelings to the far recesses of his mind again, whilst he tried to evaluate what the worm wanted from him. He realised that it could have taken him over completely just then, yet it had not. More than that, it had offered information about his son, which lifted his hopes that one day... First, he needed to find out what this creature wanted.

"So what do you want from me? Do you expect me to believe you have suddenly had a change of heart and you now want to be a loving caring parasite?" Bodolf sent, regaining some self-control.

"It is not sudden Bodolf. In a way, like you, we are slaves to Isbjorn and have been for thousands of years since we were separated from the rest of the Immortals. We were ..."

"You're telling me you were once an Immortal! That I do not believe. I know the Immortals and they are everything that you are not. They would never do what you have done, worm," Bodolf snapped. This was all too much, first the feely caring attitude and now this. The trouble was, as much as he would like to stop this thing in his head from talking, he had no control over it; so the voice carried on:

"Before our world froze, we were part of that race. Millions of Immortals died as the waters plunged to sub-zero temperatures. Some managed to make it into warmer waters further south and some were forced deeper and deeper under the ice cap. I was caught along with a few thousand others in a pocket of water trapped in a subterranean ice cavern. With very little food to eat, we were dying. Then this bear fell through a thin part of the ice above and into the cavern, badly injuring itself in the fall. As it slowly sank amongst us, we were drawn by its warmth and the possibility of food. The most senior one of us, Isba, entered his body through a wound in his side. A few hundred of us followed. As the bear lost consciousness, we joined with Isba; providing him the power he needed to take over the dying bears mind. We did not know what we had done, until we realised that we were all joined through Isba with the bear and could see what he could see, feel what he could feel.

We managed to heal the bear and dig our way out if the cavern. Our bodies did not last long within the animal, but as they were destroyed by the bear's immune system, we continued to live in its mind. Only one of us could be in control of the bear's functions, Isba. Had our colonisation of the bear's body not had any side effects, I think things would have turned out very differently; but for some reason our actions turned its coat pitch black. We soon discovered that for a polar bear, being black is not good at all. Shunned or attacked by other bears on sight, we had to learn quickly how to defend against all creatures. But with our combined power working through Isba, the bear became strong, very strong." By the end of Kirr's explanation, Bodolf's interest had been piqued enough for him to ask:

"So why is the bear called Isbjorn? And why is he… you, or whatever your combined existence is, trying to enslave the free world?" Against his better judgement he realised he was being drawn into the story, but he had to know more. Before he had travelled south to search for Banain, Bodolf had been a powerful pack leader and had heard enough stories about the black bear to give its territory a wide berth.

"The short answer is that the direct merging of Isba and the bear created a new entity, which decided to name itself Isbjorn. The rest of us tried to stop its creation and many of us died in the attempt. Those who were left faced the choice of death, or complete subservience. You have to realise that normally death is just a form of rebirth for us; but Isbjorn told us he would make sure our memories and genetic history were wiped from existence should we not obey. I never thought there was another option until we came into contact with you," Kirr said, losing his air of dominance.

"So if your bodies died inside the bear, how are you here now?" Bodolf asked, trying to make sense of the strange story.

"Although our physical bodies were destroyed, our individual and genetic memories were retained within the DNA of the bear. With that genetic information, Isbjorn was able to resurrect us. Unlike the cloned Northlings, we have the ability to move from mind to mind telepathically. When we grow old we can re-generate, but only within the body of Isbjorn."

"And supposing I believed you worm, what do you want from me?" Bodolf asked. After a long pause, Kirr replied:

"To escape…"

Chapter Twenty-Five

Torrent pressed his considerable might against the flax strap that passed around his chest and back to the sled carrying the very last load. It had taken three days of hard toil to dismantle Funchal, Neptune, and Oldore piece by piece and drag the parts up the ice ramp to the surface. However, Torrent was more than happy to swap the misery of life in the ship for this. He would rather pull a thousand ships to the top of the highest mountain, than sail in them. Reaching the top, he pulled his load to the spot indicated by one of the sailors and stretched his tired shoulders once he was free from the straps. Above him on the deck of Funchal, Garfled and a group of sailors were already connecting ropes to heave aboard the supplies.

"I think that having a woman look after you is making you weak Garfled. Before you finally decided to bed Mariana, you could have easily heaved these loads aboard on your own." He sent to the straining warrior. The memories of the incident on the ship with the Orca still made Torrent chuckle deep inside; and since then Garfled and Mariana had spent most of their free time together. Secretly, Torrent missed the company of Mariana, but he was pleased for his friend. Receiving only a glare in reply, Torrent looked around at the frenzy of activity going on around him.

Carlos and his captains had worked day and night to re-build and modify the vessels for their new role. To the side of each reconstructed hull there was now a pair of runners, keeping the ships just above the level of the ice. The rudders had been adapted, so that they could be used as brakes as well as steering devices. As he watched, a large mast was heaved upright and secured in place with stays and shrouds.

"Stop teasing Garfled and come and have some food Torrent," the gentle voice of Mariana said in his head.

"Well I am hungry, but I also enjoy teasing him," he replied, looking around for the owner of the voice and finding her standing next to a pile of dried plains grass. His stomach won the battle and within a few moments he was enjoying the grass imported all the way from the Great Plains, and a scratch behind his ear from Mariana.

Later that day, the last of the work was completed on the ships and standing on the aft deck of Oldore, Banain, Garfled, Lepe, and Carlos were looking up at a penguin-filled basket, swinging in the wind. In it rode King Aka and his advisors. As soon as their aerial carriage had landed and the gate opened, the king hurried out, sending a long burst of penguin speak to Ket, who translated to Lepe.

"King Aka say he not like to fly and want to know why you build water ships on land, he think you a little crazy Banan. I hope you have good answer for him, he not very patient penguin and flying basket trip has not helped improve his mood," he added.

"Ask the King to hold on please Lepe," Banain sent, nodding at Carlos, who turned and walked to the wheel.

"SET THE MAIN," he shouted; and watched as the crew ran around the ship to carry out his orders. As the large sail unfurled, he could feel the wind's power transferring its energy through the masts and rigging into the hull of Oldore. However, the expected sensation of movement did not come. As more of the sail caught the wind, a creaking and groaning sound started, growing louder and more disquieting every second. Carlos always had his doubts about sailing a ship on ice and now his worst fears were being confirmed. The level of noise from the straining sails and rigging had become ominously loud and he feared that Oldore would rip herself apart very soon.

"FURL THE MAIN," he shouted. Hoping the crew could carry out the operation in time. It always took longer to stow the sail then to set it, as the men would now be fighting against the force of the wind. As the noise of the tortured rigging and sails grew louder and louder, Banain ran to the side of the ship, looked down at the starboard runner and realised why they were not moving. It had been necessary to heat the metal of the runners, so they could be shaped to fit the wooden supports. Where they had been heated, the ice had melted and then refrozen again, literally freezing the ship to the ice.

Not stopping to think the situation through, Banain concentrated his mind on the frozen runner and imagined it free of the ice. The effect was instantaneous. The ship could not move forwards, because the port side runner was still frozen to the ice. The only way all that power could go was to the side. With further terrible creaks and groans and the sound of splintering wood, Oldore started to tip over.

"YOU NEED TO FREE THE OTHER RUNNER, NOW!" Carlos shouted at Banain, realising at once what was happening. He was clinging onto the wheel to stop himself from sliding down the wildly canting deck. Looking forward, he could see mayhem, as the ship tipped past forty-five degrees. Every man and animal desperately tried to find some way to stop sliding down the deck. Without the benefit of hands or four legs, the penguins were having the worst problems. He watched in horror as king Aka and his entourage slid faster and faster down towards the side. If the ship went right over, they were in grave danger of being crushed underneath her.

Banain realised his mistake and was already charging down the increasing slope of the deck to get to the port hand side, so that he could free the runner from the ice. Seeing the King in mortal danger, he grabbed hold of the main mast to stop his forward momentum and concentrated his power on a large piece of cargo netting. Moved by his will, the netting snaked down the deck and sprang up in front of the king and his aids, stopping their slide. His problem now, was that he could not hold them safely and get to a position where he could see and free the other runner without letting them go again.

Carlos watched all this happening as if it were in slow motion; he knew they only had seconds before the ship went beyond the point of no return. All his years of training as sea, had not prepared him for a situation like this. At sea, the hull did not freeze itself to the floor. However, had he been at sea and the ship was threatening to broach, he would have steered away from the wind. Out of other options, that's what he did. Grabbing hold of the large top spoke of the wheel, he hauled on it to port. At first it did not budge, but then, accompanied by a terrible creaking and groaning, it started to move. Encouraged, Carlos threw every fibre of his strength into the task and was pleased when a couple of crewmembers managed to reach him and add to his efforts.

Combined with the leverage of the hull on the port runner and the twisting of the steering runners, the forces exerted were enough to break the ices frozen grip. Freed from her bondage, Oldore shot forward, building speed at an alarming rate. With the combined weight of three men hauling the wheel to port and no resistance to stop it turning, the wheel spun wildly in that direction, tossing them aside like chaff. Still balanced at forty-five degrees and riding on one runner, Oldore careered out of the construction camp, narrowly missing the two other ships parked on the ice.

Without anyone on the helm, she continued to turn sharply to port, building more speed as she went. Carlos had been thrown some distance from the wheel and was climbing back towards it, but as Oldore's speed increased, she kept turning. As the angle of the wind came dead astern, she slammed down onto both runners again with a sickening crunch, causing Carlos to hurtle to the other side of the deck. Traveling at over thirty miles an hour, Oldore kept turning in a wide circle. In a few moments she would be headed straight back towards the ice city of Artakra.

Chapter Twenty-Six

Since the worm had told Bodolf that he wanted to escape, the wolf's world had been thrown into confusion. Of course he wanted to escape more than anything else, but from the worm and with Honi, not as the Northlings means of escape. Kirr had explained in some detail why it was impossible to take Honi with them, he had said her Northling was loyal to Isbjorn and would do all it could to stop them. Then there was the direction that they would go. Bodolf wanted to head back to the south and reach the safety of old Seville. However, the worm had told him that the city was under siege and that they should travel west to a city called Artakra, where he believed he could gain the support of the creatures that lived there. When Bodolf had enquired why these creatures would help, Kirr had said that they were the only thing Isbjorn feared and he hoped to convince them to help him fight the black bear.

"Have you decided wolf?" It was the first Bodolf had heard from Kirr in several hours. The worm no longer had any control over him, but Bodolf knew that could change at short notice.

"We have to go soon or it will be too late; we are only a few hours away from the base," Kirr continued. The pitch of his normally drone like voice rose, indicating his heightened stress level.

"I cannot leave Honi," he said, repeating aloud what he had been saying in his head. "And I still do not trust you worm," he added.

"Listen Bodolf, I know you have no reason to trust me. However, if my intentions were not genuine, why would I bother with all this talk? I could just take over your body and escape without your cooperation. If Isbjorn takes us, we will not be able to help Honi. I am sure he has sensed my doubts and he will be able to wipe them away. This is our only chance to help all of them Bodolf, our only chance!"

"Ok worm, but if you are lying to me, I swear I will find a way to rip whatever you call a heart from your living body and eat it whilst you watch. Now, what is your plan?"

"It's very simple really, you can travel at twice the speed of the bears, and Honi is smaller and slightly slower so we can outrun them," Kirr replied.

"Oh it's so refreshing to have so much intelligence helping me! I feel so much better now you have shared your master plan with me," Bodolf said. However, he was already scanning the local terrain and calculating the best exit route to get them past the bears and Honi. With one of the bears traveling behind, one in front and Honi on his right hand side, he made his choice and exploded into a full run, turning sharply to his left to give the maximum angle away from his captors. Within seconds, he had reached nearly forty miles an hour, a speed he could only maintain for a short while. Glancing back, he could see that Honi was in close pursuit and that the bears were chasing, but falling behind quickly. After a while, he had to reduce his speed, but noted that Honi had not done the same. She was about twenty yards behind and closing the gap, the white bears not visible against the stark arctic glare. Bodolf knew that she should not be able to travel faster than he could, unless her worm was forcing her body past its limits. As he ran, Bodolf made a decision that he knew the worm in his head would not like, but he had to try. Stopping suddenly, he turned to face Honi who kept on coming, the distance closing rapidly.

"What are you doing? You must keep running! The bears will not have stopped, they will be here soon, then all is lost," Kirr said in his mind. Bodolf steeled himself to try to fight off the worm, if it attempted to take him over again.

"Honi will die from exhaustion if she carries on at that pace and I will not let that happen. You need to convince her worm to come with us or we will all die here and now. Or are you just going to take me over again and run like the maggot I think you are?"

"I need time to reason with her Northling, Sarr. It is younger than me and loyal to Isbjorn; I cannot just order it to obey me!"

Well think of something and quickly, I will not harm Ho...."

He never had time to complete the sentence as Honi ploughed into him, teeth aimed at his throat. Using his years of experience and greater bulk, Bodolf managed to evade the attack, her jaws snapping the thin air where he had just been. As she turned to attack again, Bodolf realised that he could not hold her off without hurting her for long and the bears were nearly upon them.

"Honi, fight the maggot in your head, remember who you are," Bodolf sent to his mate, as she prepared to attack again.

"The cur can't hear you Bodolf and I am not a weak willed traitor like Kirr. I know all about you; your mind will bend to the will of Isbjorn. Now yield to me, or you and your mate will suffer," the voice of Honi's parasite Sarr, said in Bodolf's head. At the same time, Honi launched herself again at Bodolf, her sharp teeth missing his neck as he lowered his head to deflect her attack; but finding his left ear, which she ripped savagely before he could pull away.

With blood pouring from his torn flesh onto the pristine snow, Bodolf backed away from his mate, who was bunching for her next attack and licking Bodolf's blood from her lips. Looking into her eyes, he could see none of Honi, just the malevolent presence of her invader. In his peripheral vision, he could see the lumbering figures of the two bears and he knew they just had moments before all would be lost.

"Your feeble attempt to escape is over cur, you will return with us to...." The voice went silent and Honi stopped, her eyes changing from malevolence to confusion and then recognition.

"Bodolf, Bodolf what is happening, you are hurt? Where are we? I dreamt I attacked you, that I tried to kill you!" Honi's worried voice was almost too much for Bodolf to bear. He had dreamt of finding her again, but not like this. Her emotions and inner hurt flooded over him as if released from a dam. She was realising that what she had thought was just a nightmare, was in fact reality; her awful parasite enforced actions replaying in her head, each terrible act now tearing into her consciousness.

"Honi we are in great danger, I will explain everything to you, but we must run. RUN HONI RUN."

Years of obeying Bodolf's hunting commands took over and she leapt into position behind him as he burst into a run away from the two bears, leaving dark red droplets of blood as well as their tracks behind them on the snow covered ice.

"Did you kill Honi's worm, Kirr?" He asked his unusually quiet parasite.

"He is not dead, just subdued. I can keep him this way as long as we stay close, but not for too long; although he is not an elder, his will is surprisingly strong." The faltering voice of Kirr replied.

Bodolf could sense that the Northling was at the limit of his ability and endurance, trying to subdue the worm in Honi's head. He also realised, that her reprieve from her Northling parasite could be very short-lived. Both he and Honi were already exhausted and losing their initial burst of speed. However, for once favour shone their way, as the bears, driven past their limits by their Northling parasites, fell to the ground behind them. Bodolf reduced the pace to a manageable lope and hoped that they would reach Artakra before Honi's parasite took control again.

Chapter Twenty-Seven

Wayland stood in front of the double gates that protected the main entrance to Old Seville and went through his remaining options again; it did not take long. He either killed his fellow citizens, or retreated to the dubious safety of the castle. The massive bar holding the two oak doors closed was splintered and bowed by the relentless pressure of the Northlings mind driven rock, which had been pounding away for the last six hours. The once beautifully crafted gates were a shredded and warped visage of their former glory. The fact that they had withstood the terrible punishment paid tribute to the skills of the artisans who had created them.

Wayland had sent all but his most skilled fighters back to the castle, with instructions to defend the Immortals with every man and creature. Now he stood shoulder to shoulder with two hundred of his best men, each armed with a wide shield and club. Behind them stood around a hundred more men, armed with bows and stone tipped arrows. To either side, around a hundred and fifty wolves, plains bulls, jelks and horses, all either too old or unwilling to leave.

"Remember, our task is to stop the Northlings from reaching the castle. I know these were our friends and allies only a short while ago, but the Northlings control them and they will try to take us if they can. Try to incapacitate rather than kill and do not let them spread out," Wayland sent to his section leaders who relayed the message to the rest of the troops.

The last of his words was punctuated by the tortured groan of splintered wood, as the pummelled bar holding the shattered gates closed, finally gave way. Instead of swinging inwards as designed, what was left of the gates collapsed to the floor creating a wooden barrier, which for the moment stopped the Northling conscripts from advancing.

"ARCHERS FIRE, THE REST OF YOU WITH ME," Wayland shouted, realising that he could use the collapsed gates to his advantage. Then he charged forward to take up position behind the makeshift wooden barricade. Above his head, he could hear the whistle of arrows and in front, he could see the devastation they caused as they found their targets. However, every time a man fell there was always another to take his place. As the first of the Northlings recruits reached him, he swung his club at his legs and heard a sickening crunch as the heavy weapon found its mark. The man collapsed to the ground and Wayland lifted his shield to deflect a blow from another, who had just replaced the one he had injured. As he raised his club again to counter the blow, he looked into the eyes of the Barkeep at his local tavern. A man he knew quite well and with whom, under the influence of his beverages, he had shared many a story. The moment of recognition was enough for the barkeep to raise his weapon and bring it down towards Wayland's unprotected head. If not for the quick actions of a freedom soldier behind Wayland, who deflected the shot with his shield, it could have been a very short battle for the commander. Steeling his resolve, Wayland concentrated on his fighting, ignoring the faces of the men he faced. The ring of shield and club wielding soldiers kept them from breaking through the narrow entrance, the few who did making easy picking for the wolves and other animals guarding the rear. As the troops at the front of the battle tired, they moved back to let fresher troops replace them. After several hours of fighting, Wayland stood at the back of his battling troops accompanied by Grinstead. He had blood running down his face from a glancing blow to the head and every part of his body felt pummelled.

"I am not sure how long we can hold them Grindor, they still have thousands of reserves, and we are done. Tell the Immortals they should leave the chamber soon," Wayland said, finding it hard to talk and breath.

"They ask that you hold as long as you can Wayland, they need more time," the ape replied.

"More time for what Grindor, there are no more reserves. The only option we have left once this line breaks is to barricade ourselves inside the castle, but that will not keep them out for long. What do they…"

A series of deafening bellows came from the gateway cutting off the rest of the question and causing both of them to turn and look towards its source. Above the heads of his men, Wayland could see the heads of gigantic polar bears and hear his men's screams as the white beasts ripped into their sparse ranks.

Leaving Grindor, Wayland pushed back through his men to help battle the giant bears, but things were not going well. He watched in dismay, as man after man fell under the huge paws of these creatures. Reaching the closest bear, Wayland unleashed an explosive blow at its head. His club made contact, but instead of felling the beast, it just maddened it. He raised his shield to deflect the bear's first retaliatory blow, but it smashed the shield as though made of matchwood. He felt himself lifted through the air and flying backwards towards the wall of the gateway; as he hit, his world turned into a seething sea of pain. Unable to deal with so many injuries at once, his brain shut down and the blackness took him.

Chapter Twenty-Eight

As Oldore crashed down onto both runners, Banain was able to release his protective hold on King Aka and his advisors. Looking forward, he could see the walls of Artakra growing alarmingly quickly in front. Swinging around to face the stern, he saw that no one was at the wheel and realised that he did not have time to reach it before Oldore reached the city wall. He remembered Carlos saying that the ship could not travel straight into wind, so he envisaged it turning towards it. He also remembered that the large new wooden lever beside the wheel was some kind of brake, so he also applied gentle mind pressure on that. To his great relief Oldore started turning away from the city and slowing down. Then, when Carlos managed to stand and take control of the wheel again, he released his grip on the mast and hurried over to the group of penguins on the floor under the pile of netting. All around him, crewmembers and animals alike were getting up, the crewmen rushing back to their assigned sailing positions, most of the rest looking around to see if anyone was hurt. Banain was pleased to see Lepe trotting up to him, apparently no worse for wear.

"Lepe check if the king is ok please," Banain said, grabbing the netting and pulling it clear. Freed of the heavy netting, one by one the penguins stood up, which was no simple matter on the still moving ship. The king was the last to rise and once upright, fixed Banain with a baleful stare, which did not bode well.

"Ket say, King thinks you not able to control anything Banan, first Nust, now this ship, both disasters. He not give you army Banain, he not give anything," Lepe translated. The disappointment for his leader was clear in his message.

"Tell the King I am sorry please Lepe," Banain said, nodding apologetically to the king and turning to walk back to Carlos, who now had full control of Oldore and was navigating her back into the camp.

Please organise the disembarkation of the King and his advisors. How long before all ships will be ready to leave Carlos?" Banain said as he approached the Captain.

It will take most of the day to test the other ships and load the stores; we should be able to leave at first light in the morning. I am sorry Banain; I should have tested everything more thoroughly. I take it we will not be receiving the support of the penguins and it is my fault," Carlos said. A mistake like this for his old master would have resulted in a public flogging and losing his rank, or worse.

"The blame lies with me Carlos; I should have given you more time to prepare. I have been rushing everything recently and it looks like I have lost the support of the Immortals and the penguins." As he spoke, Banain felt a deep sense of loss gripping his chest.

"You have the support of every man and animal here Banain. I have lived my life fighting out of fear and greed; for once I feel that I am on the right side," Carlos said.

"And if they won't help us, we will just have to do it alone. There is not a man or animal here that would not lay down their life for you," Garfled said. Banain had not seen him approach, but he now stood beside the blond warrior and put a reassuring hand on his shoulder as he spoke."

"If stupid jellyfish and penguins leaders not help, then we do without them. They not warrior like you Banan. Anyway, not all penguins not help. Ket say he have friends who want fight Northling jellyfish, they gonna get on ships when dark tonight," Lepe, who had also approached without Banain's notice, sent.

"I don't want to be responsible for more deaths, this will be very dangerous, do they understand that Lepe?"

"You not responsible Banan! You start wars…No. You infest free creatures…No. You want control world…No, but be better if you did!" Lepe said and dug Banain in the ribs with his one good horn.

"I don't think I will be able to come with you unless you tell me something Banain?" Garfled said. Banain's heart sank further on hearing those words; Garfled was his friend as well as trusted advisor, if he was having doubts...

"How am I ever going to convince Torrent to get back on the ship? He has sworn that he will never set foot aboard again," Garfled said, his face now wreathed in a large smile.

"Mariana get you both on board and look after you, she boss now," Lepe replied, backing away from Garfled, just in case the large warrior decided to take a swipe at him. As Garfled scowled at Lepe, Banain realised he was lucky to have such good friends. Whatever the future held, they would face it together.

The next morning, Banain awoke to the sound of the artic wind howling through Oldore's rigging. He had only managed to catch a few hours' sleep, as he had spent most of the night making sure everything was organised properly. In the early hours of the morning, Carlos had insisted that he go to his cabin. Feeling very groggy, the worries that had been plaguing him returned and the sound of the wind did nothing to ease his doubts. He had just collapsed on his bunk without undressing, so he strode to the door and out to the fighting deck. When he had gone to bed, Oldore had been in complete disarray; with stores and rigging heaped everywhere. Now everything had been stowed, the decks were clear, the crew were at their sailing positions, and Captain Torre stood on the steering deck. Climbing the short steps to join him, Banain noted Funchal and Neptune formed up behind them.

"I see you have been busy Captain," Banain said, not a little impressed.

"It did take a little while to get Torrent to board, but all ships and crew are ready to leave on your orders," Carlos said, a slight smile on his lips."

"I take it you remembered to free the runners?" Banan jibed.

"That mistake will not happen again, with your permission, can I give the order to set sail?" Carlos said his smile fading as he turned his mind to the serious business of navigating the fleet safely away from Artakra and heading in the direction Ket had provided.

"Granted Captain, let's see what these ice ships can do," Banain said, resisting the temptation to hold onto something.

"Send to all ships; set fully reefed mainsails only and release ice brakes on my command," Carlos instructed his first mate. As most men and creatures could mind talk over some distance, signalling flags had been replaced with this much faster communication method.

Captain Torre's strode to the wheel and as a small part of Oldore's mainsail unfurled, he released the ice brake. The only clew Banain had that the ship was actually moving, was that he could see the walls of Artakra moving gently away from them. There was almost no sensation of movement, other than a quite rumble as the runners built up speed over the ice.

"Send for Funchal to release brakes and then Neptune when Funchal is clear ahead," Captain Torre instructed. As Banain looked back, he saw the two ships moving off to follow Oldore as she steadily increased her speed across the ice. Within a few moments they were travelling at over thirty miles an hour, Captain Torres issuing sail trimming instructions to his crew to keep the ship driving forward.

"This is amazing Carlos! We are doing many times the speed we can on water and with much less sail," Banain said, moving to stand by the wheel. The noise level had risen, but only to a modest whooshing sound, accompanied by the odd bump as the ship passed over harder parts of snow.

"I know our test sail nearly ended in disaster, but it did show me the difference of sailing on ice to water. There is very little resistance to slow the ships down on the ice, If we travel into deeper snow we may travel slower, but I think we should be able to maintain this speed by increasing the sail area if need be," Carlos replied, concentrating on holding the fast moving ship on course. Glancing astern, he could see Funchal and Neptune matching Oldore in speed and direction.

"I will leave you to concentrate my friend," Banain said, patting Carlos on the shoulder.

A few hours later: Banain, Torrent, Garfled, Marianna, Lepe, and Ket were standing near the bow, watching the icy panorama speed by.

"I hope you do not feel so bad riding on the ice instead of the sea Torrent." Banain said.

"The motion, or lack of is definitely preferable and the speed impressive; but where do we speed towards?"

"We search for the Northlings base; the penguins have given us an idea of its direction. I was thinking it would take at least four days to get there, but if we maintain this speed, we could halve that time.

"And what we do when we get there Banan? We only few, Northlings have whole army!" Lepe sent. The response was uncharacteristic from the normally unshakable sheep, but Banain reasoned that infestation by a Northling for such a long time must have left its mark.

"I am not sure Lepe. If we can find out where our friends and family have been taken, then we will come up with a way to save them and I hope more," Banain sent back to the group. He still found the thought of having parents other than Krask strange, even though he knew they must be human.

"I am sure you will find a way to save them Banain; I have seen what you can do. And with my Garfled and Torrent to help you, the Northlings had better watch out," Mariana said, slipping one hand around Garfled's waist and scratching Torrent behind the ear with the other.

"Yes…yes of course we will find a way Banain; but I would have been happier if you had kept your weapon. I have a feeling we will need all the help we can get," Garfled added, looking slightly taken aback by Mariana's comment.

"There is something wrong with that weapon; when I use it, it feels unlike anything I have experienced before. We will have to do without Nust or the Immortals for this task," Banain sent, a chill running down his back as he recalled the feeling of indifference transmitted from the weapon as it had killed the bears in the river.

"I know you respect Immortals Banan, but when I trapped with them in hold of ship, I sensed something, not good something. I glad we without them and weapon," Lepe said, more to himself than the group.

Banain did not reply to Lepe's comment, although he noticed the shocked response from his fellow travellers in response to it. Most people and animals held the Immortals in almost god like esteem. To hear this from Lepe was unsettling, but after his argument with Turr, he too had nagging doubts.

"I suggest we all try and get some rest. Whatever faces us, will be faced better refreshed," Banain sent and walked off towards his cabin. He was disturbed by Lepe's comments and worried about how he was going to rescue his friends and parents. In reality, he had no plan at all, save finding and somehow freeing them under the noses of thousands of well-trained enemy soldiers. In every battle so far, the Immortals had helped shape and guide his plan. Now he was alone, without even his friends Bodolf or Teague to guide him. As he entered his room and sat down, he realised how much he missed the company and advice of the wolf and how much his heart ached for Teague.

Chapter Twenty-Nine

Sitting on the balcony outside Banain's quarters at the top of the Castle, Grindor watched events unfold in front of him. From this position, he could see the battle raging at the front gates. He had made all the preparations asked of him by the Immortals and was now in telepathic communication with them, relaying the events as he witnessed them. His heart sank as he saw the bears storming through the gates and Wayland's heroic efforts to fight them, but he knew that defeat had been inevitable.

With Wayland out of the battle, the elite Northling troops swiftly brushed aside opposition from the remnants of the Freedom Army. Grindor felt terrible; although he was more loyal to the Immortals than any other living creature, the sacrifice of so many seemed senseless. However, the last time they had met, Turr had been uncharacteristically reticent, as if distracted and did not offer any advice on how to deal with the situation. With no opposition, the Northlings marched in through the shattered gates and gathered row upon row in front of the castle. The doors to the castle were strong and there were further troops inside, but Grindor knew that it was just a matter of time before they breached the last of the defences. He left the balcony and walked slowly back down to the specially constructed chamber that housed the Immortals. As he entered the chamber, an ancient Immortal was as usual floating serenely in the crystalline water. However, as he watched, more and more joined him, the magnifying properties of the water pillar making them look much larger than their real size.

"Is the Northling Army gathered outside the castle Grindor?" They sang.

"They are gathering now. They have wiped out the last of our defences and Wayland has been defeated," Grindor replied, the memory of his friend falling still vivid in his mind.

"That was inevitable, we all grieve for his torment, but you must now follow our instructions very carefully Grindor," they sang, as more and more Immortals gathered in the column of water, which seemed to be swelling and growing.

Having received his instructions, Grindor left the chamber, walked back up to the main entrance hall, and instructed the guards to open the gates. After some argument, they complied and he walked out, his small ape figure almost comical in front of the ranks of massive polar bears and wolves that stood stock still, all eyes looking ahead, bar four. These belonged to a particularly large white wolf and a muscular human, who studied the diminutive figure of Grindor as he approached them.

The mental attack from the pair would have defeated nearly any other creature in a nanosecond. However, hundreds of years of service to the Immortals had equipped Grindor to shrug it off and he continued walking towards the pair, their eyes now showing surprise.

"I am Grindor, advisor and aid to the Immortals. I know your hosts Arkta and Izotz and it saddens me to see them and so many of our citizens used in this way. Why does your leader Isbjorn make these cowardly attacks on the free people Nezz?" Grindor sent, noting further surprise at the use of its Northlings name. The Immortals had found out much about the Northlings from Rekk, who had tried to infest Banain and ended up in Lepe; including information about the leaders of the invading army.

"Who do you call a coward, ape; your forces are weak and are no match for our army. Surrender your city, or better still send a so-called Immortal to do it. Oh I forgot, they cannot leave the confines of the water can they. They are weak and will bow to the will of Isbjorn," Nezz replied.

"Never underestimate the enemy Northling. The reason your army got this far, is because most of them were our subjects. I suspect you would be quite willing to kill your own, but it goes against everything we stand for. The Immortals were not aware of your existence until recently, but they are now. I am instructed to tell you that they will accept your surrender," Grindor said, sitting down calmly in front of the massed Northling Army.

"Enough of this, ape. You may be able to perform a few tricks with the aid of your masters, but you cannot defeat our army. You and all within the walls will soon be hosts to Northlings." As he spoke, Nezz sent a message to his commanders and as one the army moved to surround the small figure of Grindor.

Chapter Thirty

Bodolf and Honi moved at a steady silent pace across the crusted snow surface. Designed to survive in this environment, they blended perfectly with their background. It reminded Bodolf of his early years here, when he had crept into Honi's packs camp and stolen her away from them. Only it was not the same. There was little sign of the Honi that he loved and knew so well. Although subdued by Kirr, the worm infesting her brain was fighting him and as time passed, it was starting to take her over again.

Bodolf tried to talk to her, but received no answer. She just followed him, a plea for release from the maggot in her head etched into every step she took. Bodolf on the other hand, was strangely comfortable with the presence in his brain, which worried him. Since taking control of the lesser Northling in Honi's mind, Kirr had also been silent. Bodolf surmised it was because of the effort involved in keeping the other Northling subdued. They had been travelling for just over a day and night nonstop and they were in dangerous territory. Slightly behind and to the right, he could make out the outline of the mountain peaks that denoted the entrance to the Northlings base. He had given it as wide a berth as possible and did not think even the keenest eye could spot them at this distance, but all of his senses were on full alert, as he pushed his tired body onwards.

"I am sorry, Isbjorn knows we are here. I could not stop Honi's host from contacting him and I will not be able to keep it from controlling her for much longer." The words were like daggers through Bodolf's heart. He could tell that Kirr was at the edge of his reserves and feel the battle raging in his soulmate's mind. Looking back, he saw the faint outline of wolves and bears moving swiftly towards them, which soon materialised into the stark reality of their hunters. There were over a hundred wolves and as many bears closing the gap with them at an alarming rate.

Bodolf scanned the horizon; desperate for some means of escape, but all that lay in front was the vast surface of a frozen ocean. Then his keen eyes spotted something moving in the far distance in front of them and his heart filled with dread. He realised they were surrounded and had absolutely nowhere to run.

Chapter Thirty-One

Arkta felt the weight of Nezz's will leave him, as the Northling concentrated all its power on the challenge it and the other Northlings now faced. It was strange to be in control of his body again and somewhat unsettling. Although the relationship he and Arkta had with the invaders was not what he was expecting when they went to raise an army, there was a strange comfort in it and the results had outweighed all of his expectations. Here they were only a few years later, standing before the last meagre city defences. He was appalled, but not surprised that his father's forces had been so easy to defeat. His father had lost his killer instincts when he saved that freak of nature Banain, instead of killing him and eating his heart. His army had been lucky to beat Lord Erador's Army, but they would not win the battle here.

As his soldiers moved towards the ape, he felt a chill in the air, accompanied by a static charge that made every hair on his body stand erect. As one, the army seemed to freeze into place, although they were not quite frozen, just slowed considerably. The ape seemed unaffected by this phenomenon and now walked normally between his frozen soldiers. As Arkta observed the events unfolding in slow motion, the doors and windows of the castle opened and fingers of water, suspended just above the ground emerged and moved towards the soldiers. Each finger was around half a meter in diameter and glowed with a radiant blue light as they snaked forward. As the first of the fingers made contact with a soldier, he fell to the ground and lay silent. Leaving a small tendril of water connected to the prone figure, the finger moved through the ranks repeating the process, as did the others. Within a short space of time, most of the Northling Army lay on the floor connected to the fingers of water. He watched as one approached him and felt the tingling sensation increase as it made contact. His legs collapsed beneath him, as an Immortal swimming in the water, entered his body and took control of his mind.

"I am an Immortal and you are safe now Arkta. I will find the Northling that has been controlling you and remove it," his new occupant said in his mind.

"You may find that a little harder than you think squid," Arkta replied and sent a message as instructed by Nezz.

During the last three months, the Northling Army had not just been infesting locals and building siege weapons. It had also been breeding thousands of polyps, which had resided in a dormant state in their members. The signal from Arkta was all that was required to wake them and within each soldier the Immortals had entered, hundreds of them woke and started attacking them. In their dormant state, the Immortals had not been able to detect the presence of more than the one active Northling in each host. Now they were not only aware of the extra invaders, they were battling for their lives against them.

With so many polyps against each Immortal, the fights were short and brutal. The invading Northlings had been genetically adapted to tear through the defences of their enemies and take over there core functions. Once achieved, they entered the tendrils of water still connecting the larger fingers and attacked every Immortal they encountered.

Nezz was in his mind again and allowed Arkta to keep control of most of his bodily functions; a favour seldom granted.

"You did well cur. The battle against the so-called Immortals is going well, but it will take much of my power to defeat the obsolete jellyfish. I will allow you to keep control of most of your mind and body to carry out my instructions, but do not fail me," Nezz said in his mind. Getting to his feet, Arkta looked around, noting that most of the army was standing again. Just behind him and now not looking so confident, the ape was starting to move towards the open door to the castle. Pleased to be in control of his body again and with all his Polyps off to battle the jellyfish, Arkta spun around and charged at Grindor, giving the shocked primate no time to defend himself. He barrelled him to the floor and closed his fangs around his neck. As his teeth broke through the ape's skin, planula invaded his blood and headed towards his brain.

Chapter Thirty-Two

Banain stood at the bow of Oldore with Lepe, the odd-looking couple scanning the seemingly endless sea of ice in front of them. To the left and the right Funchal and Neptune kept station, all three vessels traveling at well over thirty miles an hour. Krask had left to scout the way ahead again, after returning with news that had both excited and worried him.

"It ok Banan, me sure it Bodolf and Honi." Lepe sent, sensing the torment in his lifelong friend.

"Krask said that he could not contact either of them, that something was blocking their minds. He said it looked like they were either running away from an army of Northlings, or leading them towards Artakra," Banain sent back. He was not sure if he could face his lifelong friend and mentor in battle again. The memories of how they had met were not something he liked to recall. Drawn by the uncontrolled power of Banain's mind, Bodolf had come close to killing Banain on several occasions, before the Immortals had managed to convince the wolf that he should be protecting the child. Since then, Bodolf had been mentor and friend to both child and man.

"Pah, Krask not so clever, I know smelly wolf not hurt you again. He escaped from Northlings with Honi, so now we rescue," Lepe sent, adopting his normal no nonsense attitude.

"We are already too close to the Northlings base! The plan was to creep up and scout for opportunities, not charge in like this. We could lose the chance to rescue anyone if our presence is known."

"CONTACTS ON PORT BOW!" The shout was from the lookout at the top of the mast. Banain looked in the direction indicated, but could not see anything.

"I'm going to the steering deck Lepe," Banain sent, as he ran back. Carlos was at the wheel, also searching the horizon for confirmation of the lookouts sighting. As Banain arrived, the other ships veered off in opposite directions acting on a signal from Oldore.

"Krask, can I share vision?" Banain sent to the eagle flying somewhere above and in front. One of his skills was the ability to share the views of other creatures. Although he could just force his way in, he always asked first.

"Yes of course, but whatever you are planning, you need to do it fast!" Krask replied. Banain let his mind slip into that of his circling surrogate father and instantly his view changed from the deck of the speeding Oldore, to a vista high above the ice. Directly below, he could see the forms of two running wolves; just a short distance behind and closing the gap quickly, was a whole army of wolves and bears. As soon as he saw the wolves, Banain knew it was definitely Bodolf and Honi. He tried reaching out with his mind to them, but they were either too tired or scared to hear him. He could just make out the shapes of the three ships, but from this distance, they looked like another army, growing in size every second. Banain realised that they would probably think the ships something to do with the Northlings, rather than a rescue party. Bodolf and Honi turned sharply to the right and ran at an angle to both friend and foe, confirming his fears.

"Krask, you need to go down and try and get them to run towards the ships, otherwise we will not make it to them in time."

"Even if they see me, how do I tell them that the ships are not the enemy?"

I do not know, but I am sure you will come up with something, I need Bodolf and Honi to be running directly towards us, or we will not be able to rescue them… Carlos, signal the other ships to head towards either side of the army and try and draw them away from the centre," Banain sent to the captain.

All of a sudden, Banain felt extremely nauseous, as Krask went into an almost vertical dive towards Bodolf and Honi. He was unable to drag himself away from the eagles viewpoint and as the ice rushed up to meet him, was sure that Krask had miscalculated. However, at the very last moment, the world tilted back from vertical to level, the surface of the ice flashing by, a blur beneath the speeding raptor. Directly in front, Banain could see the running figures of Banain and Honi, their tongues hanging out of their mouths, their breaths leaving small clouds of vapour behind them.

Again, Banain was sure that Krask would crash into the running wolves. However, at the very last second his borrowed view tilted crazily upwards and then back down, as the eagle rose and turned sharply back towards Oldore. Banain could hear Krask keening to get the wolves attention, and through the eagles eyes he saw the recognition in Bodolf's. For a few seconds they kept on in the same direction, then as one they both turned and with a renewed burst of speed, followed the eagle towards the approaching ice ships.

With a quick, "thank you," to Krask, Bodolf pulled his vision back and assessed the situation. Neptune and Funchal had picked up speed and were now nearing either side of the Northling Army. Some of the Northling forces on either side had peeled off to face the ships, but not as many as Banain had hoped for and the main part of the force was still chasing Bodolf and Honi. Although Oldore was traveling at over thirty miles an hour, it seemed to Banain that the distance to the canine pair was closing agonisingly slowly.

"We will not have time to stop and pick them up Banain; in fact we will not have time to turn and avoid the army if we get much closer," Carlos yelled. The Captains hands were tight on the wheel, his forehead beaded with sweat, despite the freezing conditions.

"Set every inch of sail you can and have the men line the sides of the ship with any long poles they can find. Pass Bodolf and Honi to port as close as you can, we will only have one chance at this," Banain sent, switching to mind talk as he raced down towards the middle of the ship where Garfled was standing with Lepe, Torrent, and Maria.

"Garfled, attach that netting to a long rope; secure the end to Torrent and both of you move to the right hand side of the ship near the rail. Lepe, clear an area in front of

Torrent as far forward as possible. I don't have time to explain everything now, so wait for my instructions, it will all become clear in a few moments," Banain sent as he ran past the startled group. Back at the bow once more, Banain looked forward and was horrified to see that the Northlings army had almost caught the fleeing wolves. Oldore had picked up some more speed with the extra sails set, but it was not going to be enough to reach the defectors before their pursuers did. Focusing his mind, Banain sent an icy blast of air over the top of the pair into the front ranks of the chasing wolves. Although not powerful enough to stop them, it did slow them down considerably. Unfortunately, Krask, who had been flying in front, above Bodolf and Honi, had also been in its path, the force of the wind almost knocking him to the ground.

Knowing that he would receive a few choice words from Krask if they managed to pull this off, Banain looked back and focused on the netting now tied by a rope to Torrent. He envisaged it spreading out on the surface of the ice beside the speeding ship and the netting followed his commands.

"Torrent, take up the slack on the rope and be ready to pull when I say. Garfled, you will need to try to steady the net as Torrent pulls. Lepe, position some of the sailors with the long poles around Garfled and the rest around the sides of the ship," Banain sent, as he watched the distance rapidly diminish between Oldore and the labouring wolves. His gust of wind had slowed down the chasing army just enough and as the bows of Oldore flashed passed the pair, Banain dropped the bottom of the net onto the ice, leaving the top a few feet above. As Bodolf and Honi ran headlong into it, Banain wrapped it around them and lifted.

"PULL TORRENT, PULL... Garfled, stop them banging against the side of the ship. Lepe, get the sailors to fend off any borders," Banain said, releasing his hold on the netting and counting on Torrent and Garfled to bring the wolves aboard safely. Concentrating his efforts forward again, he saw that the Northling Army were just meters away.

"We cannot turn Banain; there is no time!" Carlos sent.

"Do not try; go straight through the middle of them," Banain sent back and once again focused his mind. This time he envisioned the loose snow on the surface of the ice rising up all around Oldore, whilst at the same time erecting a barrier around the front of the speeding ship. Within seconds, the world changed from a clear stark arctic day, to a grey snow laden blizzard and visibility dropped to a few feet.

"PREPARE TO FEND OFF!" He shouted, as he felt the first rank of the Northling Army make contact with the barrier in front of Oldore. He sensed rather then saw their bodies pushed to either side of the speeding ship and as Oldore ploughed further into their ranks, they made contact with more and larger enemies.

Whilst the wolves had no way of climbing up the sheer sides of the ship, the bears were a different matter. At first most were too disoriented to realise what was happening before Oldore passed them by; but a few managed to cling on and start climbing up the sides. Using the long poles the sailors managed to push most of the bears from the ship, but the sheer weight of enemy numbers was slowing Oldore down and more and more bears were gaining footholds on her hull.

Looking back, Banain could see that Torrent and Garfled had nearly managed to swing the net containing Bodolf and Honi onto the deck. However, just before it cleared, a large white claw grabbed the bottom, followed by a second one. Banain watched helpless as a massive white head followed the claws. The weight of the bear and the two wolves was too much for Torrent on the slippery deck and slowly the net started to disappear back over the side. Already using all his power to deflect the Northling Army away from the ship, Banain was powerless to do anything to help. Then a large horn poked the side of the bears head, causing it to release its grip on the net and tumble to the ice below.

"Hey Banan, Lepe save day again. I told you Mariana feed fat bull too well," Lepe sent to everyone, as he stood smugly watching Torrent pull the net back over the side of the ship again.

"Well done Lepe, but I think you should be careful what you say about animals you are trapped on a small boat with!" Banain admonished, noting the look in Torrents eyes. Then he turned back and was relieved to note that they had pushed through the ranks of the Northling Army and were picking up speed again. Releasing the shield, Banain focused on helping the sailors push the last of the clinging bears back onto the ice. Then he rushed to where a small crowd was gathering around the net containing a very agitated Honi and an unconscious Bodolf. As he approached he tried to make contact with them, but the presence of a Northling was clear in Honi and Bodolf was unconscious.

"Lepe, can you ask Ket if he can help us remove these parasites from our friends please? I will be back in a moment," Banain said as he strode on towards the steering deck and a slightly less anxious looking Captain.

"That was well done Banain; had those bears managed to board us, we would have had major problems," Marcos said, his eyes firmly glued to the heading of the ship and trim of the sails.

"I am not sure that Krask will be so complimentary, I last saw him being blasted towards the south! What is the situation with the other ships?"

"Both passed either side of the Northling Army and we are on a convergence course. We will be together again soon, but what is our plan now?"

"I am not sure Carlos; let's put some distance between us and this Northling Army and then decide," Banain said, as he took one last look behind at the receding Northling Army. Then he walked back to where the penguins had joined the group surrounding Bodolf and Honi.

"They are ready Banan, but only can do Honi now, not Bodolf as he unconscious," Lepe said, translating the information from Kirr.

Honi had stopped struggling against the net and now regarded Banain with eyes that shone with another presence, a presence he thought, which would like to rip his throat open.

"Ok Lepe, ask them to go ahead please."

As before, the penguins started chanting and rolling their heads, the sound so euphoric and mesmerising that Banain almost found himself drawn in. Mentally shaking off the effects, he watched as one of the penguins moved towards Honi and then as the chanting reached its crescendo, its sharp beak buried itself between her eyes.

Chapter Thirty-Three

The pain between Bodolf's eyes was so intense; he thought he would pass out again. He remembered banging against the side of a ship after being scooped up in a net along with Honi, but he did not think this pain was associated with that. Managing to open his eyes, they came into direct contact with another small pair, so close he could not manage to focus on them. He could hear a strange chanting, which was robbing him of the will to resist whatever the rest of the body attached to those eyes was doing to him.

"It looks like we are parting company wolf," the tired voice of Kirr said in Bodolf's mind. The words should have pleased him, but for some strange reason they did not. As his vision cleared, he saw the familiar figure of Banain and many of his friends standing above him. Honi was also there, looking down on him. Their voices were urging him to relax and let something that sounded like, "penguin," do its work. He felt another presence inside his mind, searching for the Northling, who shrank away from its approach.

He should have been happy to get rid of the worm in his head, but he realised that he could not. Summoning what remained of his mental strength, Bodolf pushed back against his would be rescuers attempt to remove Kirr, and then used his physical strength to get to his feet and shake his head. The consequences of these combined actions, was to break the connection with the penguin called Tak and send the bird tumbling across the floor, and to cause Banain, Garfled and some of the sailors to pounce on him and wrestle him back to the deck. Looking through the sea of legs and arms, he saw the disgruntled recently detached creature pick itself up from the floor and head back towards him with intent. Bodolf knew that he would not have a second chance to save the worm in his head and he still was not sure why he wanted to.

"Banain, can you hear me? It is me, Bodolf, not the Northling," Bodolf sent, knowing he only had moments to act.

After a few moments, Banain said; "I can hear something that sounds like you... However, these Northlings are very clever and this one is very powerful. If it is you just relax and let Tak to his job."

Bodolf realised Banain was sitting on the back of his neck, holding his head still for the advancing bird thing.

"I know this sounds crazy Banain; but I do not want you to remove this Northling from me, not yet anyway. He helped us escape from the Northlings and he wants to help us fight them. We need him Banain," Bodolf sent, his reasons sounding weak even to him.

"You were leading the Northling Army to Artakra, Bodolf. Honi has already told us what they forced you to do. Now just lie still for a few moments. We will talk more when I am sure I am talking to Bodolf," Banain sent with finality in his voice.

"Bodolf do you trust me?" Kirr said, deep in Bodolf's mind.

"I am not sure."

"I need to do something now, which will not go down well with your friends. If you do not agree, I will do nothing."

"What will happen if you do nothing?

"I will be.....eaten. That is the simplest way I can explain it. The penguin that approaches is a long time predator of our species. It will draw me into itself and I will die."

"Is that not what you do to others Kirr?"

"Yes."

"Then why should I protect you?"

"Because I can help you defeat Isbjorn.

As Bodolf watched, Tak approach and he heard the mesmerising chanting resume and he felt torn with indecision.

"Will my friends or anyone be harmed?" Bodolf could feel the euphoric effect of the chanting now and watched almost mesmerised as Tak positioned himself for his second attempt to free him from the Northling.

"No."

Bodolf's decision was strange really. If he had never met and befriended Banain, he would have let them rip the worm out of his head without a second thought. However, it was the teachings of the boy that influenced him now and so he said:

"You have my permission."

Banain felt torn with doubt. He, Garfled, and some sailors were using all their weight to keep the massive form of Bodolf immobile on the jolting deck of Oldore. Tak had just about regained position and was ready to try to remove the Northling again; but Banain was not sure it was the right thing to do. Since his short conversation with Bodolf, he had doubts about killing the Northling. He knew how powerful and dangerous they were, and yet... He sent a message to Lepe:

"Tell Tak to wait a minute, I am not sure this is right."

"No Banan, no wait. Kill it now, it very bad," Lepe replied instantly.

"I know they made you suffer Lepe, but I am sure I was talking to Bodolf and not the Northling just now and he did not want it killed."

"Tak not stop. He say he kill Northling now!"

Before either of them could argue further, black tendrils emerged from Bodolf's mouth and nose and quickly moved to touch all those around the wolf. As the tendrils made contact, each recipient seemed to freeze in place. As a tendril reached Banain, he felt a sensation that reminded him of his sessions with the Immortals.

Looking around, he could see that only he and Tak were unaffected by the effect. Although slowed by the tendrils, his beak was now moving towards a point between Bodolf's eyes.

"I am the Northling, Kirr, who resides within your friend, Bodolf. You have no reason to trust me, as I have committed terrible acts and do not deserve your compassion. However, there is much you need to know about us. In a few moments, the Penguin will end my life. Your friend Bodolf has told me about you Banain and if only a little of it is true, you will give me the chance to be an ally and prove that I mean no harm to you. The deep voice of Kirr intoned in Banain's mind.

"These are not the actions of an ally, let my friends go and leave my mind," Banain replied, shocked that the Northling had entered his mind with such ease.

"I will Banain, but think on this. My power is nothing compared to that of Isbjorn. I could kill you now with ease. He will rip the souls from every living creature on this planet and bend their minds to his purpose. He does not need me to defeat you or your followers and his army in the south is most probably already defeating the Immortals. Like it or not, I hold the key you need to save this planet from Isbjorn's reign."

As Kirr finished speaking the black tendrils of power dissolved and as Banain watched, Tak plunged his beak once again between Bodolf's eyes.

Bodolf felt a sharp stab, then the feeling of the other presence invading his mind once again. He could feel Kirr shrinking from this. He tried to rise and dislodge the bird, but this time they held him down firmly. Then a third and very familiar presence entered, with an intensity that surprised the wolf yet again; it was Banain. As host to these events, all Bodolf could do was observe. It was clear that the bird did not want to be disturbed in its efforts to remove the Northling, but he sensed that Banain was managing to stop his efforts to do so. Then Banain spoke in his mind:

"Bodolf, I have stopped Tak from removing the Northling from you for now. I have also isolated you from them both. As I can only keep up this level of control for a short while, is it ok if I search your memories so that I can be sure it is safe to let the Northling live?"

Trusting his friend completely, Bodolf agreed and felt the now familiar sensation of yet another entity rummaging through his mind.

After what seemed like an age to Bodolf, he experienced a sharp pain in his head and between his eyes, as Tak removed his beak and backed away from him. Then he felt the combined weight of Banain, Garfled and the sailors lift from his body. He could not feel the presence of Banain, Tak, or Kirr in his mind. His head was his own again.

Testing his limbs one by one, Bodolf pushed himself to his feet and stretched. Although he felt bruised, battered, and had the worst headache ever, he felt fine. Looking around he spotted Honi and ran towards her, overjoyed to see that she was not hurt. As he drew closer, she snarled and raised her tail, not the reaction he had been expecting.

"Honi it's me." He sent, rolling onto his back to show he was no threat to her.

"Is it? How do I know that? Why would you not have that thing in your head killed after all they have done to us? I am sorry Bodolf, but stay away from me until it is gone," Honi snarled and stalked away.

"Honi right, you stupid to keep worm in head wolf, no one trust you now," Lepe sent and walked away. Bodolf stood up again and looked at each of his friends, noting the distrust in every one's eyes, except for Banain.

"What did you do Banain, I don't feel the presence of Kirr and yet..." Bodolf sent, watching Honi and his friends walking away from him.

"He is still there Bodolf, but has agreed not to communicate or interact with you in any way, until you have had time to consider your decision to let him stay in your mind. I have informed every one of the situation and it is up to you to work out how to deal with this. Having been in contact with Kirr, I can just about understand your decision Bodolf; but others, especially those who have been affected by the Northlings, will not take kindly to having one as powerful as Kirr in their midst."

"Is there any other way he can survive, without being in me? Bodolf asked, knowing the answer.

"I do not think so my friend. The penguins do not act as hosts to the Northlings; they feed on them. The Immortals may be able to help, but I am not on good terms with them now and they are not here anyway. If you want to spare

Kirr, it may be at the expense of keeping Honi and your friends," Banain said. Bodolf noted the comment about the Immortals, but decided to discuss it later.

"Does that include you Banain?" Bodolf sent, dreading the answer.

"No my friend, I know and trust you. Now that I am sure I am talking to you and not Kirr, I will respect your decisions, as I always have. I have asked Kirr to keep himself isolated until you request his presence. But be aware Bodolf, whilst he is in your mind he is a part of you and can feel, see, smell and experience everything you do."

"I know Banain…. I know," Bodolf sent, looking again for Honi and receiving a hostile stare from her that sent shards of grief deep into his heart.

Chapter Thirty-Four

Krask flew towards Old Seville, his head full of conflicting emotions. The rescue of Bodolf and Honi should have been a joyous event; but Bodolf's decision to let his Northling parasite live, had created a large divide between him and the ones he loved. He had not had the chance to speak to Bodolf yet, but he found it hard to accept the fact that another presence was living in his friends head. He found it even harder to believe the information that the parasite had provided regarding the Northling Army taking Old Seville. As he wrestled with these unwanted emotions, a familiar voice spoke in his mind.

"Krask, where have you been? We were worried about you," Grindor said.

Although happy to hear his friends voice, Krask was surprised he had been able to make contact with him so far away.

"I am fine Grindor, how goes it with the Northling Army? We had reports that they were attacking the City," Krask replied, just able to pick out the distinctive shape of the castle in the distance.

"They were no match for us; we drove them back to the great woods. Wayland is chasing after them, killing off the stragglers," Grindor replied, then added quickly; "Did you find Banain?"

These words set off alarms in Krask's mind. Although the voice sounded like Grindor, it was saying things he knew the ape would never say.

"Let us speak together when I arrive, I am not far away."

As he replied, Krask noticed something black in the sky high above him. Focusing his powerful vision, he discerned a group of around twenty ravens.

"Have you sent a welcoming party?" Krask sent to Grindor, his mind racing through his options of escape.

"There are many Northling infested birds in the area. The ravens will make sure you arrive safely," Grindor's voice replied. Krask had known the ape for many years and all of his senses were telling him this was not his friend communicating with him. Making his decision, he deployed mental walls to ward of further communication, or worse, with whatever was in control of his friend and turned to escape the ravens. Krask was a large eagle. With a wingspan of over three meters and weighing close to thirteen kilos, he could see off most other denizens of the sky, but these ravens were different.

Even before the great freeze, ravens were one of the most intelligent aves species on the planet, able to communicate between each other with a great deal of sophistication. Recognising this innate ability, the Northlings favoured these birds over all others, as they only needed to infest the leader to control its subordinates. Seeing their prey turn away from him, the leader instructed half of his flight to descend and harry the eagle, whilst he and the rest continued to shadow from above.

Krask started a shallow dive to maximise his speed. Although he could fly a lot higher than the ravens, they had a significant height advantage on him. Once he was close to ground, he would have to fly level reducing his speed advantage. Instead of staying together, the first group of ravens took individual routes, each angling just a little higher than the next. The reason for this soon became clear, as using its height advantage, the first of the birds dove towards Krask whilst the rest waited. At the last moment Krask performed a tight loop, spiralling passed the raven, which could not slow down enough to follow the eagle through the manoeuvre. Within seconds, the second raven dropped down on Krask, this time managing to knock him downwards before Krask could perform an effective evasive manoeuvre. Time after time, the ravens attacked in this way forcing the large eagle lower with each attack. Krask knew it was just a matter of time before he ran out of sky and searched the terrain desperately for a solution to his predicament. In the opposite direction, he could just make out the range of mountains that were his home before moving to Old Seville. If he could make it there, he may have a chance.

Fending off another attack, this time by two ravens, Krask turned and used his dwindling energy to power towards the distant mountain. To reach it he would have to pass very close to Old Seville, but he had a short respite from the harrying attacks, as the raven force had expected him to try to return to the North, there forces positioned to prevent him from doing that. The respite did not last long though and with each mile gained, Krask lost valuable height. Apart from forcing him lower with every attack, the rooks were also inflicting wounds. His body was full of pain from multiple beak stabs and talon rakes. Below those injuries, his muscles, heart and lungs seared in agony from the efforts to keep him in flight.

Every now and then a rook would get too bold and Krask would feel with satisfaction his beak or talons connecting with one of the black antagonists, but it made little difference to his situation. He was passing close to the east of Old Seville and was almost level with its rooftops. The ground was dangerously close and looking towards the city, he could see more rooks streaming out to intercept him. He no longer had the energy to try to evade the attacks and it felt like he was flying through a solid wall of sharp beaks and claws. He knew his lifeblood was soaking away through his feathers and could only just see glimpses of the mountains that were his birthplace and where he had raised Banain. Realising that he would not make it home, Krask used the very last of his energy to grab the nearest rook, sink his beak into its heart, and then he fell the last few feet with the dead antagonist to the ground, hitting with terrible life robbing force. He smiled inwardly as he realised he could be with his beloved Krys again.

Chapter Thirty-Five

Far to the North, Banain felt as if something had snapped inside. He was deep inside Bodolf's mind, quizzing Kirr regarding the size and disposition of the Northling forces, when the feeling struck him with such intensity, it made every hair on his body stand on end. Along with that feeling, came another of terrible emptiness. Banain knew something terrible had happened to his surrogate father. It felt as if there was a terrible black hole inside him, where the eagle's presence used to reside.

"I am sorry chosen one, but I warned you that sending the eagle to Old Seville was not a good idea. Isbjorn's forces control everything you hold dear in the south. You need to trust my advice if you are to find a way to defeat his forces." Kirr's words were like coffin nails, each one hammering away Krask's existence in Banain's mind and confirming his worst fears regarding his surrogate father. Pulling out of Bodolf's mind, he ran out of his cabin, up on to the deck, and climbed to the very top of the main mast, passing the startled lookout on the way. He looked to the South and quested with his mind for any trace of Krask, but found nothing. He stayed there for hours, braced against the jolting wood and freezing arctic wind, the tears of his loss frozen to his cheeks. When he was just a few days old, Krask's mate, Krys, had rescued him from certain death, losing her own life in the attempt. Krask had kept him warm, fed him, protected him, taught him, and brought him to the Immortals. Krask was his eyes and ears, his mentor.....and his friend; he could not imagine life without him.

"You need to come down Banain, you will freeze to death," Bodolf said gently in his mind, He was standing at the foot of the mast looking up, his deep green eyes shining with empathy.

"He is dead Bodolf....Krask is dead. I can no longer feel him.

You cannot be sure of that; perhaps there is some other reason for your loss of contact..." Bodolf started.

"NO. KRASK IS DEAD." Banain shouted out with all his mental and audible power, cutting off any further attempts to placate him. It was a strange spectacle for the crew of Oldore; they knew something was wrong, but were in awe of the legend and power of Banain. Therefore, when they saw him burst from his cabin and climb the mast they left him well alone.

"If Krask dead, he no want you freeze, or fall of mast. You no monkey Banan, come down and behave like Krask want. He not like this." Looking down Banain could see the two black beady eyes of Lepe staring up at him, along with those of many of his friends. Knowing that Lepe would not take no for an answer, he took one last look to where his last contact with Krask had come from, and froze again!

Since rescuing Bodolf a day earlier, the free ships had been patrolling up and down between the Northlings base and Artakra. As Banain had quizzed Bodolf as to the Northlings intentions and discussed each piece of information with his advisors, a very worrying picture of the strength and purpose of Isbjorn's army was becoming clear. Now that purpose revealed itself in frightening detail. As his mind tried to take in the scene in front of him, the lookouts call took the words from his mouth.

"HUGE NORTHLING ARMY ON PORT BOW CAPTAIN!"

In a moment, Captain Torre was scrambling up to the lookout post and Banain was lowering himself from the main peak to join him. The three of them stood there for a moment mesmerised. For as far as the eye could see the horizon was full of Northling warriors. Packs of wolves ranged in front of the force, followed by teams of bears pulling gigantic snow sleds full of human soldiers. Behind them more bears pulled large siege engines, whose long wooden appendages cut dark lines into the arctic horizon: which a dark black oily smoke that was forming in the wake of the army's passage was slowly obliterating. As they watched, the closest machines arm sprang into the air, releasing a ball of fire at the small fleet. The fiery ball arced through the air and landed just short of Funchal, but then bounced along the ice, sending flaming shards in all directions. Quite a few reached her, setting rigging, wood, and sail on fire wherever they touched.

"SIGNAL THE FLEET TO TURN TO STARBOARD AND SET ALL SAIL" Carlos shouted and scrambled back down the rigging to make sure they carried out his orders. Banain turned his attention to helping the crew of Funchal put out the fires on board. He created several mini twisters, which sucked up snow and deposited it on the worst of the blazes. As he concentrated his efforts, he saw several more flaming balls arcing through the sky toward the fleet, which was now gathering speed as it turned away from the army, sails appearing on the yards in quick succession. The fleet was now in range of more of the siege machines and for what seemed like an eternity, Banain kept creating mini tornadoes to combat the growing number of fires on the ships. Realising that he could not keep on using energy at this level for much longer, he created a powerful gust of wind behind the three ships, which blew them out of the range of the siege engines for the time being. Weary from helping with the fires and from his prolonged stay up the mast, he climbed down onto the bouncing deck of Oldore; which along with Funchal and Neptune was careening along at high speed. Feeling decidedly unstable, he made his way back to Marcos, who was clinging on to the wheel, along with another two crewmembers. Looking back Banain was relieved to see the Northlings army falling behind the speeding ships.

"How far is it to Artakra?" Banain shouted, competing with the sounds of the rigging groaning under the pressure of the sails and the noise of the runners bouncing over the arctic ice.

"About six hours at this speed I recon, if the ships hold together long enough that is," Marcos replied, looking up uneasily at the main mast, which was visibly bending under the pressure of the sails.

"We have to warn the city as soon as we can, Marcos, if the Northling Army reaches them unprepared; I hate to think what will happen. I will send Kra…" Banain stopped halfway through saying the name, the grief flooding back, as he realised he no longer could call on his surrogate father and lifelong friend.

"I am sorry for your loss Banain, we all are. Krask was a father to us all and we will all miss him. I will drive the ships as hard as I can, but what Artakra can do to defend itself against such a force is beyond me," Marcos said as he fought to keep the vessel on course, relieved that the ship demanded all his attention, preventing him from having to look into Banain's grief stricken eyes.

"Unless we find some way of defeating the Northlings, Krask's death will have been in vain. I intend to find that way. Have the fleet continue to Artakra and ask every senior officer on board, to gather on the foredeck in one hour please Captain," Banain said, pushing the grief to the back of his mind and concentrating on the problem at hand. Ten minutes later, locked in mind-to-mind communication with Bodolf and Kirr, the information was flowing both ways. An hour later as he and Bodolf walked past the assembled crew, you could cut the atmosphere with a knife. Since refusing to have the Northling removed, Bodolf had become a pariah. The only person willing to go near him was Banain, so he had spent most of his time in his cabin or with the blond warrior. As the pair stopped and turned to face the crew, several of them turned to leave, including Honi.

"STOP, I want everyone's attention; no matter what you think of Bodolf and the Northling he carries."

"You mean the parasite that is eating into his brain and influencing yours as well," Honi replied, as she turned to stare at her mate.

"Honi, I know that you and Lepe have good reason to hate and distrust the Northlings. Nevertheless, without Kirr's help, our whole way of life is threatened. If we do not understand what we are facing, we are fighting in the dark. For whatever reason, Kirr has decided to help us and I fear that without that help we will not find any way to defeat the Northlings. Bodolf is one of my closest friends and mentors. I do not believe the Northlings could sway his will and like Krask, he would rather give up his life then submit to their will. If Bodolf trusts Kirr enough to let him stay in his mind, then so do I. At the mention of Krask's name, the ship was silent except for the sounds of the speeding vessel and Banain's voice. Seizing the moment Banain continued with the trickiest part of his address.

"For the last hour I have allowed Kirr access to my memories, in the hope that he can find something that I have missed, that will help us gain the upper hand over the Northlings and he thinks he may have done so. Kirr has discovered that the artefact Nust is much more than a weapon; it is in fact a type of portal to a species even more ancient than the Immortals. He believes that Isbjorn is seeking it and that he knows it lies buried within the ice at Artakra. If Isbjorn takes possession of Nust, then there will be no way of stopping him.

"How you know this worm in brain tell truth Banan? He very powerful and Bodolf just stupid wolf. Since he comes back he not the same and you should know better. I not trust Northling worm," Lepe said, moving forward to stand in front of the blond warrior and the wolf.

"Maybe I will eat you and let Kirr feed on your brain you one horned runt. Except you do not have enough meat or brain cells to satisfy either of us, Bodolf said, his bristles rising in anger.

"Ha, that's better stinky wolf. Now I know you in there somewhere. If Banan trust you, then I trust you….but not worm," The one horned sheep said, turning to face the rest of the crew with his two friends.

"I need you all to trust Bodolf on this and work with him and Kirr if we are to defeat this deadly enemy. You should leave this meeting now if you are not prepared to do that," Banain said to the rest of the assembled crew. In the silence that followed his words, he watched the acceptance of the situation settle on the countenance of all, except one. Honi stared at Bodolf for a few seconds, then turned and padded away without a backward glance. Her exit followed by surprised looks from most of the crew and one of utter dejection from Bodolf.

Five hours later the three ships once again moored in the lee of the great ice walls of Artakra. On Banain's instruction, the Penguins and Lepe went straight to warn the city about the approaching army and to try to organise a meeting between Banain, King Aka, and the Immortals. The rest of the crew started dismantling the ice ships, hoping that they would have enough time to get them back in the water again; as it looked like the sea would be their only avenue of escape once the Northling Army arrived.

Chapter Thirty-Six

"They not going to let you have Nust again Banan. King says you not able to control it," Lepe said, translating the strange cacophony of sounds that served as a language for the aquatic birds. Banain was standing with him on the ice alongside Freedom, flanked by King Arka and his advisors. The whole party was in a state of suspended time to enable communication with the Immortals.

"We are also worried about your ability to control Nust, Banain. Your recent actions have raised serious doubts about your preparedness for the role we had planned for you. Your decision to let the Northling parasite stay within Bodolf was badly flawed, none of them can be trusted. As for there being a more ancient race then us, again you have been misinformed. If they were still alive, we would know about it. Nust is simply a relic, albeit a very powerful one from a long extinct species." Turr sang in Banain's mind.

"The King say, when they defeat Northlings army, they gonna take Kirr from Bodolf as you should have done." Banain was sure he could almost hear, "I told you so," in those words from his friend.

"Tell the King that it would be very unwise to underestimate the power of the Northlings. You have seen the size of the army Lepe; try to convince them that they need Kirr's help. Also, tell them that I will not allow them to act against Bodolf's will. Our whole way of life depends on the coexistence of consenting species. If we do that to Bodolf, we are no better than the Northlings. Whilst Lepe was translating the message to the Penguins, Banain turned mentally to Turr again:

"I am sorry that you are disappointed with me Turr, but I will not go against your own teachings. You were right when you said we needed Nust, but you were wrong about why we needed it. Kirr told me that Nust is the key to finding its creators. Moreover, that finding them is the only way of ending this war without terrible losses on both sides. Kirr also said…"

Before Banain could finish the sentence, Turr's voice filled his head with a savage violence that was excruciatingly painful.

"KIRR….KIRR is a corrupt entity. It has twisted Bodolf's mind and it has tricked yours as well. With your help, it is already responsible for the death of Krask and now he leads the Northling Army to the gates of Artakra. We wasted our teachings on you Banain. We will remove the Northling aberration from his brain and any that they have infested, before they plunge this world back into darkness. We are the Immortals and there are no older species on this planet. You are a young fool Banain, we were wrong to place so much responsibility on you so quickly." The force of Turr's words left Banain mentally and physically reeling. He almost staggered to the ground under the fury of the Immortals anger, but he managed to compose himself, although the moment was not lost on Lepe.

"Are you ok Banan?"

"I am just tired Lepe, please let the king know that…"

At that moment, an ominous rumbling sound filled the air, quickly accompanied by a strange wailing sound. The

King and his entourage spoke a few words, turned and moved quickly back towards the city.

"That wailing sound is emergency siren," Lepe sent.

"And the rumbling?" Banain asked, watching the group disappear into the nearest transportation tunnel.

"He not know, but he sound worried. So what happen Banain? You nearly collapse. You no fool Lepe" The intuitive sheep said watching his lifelong friend closely.

"The Immortals are not very happy with me my friend, but I think we have bigger problems to deal with at the moment. We need to get back to the ships; I think we are all going to find out just how powerful the Northling Army is, very soon."

Getting back to the ships was not such an easy task. The first rumble of attack from the Northling Army was just a taster of what was to follow. As Bodolf and Banain ran up the long ice road towards the city and the ships, its intensity increased and looking ahead the pair could see what was causing the terrible sounds. Large cracks were spreading like fissures through the walls of the city. As they ran, the pair had to dodge and increasing number of large shards of ice that had broken away from the walls and were hurtling down the ice road, smashing through anything that got in their way. A large section of outer wall right in front of them, detached itself and started towards the pair, picking up speed as it came. The section was over ten meters wide and they stopped and watched in morbid fascination as it came hurtling towards them. Shaken out of his momentary daze, Banain concentrated his efforts on the ice below their feet, imagining a large hole beneath them. As they both fell down into the newly created bolthole, the wall segment passed over their heads, showering them with ice as it went. Banain melted steps to get them out of the hole and as they continued to run up the ice slope, they both witnessed the terrible devastation of Artakra above them. As more sections of both the inner and outer walls ripped away from the city, they left exposed the intricate web of tunnels that lay within. Along with the icy debris of the city itself, the bodies of wounded and dead penguins were also sliding down the slope, to lie bobbing in the disturbed waters below.

Reaching the top of the slope the pair ran to the ships. The scene that greeted them was no more encouraging then that of the city. Funchal, the ship nearest the Northling Army and in range of the fire cannons, was just a mass of flames, and fires were starting to spread through the rigging of Neptune. Banain could just make out the figure of Captain Fermin helping his crew to abandon the stricken ship. He quickly created twisters around the fleeing crew, which kept most of the flames at bay. However, the fire had too strong a hold to save the ship. Looking through the smoke and twisted heat ripples was a sight that chilled Banain's blood, despite the heat of his burning ships.

The horizon bristled with the stark outlines of the Northling Army's throwing weapons, already close enough to reach both the City and Banain's ships. The few that aimed at the small fleet were causing fire damage, but the ones that were hitting the city were like ground penetrating bombs. Where the fiery balls landed there was a loud hiss, and then their heat caused the ice of the city to melt under them. After a short while, they disappeared from the surface and a muffled explosion followed. Banain had already witnessed what those underground explosions were doing to Artakra.

Tearing his eyes away from the terrible devastation, Banain noted that the crews had dismantled two of the ships, but that Oldore was still sitting without rigging on her ice sleds.

"EVERYONE THAT CAN HEAR ME, ABANDON FUNCHAL AND NEPTUNE AND GET ONBOARD OLDORE NOW," he shouted aloud and mentally. Then he ran towards Oldore, sending Lepe to make sure everyone had heard the message. Two minutes later he was standing at the stern of Oldore, creating twister after twister to try shield the fleeing crewmembers of the two fiercely burning ships. It was a blessing that Oldore was without rigging, as most of the damage to the other ships had resulted through the firebombs setting the rigging alight.

Seeing Lepe and Bodolf shepherding the last of the crew on-board, the Captain released the ice brake and Banain focused his mental energy on the mass of Oldore, willing her bulk, augmented by the extra crew to move. After a few moments, Banain realised that he just did not have the power to break her free from the ice. He could see more and more flaming balls of destruction bursting through smoke from the other burning ships. It was only a matter of time before they hit Oldore.

"I can't move her Carlos; she is stuck to the ice. Get everyone off and tell them to run down the slope and try to get on board Freedom," Banain sent, knowing in his heart that by the time most of the crew got down to the dock, Freedom would either be gone, or destroyed. Assuming they made it down the perilous ice slope without the flying city debris crushing them.

"Keep trying Banain and give us just a few moments, we may be able to help," Garfled said in his mind. Looking down towards the deck, he saw the large warrior, Torrent, Marianna and several crewmembers equipped with large sledgehammers, pushing out the gangplank and running back down onto the ice. Once there the humans set about attacking the ice holding the runners in place, whilst Torrent placed his massive head against the stern of the ship and pushed. Concentrating all his energy on moving the ship, Banain felt the familiar dizzying sensation that came before he blacked out from exerting too much mental effort. Determined that this would not happen before the ship moved, he dug deeper into his reserves, remembering everything the Immortals had taught him over his years of training with them. As a student, he had always been impatient and Turr would constantly tell him to control, focus, and connect with the earth, rather than unleash his power all in one go. However, he had never really understood what "connecting with the Earth" meant...Until now. As the familiar preclude to blacking out swirled in his mind, deep inside him something clicked and it all became so clear. Within the blackness that threatened to render him unconscious, he could see a faint white spark hovering elusively in the background. He realised that it must have always been there, but he had never paid it any attention.

Now instead of letting the blackness engulf him, he used some of his dwindling power reserves to move toward the tiny beacon in the darkness. As soon as he did, it grew in intensity, moving toward him at great speed. It was as if recognising its existence had triggered a link between them. Within milliseconds, the blackness flared into something that was much more than just light. Banain realised that this was the Earths, Griseous Animus, the Immortals and Teague had kept going on about, but which had always eluded him. He could see that far from being white, the light was made up from millions of tendrils of varying shades of grey, each emanating from every living being and organism on the planet; the intensity of each tendril reflecting the life force of its host. As the Griseous Animus engulfed him, Banain discovered a completely new window from which to view the world around him. Instinctively, he tapped into several of the brightest tendrils close to him, drawing a small portion of power from each of them to bolster his own flagging supply. Then he identified those around him that were fading and connected them to stronger tendrils. The tendrils occupied by Northling parasites and their hosts drew his attention. It was as if the Northlings had no connection with the Earth and drew their power solely from their hosts. All of their tendrils were a sickly grey and he felt a terrible malevolent force controlling them.

"BANAN…BANAN… YOU OK?" Lepe's words came crashing into his mind and pulling him back from his exploration. He realised that he felt better than ok.

"I am fine Lepe. Get everyone to find something to hold onto, this could be a bumpy ride." As he sent the message to his friend, he redoubled his efforts to move the ship, sending a ripple of power through the ice holding the runners. With that and the efforts of the crewmembers, Oldore broke free with a crack and started to move forward.

"Get everyone back on board quickly Garfled," he sent, as the ship started to gather momentum. Satisfied that Garfled had the situation in hand, Banain turned his attention back to the immediate dangers that were coming from the destruction of Artakra. The exploding fireballs were now creating havoc in the besieged city. As he watched, another massive section broke away and joined many smaller sections sliding down the ice slope to smash into the sea below. As the full view of the ice bay came into view, he was pleased to see that freedom had slipped her moorings and was moving away from danger, which was a good thing, as the harbour was buried under many tons of smashed ice. Looking down the slope, Banain could see one small gap in the water free of ice, which may just provide an avenue of escape, if they could reach it in time. Using his newly found powers, he immersed himself half way between his inner vision and the images his eyes were sending his brain. To anyone watching him, and there were a few including Lepe, he looked almost ethereal: standing almost still on the now bucking deck of Oldore, with both hands slightly in front of his sides, palms facing forwards. However, it wasn't just his stature that was grabbing the crew's attention; he was emanating a palpable aura of calm. It was as if he was immune from the carnage going on about him. As Lepe and the rest watched transfixed, a massive part of the city exploded and flew straight towards the ship. Just before it reached them,

Banain raised one hand and waved it to the side. Thousands of tons of hurtling ice ignored the force of momentum and gravity; surrendering to his will and falling harmlessly to the side of the ship. As Banain focused more of his renewed energy on his inner visions, he started concentrating on the sparks of life he could see were in danger, as well as guiding and protecting the speeding Oldore.

Chapter Thirty-Seven

On the ice, Garfled pushed Mariana up Oldore's gangplank, which was now bouncing madly along the surface as the ship gathered speed. Now just he and Torrent had to climb aboard. Realising that the ship was already traveling at near his maximum speed, he called Torrent, who immediately turned to run alongside him. Years of working together had honed the two into a single fighting unit and Garfled jumped easily onto the massive planes bull's shoulders. Torrent made a sprint towards the gangplank, which at that moment hit a large chunk of ice. The gangplank shattered, its components joining the ice debris already gathering speed alongside Oldore. Looking up Garfled could see Mariana, open mouthed with shock, as the realisation of the pair's situation registered in her mind and Oldore started to outpace them.

Garfled mentally braced himself for the crushing impact that was sure to come, as he watched a massive chunk of ice tear across the sky towards them. Then let out a mighty sigh of relief, as it veered to the side and smashed harmlessly on the ground. Torrent was doing his best to keep up with Oldore, but as the ice slope steepened the ship accelerated, pulling further away from the tiring bull.

Then, just as Garfled was about to jump from Torrents back, the bull put on a spurt of speed and started closing the gap again.

"Are you ok?" Garfled sent, holding on tight as Torrent raced down the ice hill at breakneck speed.

"Yes… Suddenly I have lots of energy! I don't know how, but I feel like I could run forever!" Torrent sent back. The next few moments were more than surreal for Garfled. Only his years of fighting on and with Torrent, allowed him to maintain his position on the weaving and jumping bulls back. From his precarious position, Garfled could see the figure of Banain standing as if inured to the mayhem. By rights, the icy wreckage from the disintegrating city should have wiped all of them out. However, all that threatened the ship, Torrent or Garfled bounced harmlessly away, as if deflected by something. As the small convoy reached close to the water's edge, the slope steepened considerably and the ship almost nosedived into a small area of water free from larger chunks of ice. The water slowed the ships momentum instantly and before Garfled realised what was happening, Torrent made a mighty leap towards her stern. Garfled watched for what seemed like a lifetime, as they flew across the widening gap of water between the ice and Oldore. Then they landed almost gently on the aft deck, right next to Banain. As soon as Torrent came to a stop, he seemed to sag and then crumpled to the floor. Garfled jumped clear and ran to the front of his friend, desperate with concern for his friend.

"Don't worry Garfled; he will be fine; he is just sleeping. I need the energy I was diverting to Torrent to help protect King Aka," Banain sent. Looking around, Garfled noted that Banain was standing a few paces away from him and was amazed how different he looked. In the past when Garfled had witnessed him using his powers, Banain had not been able to sustain his efforts for very long, becoming quickly drawn and pale. The Banain he was looking at now was exhibiting none of those signs. In fact, he looked relaxed; despite the fact that Garfled was sure he was expending vast amounts of energy containing the situation around them. At the dock, he could see King Aka and his entourage leaping into the water surrounded by thousands of penguins. All around them, massive slabs of ice that should have been causing mayhem bounced harmlessly away. It looked like a massive protective bubble moved over the penguin population as they swam to the safety of the entrance to the harbour.

"What has happened to him Lepe?" Garfled asked, as the sheep moved over to stand next to him, also staring in consternation at Banain.

"I not know if to be pleased or worried. Something changed in Banan, he like different person...not boy anymore I think."

"Stop standing there with your mouths open, you will catch flies. There is nothing wrong with me. I just learnt how to use my powers properly; if I had listened earlier, I could have done it ages ago," Banain said looking at the bemused pair, who were both in the grasp of Mariana, who had just run up on the deck, tears of joy and relief streaming from her eyes.

"Oh yes you ok Banan. It ok, Krask not here to tell..." Lepe started to reply and then stopped, remembering that his friend and Banain's surrogate father was dead.

It is Ok Lepe. It's what Krask would have said if he had seen the expressions on your faces. Now, I need to speak to king Aka and Turr as soon as possible." Banain said as he smiled at Lepe. However, years of friendship and shared experience, revealed the torment Banain was going through over the loss of Krask to his lifelong friend.

Chapter Thirty-Eight

Fifteen minutes later: Banain, King Aka, Bodolf, Lepe, and Ket were all crammed into the cabin in the bilges of Freedom, in front of the gently undulating form of Turr. Banain waited patiently as the King had a long session of squeaks and squeals with Ket, who then relayed the message onto Lepe.

"The King say he and many of citizens of Artakra owe you their lives. He not know how repay you," Lepe translated.

"Please ask the King if it is ok for me to enable us all to understand each other?" Banain replied, waiting patiently for the reply.

"King say of course, but he not sure how you do it…. I not sure how you do it!"

Banain tapped into his newfound skills and identified the sparks representing those in the room. He was amazed to see that rather than a spark, Turr was more of the tip of a tendril of light, that disappeared down below to the flooded chamber where thousands of other Immortals were gathered. He mentally ran a small thread of communication between them and then sent a message.

"Can you all understand me?" As the words left Banain's mind, the King and his entourage visually startled at the unexpected communication.

"Yes…I can, but how is beyond me, blond one. I was not aware of your abilities before, why did you deceive me

- 224 -

by letting me think you could not communicate with us?" Before Banain could answer, Turr's melodic voice interceded.

"He could not do much of what he has demonstrated in the last hour before, although we have been trying to teach him some of these skills for some considerable time. What he has managed is far beyond our expectations. How have you managed to master these skills so well Banain?"

"It is not a long story, but I do not have time to tell even the shortest version of it now. As we communicate, Isbjorn is destroying Artakra, not for the pleasure of doing so, but in order to find Nust. If he achieves this objective, his power will grow to a terrible level and this world will fall to him. You need to let me retrieve Nust before Isbjorn finds it."

The responses from both Turr and the King were predictable. Banain kept silent as they both reiterated how dangerous Nust was and even with his new found skills Banain was not equipped to deal with its powers. As they agreed not to let him have Nust again, Banain studied their aura's, noting how strong the kings spark was and how different to the glow of light emanating from Turr. Then he noticed something strange with Ket's Aura. Then he realised what it was.

"I appreciate that you think you are acting in the best interest of all, but suggest you consider further. Turr, you need to travel back to Old Seville and try to help with the situation there. From what Kirr has told me, the Northlings plan was to take over everyone in the city and drive the Immortals from their enclave beneath. They might be able to hold out until we can find a way to defeat the Northlings, but if Isbjorn arrives there, all will be lost. King Aka, what happens to Northlings when you remove them from their hosts?" Banain asked, not giving Turr time to intercede.

"They die!"

"I don't think that is so for the ancient ones. I have noticed a faint secondary spark of life residing in Ket. I know that he removed the Northling from Lepe and I believe that it is still alive. I also believe it is in communication with Isbjorn, which would explain how he has been able to predict our actions so well. If I am right, every penguin that has removed an ancient Northling from its host carries it. They may not be able to take over there host, but it seems they can communicate with others of their own kind. I have a way to test this theory, please give me a moment."

This time when Banain stopped talking, both King Aka and Turr stayed in shocked silence.

"Kirr, please see if you can communicate with the Northling in Ket," Banain asked, making sure all could hear his request and Kirr.

"Ket... The game is up. Banain knows you are still in there."

After a few moments, Ket's voice was in everyone's mind:

"Your petty discovery will make no difference. We are everywhere and Isbjorn hears all. I know you Banain and I know you Lepe, I have seen the fear in your minds. You are weak and cannot defeat us."

The familiarity of Ket's voice sent a shiver down Banain's spine as he remembered its brief invasion of his own body.

"It would seem that Bodolf is not the only one to harbour an Ancient Northling. You will need to gather all the penguins that think they have killed one and I should be able to prevent them from communicating to Isbjorn. Whatever you decide regarding Nust, I will be dropped off with Bodolf further up the coast at first light, so that we can get behind the Northling Army. Then we will find and rescue Teague and my parent and try to find the Ancients. It may be impossible without Nust, but we have to try. I do not believe there is another way to defeat Isbjorn. Before anyone in the crowded space could utter a word, Banain turned and climbed the stairs up to the deck. He strode to the rail and gazed across at the icy ruin that until a few hours ago had been a breathtakingly beautiful home to the thousands of penguins, who were now swimming around the two ships, nervously watching for any bears entering the water.

"Captain, let's get out of here before the Northlings manage to bring their catapults within range of the ships," Banain said to Carlos, who had moved up to stand within earshot of his clearly troubled leader. Not for the first time Carlos was taken aback and not a little in awe of the blond warrior. In his short time as Captain of the Freedom

Armies fleet, he had witnessed things that would have earned him scathing mockery, should he have mentioned it in a harbour side tavern. Now as he also watched the aftermath of the latest events, he wondered what else could happen. His fleet was reduced to two ships and he was saddened with his orders to leave one behind with Banain and a skeleton crew and return to Old Seville with the Immortals. "Captain?"

Jolted out of his musing, Carlos realised he had not responded to the instructions.

"I am sorry Banain; I will get the ships moving as soon as I can. Crewmembers are removing the ice rails as we speak. We have been able to disconnect them from inside the ship, but we will not be able to retrieve them. Will we have the assistance of the penguins?"

"Yes I have requested their help."

As Banain spoke, the penguins formed up around the two ships and started to move them towards the long ice fissure that connected Artakra's inner harbour to the outer one and the open sea. Banain watched the tops of the sheer walls for signs of attack by the Northlings, but he was confident that they would not have had time to make the long traverse around the harbour with catapults yet.

The squeak of the winch system, that allowed the transport of those creatures not equipped to climb ladders and supplies to the hold that housed the Immortals stopped, signifying that it had reached its destination. A few moments later Lepe and Bodolf joined him at the rail.

"Hey Banan, I go with you to find Teague and your parents. They need know what bad big head you are. You not just go with stinky wolf." The small sheep sent, doing his best to scowl at Bodolf.

"I am sorry Lepe, but you will not be able to keep up on the ice and Bodolf and I will travel faster alone," Banain replied, trying to ignore the scathing stare.

Pah, I always beat you Banan, on snow, on ice, on mountain… I always beat you, you only got two legs! What you mean, I slow you down?" Lepe fired back, moving within poking distance.

"It's too dangerous Lepe. I don…"

"Don't do, too dangerous with me Banan. And don't think you sneak off like Gibraltar that time. I go, anyway you get lost without me," Lepe interrupted, using his one good horn to jab along with the last few words.

"Well you are not going without us," Garfled sent.

"Or me," Honi added.

Whilst Lepe had kept Banain's attention with his jabtalk, Garfled, Torrent, and Honi had arrived and were all looking angrily at Banain.

"It looks like it will not be just me and Bodolf then," he said, looking towards Bodolf for confirmation. However, the wolf's eyes stayed firmly fixed on Honi. Banain doubted that he had even heard him.

"You will not be traveling without Nust either. We have agreed with King Aka that the advantages of you having Nust outweigh the risks, given your newfound skills. Nevertheless, we urge you to give up this idea of finding the Ancients. After you have found your birth parents and Teague, you should come to Old Seville and help us to defeat Isbjorn and his army."

"Thank you Turr, I will consider your advice," he replied. But they both knew he had considered already and was set on his own course of action.

Chapter Thirty-Nine

A weak dawn sun peeked over the distant icy horizon, illuminating a dismasted ship standing into a small ice harbour some six miles north west of Artakra. The water around her was disturbed by the slicing dorsal fins of over a hundred killer whales and the air was misted from the frequent spumes of warm air, ejected from a multitude of blowholes. The normally pristine white shoreline heaved with a black and white throng of penguins. Those nearest the water looking nervously towards their most feared predators. Freedom had left an hour before, but her sails were still visible on the horizon. The skeleton crew would be kept busy re-rigging Oldore after Banain and his expedition force left.

Banain was standing beside a growing pile of equipment, getting more and more frustrated as each apparently indispensable item was brought from ship to shore. Nust was in its specially designed holder on his back again. Retrieving it had been a simple matter, once he had received permission from both the King and Turr. The three had joined their minds and commanded its return. It had flown silently back into his hand from its temporary resting place without fanfare. Using his newfound vision to seek out its spark, he was surprised to find that whilst very bright, it did not feed into the earth like the others; it simply disappeared into the sky. He had hoped to discuss this with the Immortals, but there had not been enough time.

"How much more is there Lepe? The whole point of this mission was to travel light and fast. At this rate, we might as well just pull Oldore along and be done with it!"

"Oh you be grateful when we nice and warm with food in bellies at night, instead of freezing and hungry Banan. Ships carpenter spent all night making sled for us. You see Banan, everything gonna be great. Much better then travel alone with stinky wolf!"

"We are not going to need extra food if you keep calling me that. Sheep is very nourishing, even though it would be tough and stringy coming from you," Bodolf joined in, turning to glare at Lepe.

"Enough both of you, it is going to be a difficult enough journey without your bickering every step of the way, and what is that terrible noise?" Banain said, turning to look towards Oldore. The noise was coming from Torrent, who was being lowered down into one of the two dories that were being used to ferry men, animals, and equipment ashore. All conversation and penguin related noise stopped, as every head turned and watch events unfold.

"I AM NOT GOING TO FIT IN THAT TINY THING GARFLED, PULL ME BACK UP NOW!" Torrent's roar of protest transmitted to every being within range, including the whales, who came over to investigate the commotion, their waves churning the already disturbed water around the little boat.

"It will be fine Torrent; the captain has assured me that this vessel is quite capable of taking your weight, as long as you don't move around too much," Garfled sent, in an effort to calm his friend. He was perched right at the end of the small craft and was already soaked from the splashes caused by the nearest whales.

DO NOT MOVE AROUND TOO MUCH, I WONT BE ABLE TO TAKE A BREATH IN THAT THING WITHOUT SINKING IT!

"Garfled you will be fine, just relax and in a short while you will be ashore. I have some of your favourite apples for the journey over. The soft voice of Marianna interceded. After he kept her warm that first night in the old forest, they had shared a unique bond. She loved Garfled with all her heart but she reserved a special place in it for Torrent. Hearing her words he relaxed a little and allowed the struggling sailors to winch him down to the small boat. Just as Captain Marcos had stated, the small vessel did take his weight, but only just. After Marianna joined them, the trio started their journey towards the shore, propelled by two of the Orka's.

"Apples, you told me the supply had run out ages ago; how can you now have apples?" Garfled quizzed, trying to avoid and see past Torrents swishing tail, which normally only swished when he was doing, or eating something he enjoyed.

"I saved them for him, as he needs to keep his energy up. To be honest, you could still lose a few pounds Garfled. I know you have been eating with the crew of Oldore, as well as eating the food I prepare for you; so I saved some treats for poor Torrent, who has to carry you everywhere."

"Oh this is worth all the effort of pulling and pushing your floating boxes. If I die today, I will sing a whale song of joy telling of this moment," the voice of Kia boomed in Garfled's head. Looking around behind the tiny boat, Garfled could see a dorsal fin larger than the others streaking towards the small craft. As it came alongside, the large head of Kia came above the water and for a second one eye fixed on Garfled, then disappeared below again. Just before Kia's tail disappeared beneath the waves, it slapped the water, sending a substantial amount towards Garfled. The deluge hit the warrior with uncanny accuracy, missing Marianna and Teague completely.

"KIA, you stop that right now. This boat is unstable enough without your messing. Garfled has to spend god knows how long in the freezing cold, thanks to you he could catch his death. Now go away or I will be talking to Kaska and not for the first time about your antics," Marianna sent.

"I think he will be fine Mariana. After all, he has you to fight his battles for him," Kia sent to all.

"I am sorry my love, I should not have interfered. That overgrown fish may be king in the water, but you are my champion. Here, catch."

She threw the last apple to Garfled; much to the consternation of Torrent, who had been watching it with intent as Mariana waved it about during her rant at Kia.

Catching the apple deftly the disgruntled warrior muttered something unintelligible about Okra's under his breath; shook most of the water from his long hemp jacket and took a bite from Mariana's peace offering.

A little while later, all the expedition force were safely ashore, and receiving instruction as to the assembly of the large sled made by the ships carpenter. Banain was standing with Torrent and Garfled, listening to their complaints about the journey in the small boat.

"It's a shame you didn't ask for my help. I could have created an ice path all the way to the ships and you could have simply walked ashore."

Although he made light of the revelation, he realised that he could have saved a lot of time had he done so. In truth, he was so preoccupied with the rescue of Teague and his parents, that he was not thinking straight. He would need to rectify that, if this mission was to succeed.

Chapter Forty

"I know she is there Banain, but so are a thousand enemy soldiers who will not just let us take her! I thought the plan was to sneak around behind them, go to their base whilst the army was still away, and rescue your parents," Bodolf whispered in Banain's mind.

After quick farewells, the group, which consisted of: Banain; Bodolf and Kirr; Torrent; Garfled; Honi; Lepe and Marianna, had packed the sled, harnessed a grumbling Torrent to the front and set off towards the Northlings base behind Bodkirr; as Lepe had taken to calling Bodolf and his resident Northling. The specially constructed shed had allowed for surprisingly fast travel and even Torrent had cheered up when he realised how easily it glided over the frozen surface. Banain had been worried that the massive bull would not be able to travel fast enough on the Artic surface, but he seemed to compact the snow under his huge hooves and only sink a few inches before finding firm footing. Banain, Garfled and Marianna were equipped with special attachments that clipped onto their boots to help stop them sinking into the snow, but with Torrents coaxing, Marianna soon took a seat on his massive shoulders. All was going to plan and the small force were skirting past the front of the Northling Army, who were moving back towards their base. Then Banain called a halt, saying he could sense Teague nearby.

"Bodolf is right Banain, to try and attack the main army would be suicide. We should get to their base and rescue your parents, and then we can work out a way to help

Teague," Kirr said. The huddled group acknowledged the Northlings words with nods of agreement.

"I know that was the plan, but we may only have one chance to rescue her. Isbjorn will concentrate all his efforts on finding us, or more importantly Nust. Had my parents and Teague been together, it would have been as planned, but we do not even know what has happened to my parents, or if they are alive. Teague is here and those of you who have been the host to a malevolent Northling know of the terrible torment she is going through. Although the army is large, it is spread over a long distance, they are not expecting an incursion, and they don't even have scouts out... I have a new plan."

Banain sat on Torrents shoulders and studied the ranks of the Northling Army as they filed past his position. Even though he knew the shield he had erected around pair of them would render them invisible, it would not stop a wolf or bear from smelling them. Luckily, the Northling Army marched in species formation, with the wolves in the lead, followed by the bears and then the humans. Getting the rest of the small expedition force to set off towards the north, pulling and pushing the sled more slowly without Torrent, had been no easy task. However, in the end, his reasons added up and his plan was grudgingly agreed.

As the pair waited silently, not even daring to communicate mind to mind, it reminded Banain of the times he had sat astride Star, his warhorse and companion. His heart sank as he realised just how many of his friends and species who relied upon him were in trouble, or dead. If only he had stayed in old Seville and not come on this fools mission, he may have been able to save the City, its inhabitants and Krask. Now, here he was again, risking the lives of those who cared for him.

"Be strong Banain, it is your destiny to be here now, Soon it will be time," a voice, or more a mix of voices whispered in his head. He was sure that he could recognise the voice of Krask and a similar sounding female voice. As the last of the message resonated in his mind, he felt Torrent tense beneath him. Focusing back on the job in hand, he saw the reason. Towards the end of the marching army, came the enslaved humans. They differed from the local Icelanders, in that they had no uniforms, just very basic animal skin robes. Around two hundred of them, split into four groups of fifty, were pulling the four catapults used to blow Artakra apart. Banain also tensed when he spotted the familiar stature and partially hidden face of Teague, who was walking along with a few other slaves. Tapping Torrent on the back of the neck as arranged, Banain drew Nust from its holster and held it above his head. After a few seconds, it flew from his hand and streaked away towards the front of the Northling Army. A few seconds later, what looked like an arctic storm appeared and moved quickly towards the marching army. The well-trained soldiers were used to sudden storms and immediately began to dig snow shelters, whilst the wolves and bears stopped, waiting for it to pass. The humans pulling the catapults ran to shelter under them. Within seconds, the front of the roiling snow laden Nust induced storm hit the Northling Army and their world turned white.

As the storm turned a clear day into a whiteout, Banain looked inside his head for direction. Now that he had mastered the skill, it was like opening a third eye, which sent a strange monochrome picture of the world to his mind. He quickly identified the dual sparks belonging to Teague and her parasite. Using subtle body movements learnt from years of riding Star, he guided Torrent around the soldiers and slaves, until they were standing next to Teague sheltering behind the rear wall of the last catapult. They were undetected so far, but if he used any of his mental communication skills, the Northlings would detect them straight away. As he slid down from the back of Torrent, he pulled off one glove and reached inside to an inner pocket of his tunic. He located the cloth, steeped with a form of chloroform the healer on-board Freedom had prepared for him. In one quick movement, he grabbed Teague's hood, pulling it back from her face and replaced it with the infused cloth.

As Teague struggled, Banain prayed that the chloroform would be strong enough to knock her out without hurting her. He also hoped that the Northling within her would be helpless to do anything whilst she was unconscious. Within seconds, she stopped struggling and Banain felt her neck for a pulse, which thankfully was still strong. Torrent had already lowered his bulk to the ground, so it was easy for the strong warrior to lift Teague and place her gently on the bulls back.

Just as Banain was about to climb on behind Marianna, he noticed something strange about two of the life sparks emanating from a couple of prisoners chained to the next catapult up. Apart from Nust, all creatures' sparks had bright tendrils of light that went into the Earth, and sometimes fainter ones that connected them to blood relatives. The two sparks he was looking at in his mind now, both had tendrils of light connecting directly to him.

Chapter Forty-One

Far to the south, something amazing was happening in a valley hidden deep inside the mountain range, close to Banain's childhood home. Most of the escapees from Old Seville had gathered and were facing towards a raised bluff that fronted a large cave. Thousands more were streaming into the valley. Standing facing them on the bluff was Star. To an outside observer, it would be more than a little strange to see thousands of horses, plains bulls, wolves, and Jelks, all eerily quiet and staring at the large warhorse. However, for those equipped with the ability to communicate, the noise was deafening.

"Why you want to fight for the humans? They will only try to enslave us all again. At least the Northlings are not led by humans," One of the Jekals sent over the noise of all the others. He received an equal amount of cheering and booing to his comment.

"If you think that humans are bad, I can tell you that the Northlings will be much worse. Now they choose species that are most useful to them, but if we do not stop them and their numbers grow, they will need more and more hosts. Not one of you or your families will be safe. At least under Banain's leadership, animals have the choice to live under community rules, or as you have always lived," Star answered, not enjoying his role as leader at all.

"And what are we supposed to do? The Northlings have the City and we do not have the machines, or the weapons to take it back. The skies above old Seville are full of ravens, all under the control of the Northlings." This time the comment was from one of the many rooks grouped in the trees near the bluff.

"We may have a solution for that. Far to the south is Gibraltar. It is an outpost for the Immortals, a very ancient and powerful species. I sent a messenger there some time ago and yesterday he returned with some help," Star sent to the gathered, his last word sounding more like a question than a statement.

He turned to look behind him and from the cave entrance, a tall thin man walked out to stand beside him. He was dressed in a long flax hooded tunic that reached all the way to the floor. The tunic was the same colour as the Freedom Army uniform, but it had no bird emblem, or emblem of any kind emblazoned upon it. His hood was down, revealing a thin face and a long hawkish nose. In his left hand, he held a long white staff adorned with an intricate carving of some type of sea creature. Along with the man, around one hundred apes also exited the darkness of the cave to stand just behind him, except for one, who joined the pair facing the startled onlookers.

This is Lord Erador; some of you may remember him from when he ruled Old Seville. He lost the war against the combined forces of the animals on the slopes just outside this mountain range," Star sent.

He did not share the Immortals view that sending this mortal enemy of the Freedom Army to help them was such a good move. In fact had it not been for the arrival of this ape with the human, he would not have past the sentries guarding the entrance to the valley.

"This ape is called Jabber, although I never met him before, I feel as though I know him from the stories told by Banain and others. Everyone thought he died trying to save the life of Teague, after the great battle. In fact, he managed to evade capture by Lord Erador's soldiers, only to be taken by slavers as he tried to make his way back to Gibraltar. I am sure many of you will hear the full story, as I did, several times last night. But the point is, if Jabber vouches for the lord, then we should at least listen to what he has to say," Star sent.

Jabber had indeed regaled him and several others with every detail of his defence of Teague; his escape from the soldiers; his subsequent capture by the slavers; his life as a toy for a rich family across the water, and his subsequent escape and journey back to Gibraltar. Star was ashamed with himself, as the thought had crossed his mind that Jabber's captors might have let him escape on purpose, just so they could get some peace. He nodded at the Human who took a step forward.

"We do not want to hear the words of this killer, I have heard about what he did. Thousands of us have suffered or died at his hand," a large half-breed wolf snarled above the clamour of the rest.

"Yes, send him down here and we show him how he not welcome. Why he in our valley anyway?" A relative of Lepe added her opinion and her own angry stare to hundreds of others.

"I know many of you have reason to hate and distrust me, but the man I was, has gone. I have been reborn and I am here to help, if you will have me." His voice was almost hypnotic and Star, along with the rest of the gathered animals fell silent as he spoke. His voice was very similar to that of the Immortals, in that it was as if there was more than one person speaking.

"For the last five years, I have grown up with and been mentored by the Immortals. I have no memories of my life before rebirth, but I have heard enough from those I have met, to know that I was a very bad person. I am not a Lord, just a surrogate child of the Immortals trying to carry out their wishes, so please just call me Erador. I have some inherent skills and have been trained by the Immortals on how to use them."

"Oh great, not only is he inside our secret base, he also has the power to kill us all!" Another voice said, but it was quite subdued. Then Jabber sent:

"I have been a servant of the Immortals all my life and love Banain as a brother. I would not have brought Erador into your midst, if I thought he would do harm to any Banain holds dear. I also trust the wisdom of the Immortals and they believe that with Erador's help, you can win back Old Seville. We will leave you to decide if you wish us to stay and help, or go back to Gibraltar."

"That was short for Grindor....but effective," Star thought to himself, as the apes and Erador disappeared back into the cave.

"This is a difficult matter for us to decide. Let each senior species member, gather and agree the decision of their kind and let me know by the suns rise," Star said, turning to go and gather the horse council.

Chapter Forty-Two

Banain had never experienced more division between his emotions and his common sense. His feelings were yelling at him to rescue his parents, but he knew that the chance of them all escaping would be slim if he did. Torrent was already carrying the unconscious form of Teague, and the success of his plan relied on a quick escape and the ability to catch up with the rest of the expedition quickly. Torrent stamped his hoof gently, in an effort to relay that they should be moving, but Banain just stood in the whorl of snow, frozen in indecision. Hundreds of thoughts tumbled through his mind as he tried to come to a decision. If he did not rescue them, he knew that Isbjorn could use them as hostages. He was surprised that the Northling leader had not threatened to do so already. His decision surprised him almost as much as Torrent, as he nudged the bull to get his attention and ran towards the prisoners harnessed to the first of the four catapults. Using his third eye, Banain could see that the Northlings possessed none of them, so he signalled to Torrent that he should move to the front of the row of slaves. He undid the harness where it connected to the machine, cut off a length of rope, and connected it to Torrents pack. Then he ran back through the cowering humans, quietly telling them to get up and follow the person in front. Months of brutal conditioning meant that they accepted the order without question, and when Banain signalled for Torrent to move to the front of the next group, they all fell in line behind him. They repeated the routine until all two hundred humans were standing in a very long row behind Torrent. As Banain had reached Judoc and Nimean, his birth parents, he had received no signal of recognition from either of them. Just the same blank resigned look shared by the rest of the captives. Banain was disappointed they had not recognised him, but he reasoned that in their minds he would only be around eight years old, and his face was almost completely covered with his hood. As Torrent started moving at an angle away from the column, the captives started moving, almost as one, in formation behind him. Banain rushed up and down the line to check that everyone was ok. He was already at the limit of his control over Nust, so he instructed the ancient weapon to continue the storm in the wake of the escaping prisoners, keeping the abandoned siege weapons concealed as long as possible and erasing all tracks of the escapees direction. Running to the front, he leapt onto Torrents back and took Teague in his arms. He was not sure how long the potion he had used on her would last, or how it would affect her Northling, so he entered her mind very carefully and checked for her vital life signs, which were weak but steady. Almost immediately, he was assailed by a very strong presence.

"So... You are the overgrown baby, Banain, who thinks he can defeat Isbjorn and the Northlings army. I know everything about you child and believe me, you are no match for Isbjorn. I find it hard to believe this female thinks so much about you, the familiar gravelly Northling voice sent.

"And I can't believe such an ancient, noble and knowledgeable species, would act in the way you have, Sklak. Yes, I know your name and much about you as well. Kirr tells me that you were once in the Immortals high council and that you have voiced doubts to him over the sanity of Isbjorn." His exchange was just supposed to stall the powerful entity, whilst he tried to figure out a way to disentangle his hold on Teague's brain without hurting her. However, something in the Northlings manner caused Banain to pause in his attack.

"Kirr is alive? I understood they killed him and his patrol. These are lies you are telling me boy. Lies to try and save your precious female."

Banain did not answer the accusation, giving the Northling time to consider the information. Kirr had told Banain that Sklak was part of a secret group of Northlings that were trying to overthrow their tyrannical leader.

"If what you say is true, then all may not be lost. I can sense you have great power, but you know that I can damage her beyond repair before you can defeat me," the gravelly voice continued.

Banain considered his options, which were not that many. If he tried to silence the Northling, Teague could well be hurt. If he did nothing, Sklak could still hurt her and send their location to the Northling Army. In any scenario, if he did not act soon, they would be tracked down and killed by a vastly superior force.

Chapter Forty-Three

In Krask mountain Jabber was outlining his plans to the representatives of the animal clans for the umpteenth time.

"I know this sounds strange, but I hold some of Erador's memories relating to Old Seville. He and his predecessors rebuilt the city and the castle after the great storms. A secret passage leads to a chamber in the cellars of the castle. It emerges very close to the new Immortals chamber. The Immortals are in a stalemate with the Northlings, neither side being able to gain an advantage. The initial battle was frighteningly brutal, with thousands from both sides dying. If we can get Erador into the Immortals chamber, His training will enable him to provide a conduit to channel the Immortals power. The problem is that the entrance to this tunnel is within the expanded city walls, which are, as you know, heavily defended."

Most species had already agreed to help, but a few wanted more information, and to know what the risks would be. Jabber was doing his best to explain, but after several hours, even his normally inexhaustible well of information was running dry.

"And who will decide who does what and has greater risk?" A large male Jelk, who had questioned most of what Jabber had told him several times sent.

"As Jabber has already told you several times Narek, there are enough members of the existing freedom council to form a war council. It will be their job to designate responsibility for the different elements of the army, relative to their skills. I do not believe there is any further information Jabber can provide. If any of you do not wish to assist with the retaking of Old Seville, then that is your right," Star said, fed up with the whining of some of these species. When he had put the plans to the other horses, there had been unanimous agreement. Like him, many had felt terrible shame when instructed to desert their friends and riders in Old Seville.

"Ah, so if we don't go, the Jelks and any others who do not join in, will forever be seen as cowards; is that what you are saying?" Narek continued, undeterred by the obvious irritation in Stars voice.

"I cannot foretell what history will make of any of our actions Narek, it very much depends on who is left to record it. Whatever you and the rest decide, the army will leave at noon tomorrow," Star sent. He stood looking at Narek for a moment, then turned, and left, followed by the rest of the council members.

Chapter Forty-Four

Banain sat on the back of Torrent holding Teague in his arms, still undecided.

"Trust him..." The words were spoken so softly that he was not sure he had heard them at all. It was the same mix of familiar voices he had heard before. Whereas normal mind-to-mind communication felt like it originated inside his head, these words seemed to come from everywhere....and nowhere.

"You do not have to take my word for it Sklak. Kirr is less than a few hours travel from us; we just have to get to him. My original plan did not include the rescue of two hundred slaves. I can only confuse the Northling Army for a while and then they will have all of us," Banain said.

"Isbjorn told us that you have the ancient weapon known as Nust. If that is true, it is capable of defeating these soldiers, as they are not protected by his power this far from him. Why not just use it as you have before?"

"What I did before was a mistake; despite its capabilities I do not believe Nust was created to kill. I do not know his true purpose, but I know that using it to take life is wrong. I will not do it again."

"And I know that should Isbjorn capture Nust, he would have no such moral dilemmas. For some reason you response pleases me, although it will also probably kill me. I can help you to escape from the Northlings, but you will need to let me communicate with them."

Banain was not sure what Sklak was planning to do, but he did not have time to debate this further. With the two words, "trust him," still at the forefront of his mind, he released control over the Northling.

Instantly Sklak shouted:

"I HAVE BEEN CAPTURED BY BANAIN. HE IS HEADED BACK TOWARDS THE COAST,"

Chapter Forty-Five

"We only have one chance at doing this Jabber; if the gates do not open the cause is lost," Star sent to the ape sitting astride his withers.

He was standing just at the edge of the tree line, along with fifty other ape-mounted horses, around a mile south of the old City. All were looking towards the north for the sign that the battle had started. "

Get us to the walls and we will do our bit, if we are seen before we get there, things could get very ugly, but we apes are great climbers you know. Did you know that we can climb almost anything and that I still hold the record for..."

"Climbing to the top of the Gibraltar Mountain faster than any other ape? Yes you did tell me," Star finished for Jabber. More times than I can count, he thought.

Then the sky darkened, as thousands of birds of every kind came into view from where they had been gathering to the north of the City. Almost immediately, a second cloud rose from within and around the city and headed towards the first. Even from this distance, the cries of the aerial armies carried on the wind to the ears of the stationary hoof, foot, and paw soldiers. As the two clouds clashed, Star trotted out from the cover of the trees, looked back to check the others were following and then increased his gait until he was at a full gallop. Holding on was no easy task for Jabber or the other apes, as the charging horses swerved around shrubs and small trees and jumped in and out of canyons and riverbeds to try to keep their approach concealed from the city.

Looking back, Star could see that some of the apes had not managed to hold on; their mounts having to stop so they could leap back on. On his own back, he could feel Jabber almost lose his balance as he leapt over a riverbed.

"Apes are not born to ride, are they Jabber. As I recall Grindor was not the best passenger. Be ready, we will be at the wall in a few moments."

As Star jumped the last small river, the ground in front was devoid of any further cover. The walls of the city rose in front of the fifty galloping horses, who now marshalled the last of their reserves to close the gap as quickly as possible. As planned, the bird invasion from the north had drawn the cities defenders to that side of the city. In fact, the birds had already driven off any aerial threat and were now harrying the troops on top of the city walls. As Star reached the wall, he slowed to a canter and Jabber leapt from his back onto its almost smooth face. Most other creatures would have simply slid down its surface, but he found toe and finger grips, where it looked like none existed. As more apes arrived, they also leapt from their mounts and followed Jabber, who was making quick progress towards the top of the wall.

Star looked back towards the south and was pleased to see a dust cloud moving towards a large pair of gates, just to the east of his position. Underneath that cloud was the bulk of the freedom animal army. If Jabber and the apes did not manage to do their jobs, they would have nowhere to go when they reached the wall.

Chapter Forty-Six

For a few seconds it felt like a crushing weight had landed on Banain's chest, as Sklak's warning rang out. Then he realised that the Northling in Teague's brain, was misdirecting his own army members and was sending them in the wrong direction. After making sure Teague was secure on Torrents back, Banain slid to the ground and ran to the rear of the two hundred rescued prisoners. If the army did pick up their trail, he wanted to be between them and the Northlings. It also allowed Nust to range further behind the retreating group, keeping up the appearance of a storm for as long as possible.

Using his inner eye vision, he could see that a large part of the Northling Army had taken Sklak's bait and were heading off quickly in the opposite direction, whilst the rest were continuing on course back to their base. When he was sure they were far enough away, he called Nust back to him, as he was channelling energy from the rescued prisoners to feed its voracious appetite, and they needed all the energy they could get. He had already decided that he would not let them know their situation, until they were much further away from danger. Partly because it would be safer that way, and because he did not know what to say to, or how to deal with his birth parents. He was also worried about how he was going to feed them all. There was enough food on the sled to keep the original six members of the expedition force fed for around ten days, but two hundred! He really had not thought this through.

"Teague is waking Banain; I am worried she will be disorientated and fall," Torrent sent. Pushing all thoughts other than Teague's welfare aside, Banain ran back to Torrent and leapt onto his back. He was just in time to steady Teague, who was trying to sit up.

"Are you ok?" He sent.

"You cannot fool me Sklak, you do not even sound like him. What have you done to me this time?" Teague replied, her words slurred by the lingering effects of the chloroform.

"It is not Sklak, it is me, Banain. Open your eyes Teague," Banain spoke this time, as he pulled her closer to him, steadying her head against his chest. Slowly her eyes fluttered open and then settled on Banain's deep blue almost black orbs.

"Banain," she said, a smile starting to crease the sides of her lips. Then her eyes widened and the slight trace of a smile was gone.

"I can still feel that thing in my head Banain. It tries to tell me that it is my friend and that it wants to help me. But I have seen what they have done Banain, terrible, terrible things. Please get it out now!" Teague sent, her eyes locked imploringly onto his. The words wrenched at Banain's soul, he wanted nothing more than to do whatever she asked, but he could not.

"Listen Teague, at the moment he is helping us to escape from the Northling Army. You need to be brave and endure his presence until we are safe," Banain sent, noting Teague's eyes narrowing in anger and frustration as he communicated.

"I know that he will tell you anything you want to hear. Try to act like a man and not a boy Banain. Rip this thing out of my head and fight instead of running." She said aloud, her words as cold as the stare now levelled at him.

"I am sorry Teague, but for the moment you will have to endure his presence. Sklak has promised he will not harm you and I cannot remove him now. Please stay on Torrent," Banain sent, as he jumped to the ground. Her words had wounded him deeply, but he had to ignore this new pain for the moment and concentrate on getting everyone to safety.

Chapter Forty-Seven

Jabber stopped on a small ledge just below the top of the outer wall of Old Seville, and waited for the rest of the troupe to gather along both sides of him. The distraction provided by the birds was doing its job and none of the defenders had noticed them yet. Peering carefully over the top of the parapet, he could see around twenty soldiers, all armed with bows and short swords on this part of the wall. They were all firing at the mass of birds that had driven off the aerial contingent of the Northlings army. Fortunately, the birds were staying just out of range of the arrows, which posed more of a threat to the defenders as they clattered back to earth within the city.

Sending instructions to the other apes, Jabber leapt for the top of the wall and then towards the nearest soldier. He and two others reached the man at the same time and three pairs of hands and feet quickly disarmed him, his weapons joining many others thrown over the wall. With no defence against them, the birds wheeled down and started harrying the startled soldiers, allowing the apes to move on towards their main objective. Running along the top of the wall, he looked down into the main yard and noted it was full of caged prisoners. The Immortals had told him that the battle between them had depleted the Northlings stock of polyps. He guessed that they had yet to infest these prisoners. Focusing back on his main objective, he scanned the area in front of the gates for enemy soldiers and was relieved to see that it was clear. Almost as one, the troop swarmed down the inner wall and ran up to the gates. It was here that the plan fell to pieces. When the Northlings had repaired the gate after taking the city, they replaced the three large wooden locking bars with one huge one. As the fifty apes wrestled the massive piece of timber, Jabber realised that they were just not tall enough to get the purchase they needed to lift it clear of its retainers. He could hear the shouts of the defenders drawing closer on both sides, despite the best efforts of the birds. If they could not get the gates open soon, the retaking of Old Seville would come to an abrupt stop.

Chapter Forty-Eight

"How are we going to feed all these people Banain?" The question came from Bodolf, who was staring in shock at the large group of humans who had emerged from the weak morning arctic gloom and shuffled into the expedition forces night camp. Banain had sent him a message several hours earlier, saying that he was returning with Teague and some rescued prisoners, but he was not expecting this.

"Let's worry about that later Bodolf, for now, we need to give them what help and food we can. Garfled, share what rations we have between these people and get the ropes off them," Mariana sent as she ran towards the bedraggled group. As she approached Torrent, he lowered himself to the ground, allowing her to reach Teague, who was just sitting staring without focus on anything,

"Teague it is me, Mariana. You saved me from my village. Do you remember?" She asked as she helped Teague to the floor. Leading her towards the sled, she sat her down, took both her hands, and looked for signs of recognition in her eyes.

"It's in my head and he won't get it out," Teague whispered, turning her head to look at Banain.

"I am sure he will Teague, just as soon as everyone is safe. Sit here for a moment whilst I help with the rest."

Mariana left Teague staring at Banain and walked over to the blond warrior, who was deep in discussion with Garfled and Bodolf.

"Banain, are your parents and the rest of them ok?" She asked, looking towards the group, who were standing as if in a trance.

"I thought it was best to just keep them as they were until they were safe, it was easier to guide them when they all moved as a group," Banain said, breaking away from his conversation and looking towards the ex-captives, a frown creasing his face.

"And your parents, you have spoken to them...? Oh Banain come on, you need to tell them who you are. Where are they?

"They will not recognise me; I should be a ten year old boy!" Banain said, the frown deepening on his face.

"They are your parents Banain, let me go and speak to them so that they understand what you have been through before..."

"NORTHLINGS..."

The mental shout that interrupted Marianna came from Garfled, who was running towards the rear of the file of prisoners, drawing his sword as he went. Banain snapped into his third eye view and was appalled to see hundreds of Northling soldiers moving swiftly towards them.

"Is this your doing Sklak?" Banain sent to the Northling in Teague's head. However, before Sklak had time to reply, another, much more powerful voice invaded Banain's mind.

"It was his doing child, but he did not know he was doing it. Both Sklak and Kirr have unwittingly been working for me since they made their pathetic bids for freedom. Your escape with my weapon from the penguin's city was a slight setback to my plans, but in the end your capture and its journey to me was inevitable. Now give Nust to me and we can end this before you or your friends get hurt."

With his third eye, Banain could see an entity shining far brighter than the rest moving towards the front of the Northlings army. Its light, although brighter, seemed flecked with darkness. It looked sick, as though polluted with evil. Through his eyes, Banain watched as rank upon rank of wolves, bears, and human soldiers emerged from the arctic gloom and stood in a semi-circle around the enlarged expedition force. At centre front, stood a massive black bear encased in black sealskin armour. On its front left upper leg was an empty scabbard.

Banain walked slowly towards the massive bear, until positioned between it and his own group. As he walked, he gently tried to probe the bears mind, but immediately Isbjorn repelled him, the brief contact jarring him to his soul. When he was close enough to look directly into Isbjorn's eyes, he encountered the same cold black orbs that Arkta had five years before. They were a conduit to a soul bereft of love or compassion. He found only a fierce will to survive and rule at all costs. Banain knew he could not influence or best this creature. In fact, he was not sure if he could even slow it down. He knew it wanted Nust and could already sense its intense concentration on the weapon.

"If I give you Nust, you will enslave the whole planet and I cannot let that happen. If you do not leave now, I will use it to defeat you and your army. If you know about Nust, then you know it is capable of this," Banain sent. He knew he would not use the weapon this way after what happened in the river, but hoped his bluff would work.

"I know what Nust is capable of child and I know you will not kill anyone. Nust wastes its power on you. It exists to assist a ruler, not a child with fantasies of a utopia where all are born equal. Some are born to rule, the rest to serve or die as rulers see fit. Man nearly killed this planet once, and with Nust, I will ensure he is not able to do it again. Is that not what you want? Is that not why the Immortals trained you? Let me take the weight of this responsibility from your shoulders. Once every creature on this planet is host to a Northling, there will be no more fighting, no more wars, no more killing. Isn't that utopia child?" As he spoke, Banain felt the latent power behind the words channelled through eyes that seemed to be drilling into the depth of his being.

"My utopia is not based on cruelty and slavery; it is based on love, trust, and respect for each other. The Immortals told me that that the enslaved always find a way to break free of their bonds, however imposed. You are right I will not use Nust to kill, but it has other powers." As he spoke, Banain reached behind his back, pulled Nust from its scabbard and threw it into the ice between him and Isbjorn, focusing on its objective as he did so. When Nust hit the ice a massive wall formed, which quickly extended as the weapon travelled from side to side faster than the eye could follow.

"Bodolf, do you know anywhere we can find shelter and a defendable position?" Banain sent, desperate for any chink of light in the darkening situation.

"I am sorry Banain, I have hunted here before, and it is a desolate and barren place. There is nothing that will help our situation," the wolf replied.

"You're little tricks will not work against me child; give up and save your friends. The wolf is right; you have nowhere to go. As he spoke the ice wall exploded, allowing Isbjorn and his army to march through its powdered remains, spreading out as they came so that they could encircle Banain's small force.

Chapter Forty-Nine

Jabber knew he only had moments to get the gates open before his small force was overwhelmed, but the wooden locking bar was simply too high and heavy for the apes to manage. With a sinking heart, he tried one last time to move the bar, but had to concede that even with a hundred more apes, they could still not shift it. It looked like they would now need rescuing, as well as the rest of Old Seville.

"Follow me," he sent and pulled himself towards the top of the wall once more. He had agreed an exit strategy with Star, but had hoped he would not have to use it.

"Don't go… Free us… We can help... My husband has the key."

For a moment, Jabber was not sure where the message had come from; then he looked back towards the yard and his eyes locked with that of a woman in one of the cages. She was gripping and shaking the gate of the cage so hard, that one of her hands had turned white. The other was pointing towards a large man who was fending off attacks from several large crows. Jabber could see that whilst some of the captives were in shock or wounded, many were also attacking their cages, trying to find a way out. Jabber leapt back to the floor and loped towards the large man, the troupe obeying his last instruction and following behind him.

"Please don't kill him!" The woman sent again.

Jabber leapt at the man, who was still fully occupied with the attacking birds and, along with a few more of his allies wrestled him to the ground. On the man's belt was a large key, which Jabber grabbed and carried over the cage containing the woman. The lock was of a simple design and he soon had the gate open, allowing the prisoners to rush out. The woman made sure her man was ok, then ran back and grabbed the key from the lock, setting off to free the other prisoners. Jabber sent a general message to all that could read him, to open the gate and twenty or so prisoners immediately ran up to it. This time the bar moved, although grudgingly and with a final heave it fell clear, allowing the gates to open. The timing could not have been better, as Star and the horses, followed by the rest of the reformed freedom animal army, thundered through the gates, sending what remained of the defending forces running in the opposite direction.

The battle to free Old Seville was very unlike a normal clash of armies. Whilst infested residents had no compunctions about killing friends and neighbours, the un-infested had to fight without using lethal force. It was inevitable that deaths on both sides would occur, but in the six hours of hand-to-hand, tooth to sword and horn to hand fighting that followed, the incapacitated, and infested were locked safely away in cages. Having liberated most of the city, Star and the newly reformed Freedom Army, moved into the large courtyard; where they found the bulk of the Northling Army ranked up in front of the entrance to the castle itself. A little way in front of the army, stood Grindor, Arkta and Izotz, accompanied by a large polar bear.

"Your battle to reach this far was impressive but futile. You might be able to subdue a few townspeople, hosts to lower rank clones; but you cannot defeat the army that stands in front of you, and even if you could, you would be killing your friends. Very soon, we will have enough polyps to become one with all of you. Your coming here has saved us all much trouble. To help persuade you, this is what will happen to all your friends if you attack or if you leave." The message did not seem to come from any person or animal in particular, but reached the minds of every animal facing the Northling Army. As the words ended, so did the life of Grindor.

Chapter Fifty

"Garfled, move everyone north, I will hold them until you are safe," Banain sent, sending Nust back to form another ice barrier.

"There is nothing to the north but more ice Banain. What can you hope to achieve?" Bodolf said, the sadness and pain he felt for the hopeless situation evident in his tone.

Banain was not sure what he could achieve, in fact he was not sure what was happening at all. He was hardly able to delay Isbjorn and his soldiers for a few moments, let alone give the rescued prisoners and his friends the opportunity to escape.

"I don't know my friend, but please do as I say Garfled

"You not gonna beat fat bear on own Banan. Not sure how we help, but we stay," the familiar voice of Lepe said in Banain's mind.

"We need to keep following Teague and the rescued prisoners Lepe. It is difficult for me to keep fighting and follow them at the same time. Can you guide me?" Banain sent. Once again, the sacrifice his friends were making humbled him. For the next few hours, Banain kept up the relentless battle of wills against Isbjorn. For a while, it looked like with Nust and his friends help, he could keep reconstructing the ice walls without spending too much energy. Then Isbjorn changed the rules of engagement.

Like Banain, Isbjorn was also drawing on the life force of those around him to destroy the ice walls. However, instead of using any of his own energy, he was drawing it from individual soldier's one at a time. Banain realised that even his passive retreat was resulting in death. In his third eye state, he could see Isbjorn's malevolent tendril of light connect with soldier after soldier, sucking their life forces from them and leaving their bodies to freeze on the arctic ice.

"Do you see Banain? Do you see how pointless your ideas are, your beliefs are, your compassion is? You cannot save them all: no matter what you do, they will die. Unless you give me Nust."

Isbjorn's voice was like a sickness in Banain's head, mocking and taunting him. The worst of it was that this monster was right. It was then that he decided he could not let this happen. Gathering his strength, he concentrated on the tendril that was channelling energy from his latest victim and mentally cut the connection. As the severed tendril recoiled, he mentally grasped it and held on with all his mental power.

"FOOL BOY FOOL. NOW YOU WILL DIE." The words rebounded in Banain's head as his inner vision turned black. To his friends watching, it appeared as if the world had frozen in time in front of them. For a few seconds Nust hung motionless in mid-air, the latest ice wall froze in the middle of exploding, its suspended fragments glowing with a rainbow of colours. Then everything resumed, except for Banain and Nust, who both fell lifeless to the ground. They watched, frozen in horror, as the large black bear stalked up to the ancient weapon and picked it up with his mouth. As his jaws closed around Nust, his whole body emanated black flecked light. Then he reared up and roared:

"I AM CHOSEN. MY DESTINY IS MORE... SO MUCH MORE...

Not even bothering to look at Banain or his small force, Isbjorn bounded off in the direction taken by Teague and the prisoners, what was left of his army following behind him.

Chapter Fifty-One

Star had no time to consider the Northlings message. As Jabber and the other apes witnessed their leader and mentor scream in pain and collapse to the floor, they acted. As one, they swarmed towards the Northling Army, ploughing into its ranks and surrounding the body of Grindor in a protective screen. He and the rest of the army then stood rooted in shock and indecision. If they attacked, it would mean that they would be killing their own friends and leaders, if they did not, the Northlings would infest every creature on the planet.

"There threat is hollow Star, they sacrificed one of their clones to kill Grindor, but they will not sacrifice themselves. I have reached the Immortals and am as one with them; we have already defeated the clones within the walls, but you must defeat their army. I will do what I can to help." It was the voice of Erador.

They had managed to smuggle him in through the tunnels as planned and now looking up, Star could see him standing with his arms wide open on the balcony over the main yard, flanked by two wolves. Star could feel his power, as it washed over him and the rest of the Freedom Army. All the fatigue from the hours of fighting was suddenly gone and followed by the rest of the invigorated army, he charged into the ranks of the Northlings.

The problems for the invaders doubled, as from behind them, the doors to the castle opened and the wolves and jelks that had entered through the secret tunnel streamed out to attack their rear.

Taken by surprise, opposition crumpled very quickly and without too many casualties. The worst part for the invading force and those freed to help fight the Northling Army, was sorting out the aftermath of the battle. Although they had tried to minimise casualties, over one hundred men, woman and animals had died and were laid out side by side, just outside the gates of the city. Except for the jelks, who ate their own dead, as it was their belief that the departed soul would then pass back into the pack. The bodies would be left for a day, to give all a chance to say, sniff, or lick farewell. There was to be a mass burning ceremony of the fallen the following day. They took Grindor's body to the Immortals chamber, where he was prepared for yet another re-birth.

Dealing with the living had been almost as hard. They placed those infested with Northling clones in guarded houses in the city and those with ancients in the dungeons of the castle. This allowed the Immortals to keep them subdued. Many Freedom Army members left the city to return to their own territories, others moved back into abandoned homes, stables, stalls, and lairs within the city. Despite winning the battle, there were no great celebrations of victory, as so many friends and fellow species were still possessed by the enemy.

Chapter Fifty-Two

"He dead Bodolf?" Lepe asked again, as he trotted around and round the crumpled form of Banain.

"I don't know Lepe and I can't hear a thing with you trotting around like that...I'm sorry my friend, I know how much he means to you... to us all."

His head was pressed to Banain's chest, listening for any sounds of life.

"I sense something within him, but it is very weak. I can try to sustain him, but I am no healer," Kirr sent.

"Please, do what you can for him Kirr. Lepe go and see if Teague and the prisoners are ok and if so bring..."

Bodolf never had chance to finish the sentence, as Teague came running out of the gloom, followed by some of the prisoners.

"Teague, what happened? Did Isbjorn attack you?" Bodolf said, moving aside to let her kneel beside the still body of Banain.

"He just ran right past us! I realised something terrible must have happened for the bear to break through, so I ran back.

"Teague took up her healing stance and concentrated on finding Banain's spark. His aura was like nothing she had seen before; every part of him glowed so brightly with pure white light that was almost blinding. A quick survey of his vital organs showed that all was ok and his heart was beating, but very slowly. It was as if he had gone into hibernation. Normally she could determine the problem by the changes in the brightness of a patient's life force, but she could find no darkness anywhere and therefore nothing to heal.

"You need to look deeper Teague," the voice of Sklak said inside her head.

"I didn't ask for your help and you said I wouldn't know you were in my head, but here you are!"

"Banain is in shock, he was in direct contact with Isbjorn, who unleashed the combined power of many Ancients against him. Any other would be dead already, but somehow he has survived. His brain has shut his body down to protect him from harm. You must revive him, he is needed," Sklak continued, despite Teague's remonstrations.

"If he is in no danger, then he needs to rest and recover. I will not put him at further risk; he has done enough already. Now stay out of my thoughts," Teague sent. Then she withdrew from Banain's mind and stood up next to him.

"He ok?" Lepe asked, looking in distress at his friend still lying lifeless on the floor.

"He is in shock but alive. He needs time to recover Lepe… We will put him on the litter and get him back to the ship."

She turned to look for Torrent, but met the steady stare of Bodolf instead.

"You know this is not what he would want Teague. Banain has a job to do and if he cannot do it, everyone will suffer. He will not thank you for protecting him. If you love him, you will help him to do what he must."

He sent his message to the entire group standing around Banain, but his eyes never left hers.

"The maggots have been talking to each other then have they? Why would you believe them Bodolf? You know they have been working with Isbjorn all this time: they are just lying again. Honi, tell him he is being used by that thing in his head."

"I don't know Teague. Like you, I have had one of those things in my head and I was so angry with Bodolf when he would not have his removed. However, for what reason would they want to revive Banain, the only threat against Isbjorn? If you are able to revive him now without harming him, then you should."

"You need wake Banan Teague. He not gonna like sleep through main battle. He gonna be mad!"

Looking around the gathered group, all Teague could see were nods of agreement from everyone as Lepe finished. Sighing in resignation, she sank to her knees once again and re-entered her healing state. As before, Banain's aura was a brilliant white; but this time looking more closely at his brain, she could see a strange area where the white seemed to be swirling around something, as if trapping it in place. Whatever it was, Teague could tell it was very powerful and malevolent.

"Honi, could you help me like you did with Yrik please?"

She soon felt Honi's presence and with the wolf concentrating on an image of Banain in full health, she gently probed the strange area she had identified with her mind. The jolt of pure malice she received on contact, nearly threw her from Banain's mind completely. She would have tried again, if not for the howl of pain and terror from Honi, who had collapsed to the floor beside her. Much to everyone's relief, Honi recovered almost instantly and stood up, shaking her fur as if touched by something foul. Bodolf was licking her in an attempt to take the hurt away, although he could not see where it was.

"Thank you Bodolf, I am ok now. I am sorry Teague, but whatever that is, it is too strong for me." As she sent, she backed away from Bodolf's rasping tongue as gently as possible.

"Now what Sklak?" Teague asked, almost spitting out the Northlings name.

"Banain is being protected by his brain, which has recognised that there is great danger residing within him. There is a tendril of malevolence left by Isbjorn, which draws its power from Banain. Unless you can get to Banain and get him to fight this thing, it will keep feeding on his energy, until he dies."

"You didn't say he was in danger before! Now he is going to die?... Make up your mind."

"Until you made contact with the tendril, its existence was shielded from me."

"So... What now?"

Chapter Fifty-Three

"BANAINNNN, BANAINNNN"

He recognised the name; it was his own… And the voices, he knew the voices. There was Teague, Honi and two others, familiar, but not heard for a long time. The voices triggered memories in his comatose mind. He was staring into the sky, all around him strange sounds; the rhythmic swishing sound of a mowing scythe, the gentle singing of a woman's voice.

Are you ok my little man, sitting under the tree.

Are you ok my little man, just wait there for me."

She had sung to him. Then … a scream of pain that had invaded his tiny mind. It had come from a man this time, a man he also knew.

The woman had been trying to reach him, but something lifted him high in the sky over the heads of wolves, her screams of anguish loud in his mind. He recalled looking up and seeing a strange creature carrying him and knew he should trust it.

Then he could just hear those voices shouting, as though from a long distance away:

"BANAINNNN… BANAINNNN…"

"MOTHER?… FATHER?…"

Now he recognised the voices, older, but unmistakeable.

"BANAIN, LISTEN TO TEAGUE, YOU ARE IN GREAT DANGER."

The voice of his mother said. His mother was here…All was well…He could sleep now.

"BANAIN, LISTEN TO YOUR MOTHER!…"

He knew that tone, the tone of command. His father had only used it a few times with him. Once, he remembered, he had managed grab hold of a small flying creature and was about to eat it when his father had used that tone on him.

"Yes father… Teague?"

Banain though, trying to crawl through the blackness that surrounded him. It was like treacle, sticking to his mind and stopping him from thinking. Teague… He knew the name and the voice. He could hear another voice, very distant, but it was her voice. He loved that voice he realised; he loved the person behind the voice. He could picture her despite the treacle blackness that surrounded him. She was so beautiful, so clever. He had to find her.

"TEAGUE I LOVE YOU… WHERE ARE YOU?"

He shouted into the blackness.

"I am here Banain, you need to focus your mind and attack the tendril left by Isbjorn. Sklak and Kirr are here to help you. With them you can destroy it and free yourself."

He could hear her voice more clearly now, although she was not shouting.

"I love you Teague, I have been a fool. I always loved you but I did not know how to tell you... Do you love me?"

He thought he could see a faint glow at the edge of the treacle darkness.

"Banain, you need to focus on coming back to us, and then we can talk of such things."

The rejection in those words drove the will to leave the safe comfortable treacle blackness from him.

"What the matter with you Teague? Of course you love Banan, everybody know that. You mope about all time not near him and you all angry when you are. Why you not tell him?"

Banain recognised this voice straight away; it was his best friend Lepe. The voice of his friend brought him back towards the glow again, just near enough to be able to hear what her response would be.

"These are matters of the heart Lepe and not to be taken lightly. Banain needs to be focused on fighting Isbjorn, not on... other matters."

Banain recognised the voice of Bodolf. He moved a little closer, the glow turning into several sparks. But it was as if he was looking at them through a thick dark fog.

"Pah, you not best one to talk, stinky wolf. You like exited puppy with Honi just now. Now it take nasty black bear to get Banan to say he love Teague. You love Banan Teague?"

For a moment, Banain could hear nothing, the silence almost a roar in his mind. He looked towards the specs of light through the fog, trying to identify which was which. Then he slowly started to retreat, until all he could see was a faint glow. Her voice, when it came, was accompanied by a flare of light.

"Of course I love him Lepe. From the first time I saw him, as I was lying on that floor wounded, he stole a little piece of my heart. Over the years, he has chipped away at the rest. There is not a part of me that does not love every part of him.

However, I did not think he loved me. I hoped he did. I prayed he did. He was always so aloof and dismissive... I never believed we would be together...

She stopped for a moment and then shouted:

YES I LOVE YOU BANAIN YOU IDIOT..."

With every fibre of her being.

It was as if her words had unlocked a light trapped within her, which now burst into the darkness seeking its true home. It shot through the fog and treacle, illuminating the darkness for the briefest moment. In that moment, Banain saw the nature of his love... and his captor.

The tendril that Isbjorn had imparted in that brief, but violent joining of minds had only one purpose, to feed on Banain. It was akin to a long worm with many mouths, which was feeding on the energy produced by Banain's mind. As it consumed energy, it spewed out a numbing fog that was acting like a tranquiliser on Banain, robbing him of the power to fight. It was also robbing him of his ability to communicate properly, which was why he could only see and hear his friends as if through a thick fog.

The brief flash of light identified the horrible reality of the creature inside his mind and galvanised him into action. Fighting through the nauseating numbing fog, he tried to imagine the creature gone. For a moment, it worked and as the fog in front of him cleared, part of its body dissolved... However, he realised that he could not see it all, and as quickly as he removed what he could see; it re-appeared elsewhere.

"Clear a path to the light Banain, help is there."

Banain recognised the voices of Krask, Krys, and Grindor.

"I can't fight it… It is too strong and I am too tired…"

"You can, you always could. Concentrate your mind. Use your gift Banain…"

With those words of encouragement, Banain focused his mind on clearing a path through the fog and the writhing body of the worm. Ignoring the many mouths that tried to bite and tear at him. Slowly he could see the light becoming brighter, until he could make out the individual sparks of his friends. With a final push, he broke through the last of the fog, into what felt like a small clearing inside his mind. In front of him seven sparks of life hovered, gently undulating from side to side.

"Well done Banain, but the battle is not over. You must remove the tendril from your mind completely. We will help you if you will permit us?" The joint voices of Kirr and Sklak said. Out of the influence of the worms mind numbing fog, Banain felt his power and realised it was slowly ebbing away. He also realised that the Northling ancients were correct and that he had to find a way to destroy it.

"How can you help?"

"Open your mind to us. Join with us. Be one with us," they both intoned.

As Banain opened his mind to the Northlings, they floated closer, until the three of them merged into a single bright orb of light. Banain felt their power flooding through him and in that moment, he knew them completely. It was unlike any joining of minds he had experienced before. It went so much further, so much deeper.

"Now we are one he realised; now they are part of me. Now their power is my power, there sorrows my sorrow. And there was much sorrow. But that was not for now, that was for later, after this, after they dispelled all Isbjorn's darkness. Turning away from the five sparks of light floating in front of them, the melded trio moved back into the fog and darkness. As they moved deeper into the fog, a thousand hands and tentacles flashed out grabbing hold of the worm, ripping it piece by piece from Banain's mind.

Chapter Fifty-Four

Banain's eyes literally popped open as he regained consciousness. He was lying on the ice, with his head resting on Garfled's folded coat. Lying in a circled around him, were Teague, Honi, his Mother and Father, Bodolf and Lepe. Mariana was fussing over the rescued prisoners.

"Welcome back Banain. Do not worry about them; they are recovering from their journey into your mind. On advice from Sklak and with agreement from the rest of the expedition force, Teague managed to take them in to fight whatever was attacking you. It seems they were successful. Teague assured me they would awaken soon, before she fell to sleep as well."

Banain stood up, went to each of his friends and relatives and hugged or kissed them, whichever was most appropriate. He saved Teague for last and sitting down again, cradled her head on his lap. He wanted to sit like this with her forever, to tell her he loved her as her eyes opened. He wanted to speak to his parents lying next to him. He wanted to tell Lepe and Bodolf how much they meant to him. He needed more time!

"We are sorry Banain, but it will be a while before they recover from their efforts and you must go now," Kirr said in his head.

Banain sighed inwardly, gently laid Teague's head back down, and stood up.

"Torrent will you take me to fight Isbjorn please?"

By way of reply, Torrent moved up to Banain and lowered himself to his knees.

"We are always with you Banain, where do we go?"

Garfled asked, preparing to leap on Torrent.

"You cannot go Garfled; you are needed here and besides this will not be a battle that a sword can win. Should I not come back, I know that you will look after Teague and uphold the values of the protectorate." Banain said, clasping Garfled's arm in his own and looking deep into his friends eyes.

With that look, it seemed to the warrior that all of a sudden he understood what Banain had been saying when he had tried to explain his beliefs about the world. He had never really understood before; but now it was as if a door in his mind was at last open to him, and he stepped through. As he stood there mesmerised, Banain leapt onto Torrent who stood up, walked over to Garfled, shared air with his friend and fellow warrior, and then turned to follow Isbjorn.

Imbued with Banain's power, Torrent carried the blond warrior across the ice at great speed. They left a plume of snow swirling in their wake as they followed the trail left by Isbjorn and his army. Before long, they came across the first of Isbjorn's soldiers lying exhausted in the ice. The warrior, a man, hardly had the energy to look up as the pair thundered past. Without slowing, Banain sent a burst of energy to the drained warrior. Over the next hour they past hundreds more men, then bears, and finely wolves, all left exhausted from trying to keep up with their leader, and Banain helped them all.

Now they followed just a single track and they kept following it for hour after hour. They ran through the night, Isbjorn's trail illuminated in Banain's third eye vision. Then, just before dawn, they saw what looked like a whirlwind, smudging the brightening sky in front of them. As they came closer, they could see it was a maelstrom of snow and ice, thrown into the air by Nust. It was creating a massive hole in the ice. Isbjorn stood on the other side, looking down into the newly forming crater.

Banain jumped down from Torrent and placing his forehead to that of the large plains bull said:

"Thank you my friend, you must go now. I have implanted the way back to the others in your mind. Be careful of the soldiers on the way."

"I would stay if you need me, he is more my size then yours Banain."

Torrent said, glaring at the large black bear in the distance that was ignoring them, for the moment.

"That is true my friend, if this battle were to be fought by might alone, you would be my champion. But it will be a battle fought in the minds, and I am afraid all your strength, skill and honour, will not protect you from the evil that waits across whatever that hole in the ice is," Banain said, trying to discern what Nust was creating. As he watched, Isbjorn disappeared from view.

"Go back now please and care for the others Torrent, I can be responsible for no more deaths and I must face Isbjorn alone," Banain said, running towards where the black bear had disappeared.

"And who cares for you Banain?" Torrent said to himself, as he watched him go.

Chapter Fifty-Five

The hole created by Nust was perfectly round and covered an area of around twelve thousand square feet. A circular stairway carved out of the ice wound around and down to the ground some three hundred feet below. The ground was bereft of ice or snow, revealing a green kidney shaped structure. Looking down, Banain could see Isbjorn loping down the steps; he was over half way already. Without hesitation, he followed, taking two at a time. The two of them were evenly matched in speed, but Isbjorn had a head start. The strange thing was that Banain was not sure what he was going to do when he caught up with the bear. Even stranger, he was not sure it mattered. The closer he raced towards the strange structure, the more it drew him. It was as if this was the place he had been seeking all his life.

"Do you feel it child. Does it call to you?" Isbjorn said in his head. He ignored the voice and concentrated on the scene unfolding in front of him as he descended. From the top, the structure had looked flat, but now he could see that it was in fact a large dome, set on top of a small hillock. The green colour was grass, frozen in growth on its roof by the ice. As he descended, he could see that it had a stark white wall, with dark flecks covering half its circumference. There seemed to be some type of entrance towards the centre of the white portion of the building.

"You don't know child, do you? You do not know what this place is. You feel it but you do not understand it. I know... Do you know how I know? From you child and all like you. You do not know your own minds, but I do. I searched them all, thousands of them, gathering small bits of information here and there. However, you were like and encyclopaedia Banain, the font of all knowledge and you did not even know. Then when I finally touched Nust, it all became clear to me. You will die here Banain, and I will rule all. Not just the Earth Banain, everything you see, will be mine."

Banain ignored the jibes and continued to run down the ice steps. Isbjorn had reached the ground and was running towards one of four large standing rocks near the structure. This rock stood a little way from the other three, which was almost opposite the entrance. As he reached it, he stopped, pressing a large claw to its surface. Bodolf heard roars of frustration from the bear, as he went from stone to stone repeating the process. Then a crushing weight hit him like a sledgehammer, throwing him from the steps. Banain erected a tight shield around himself to protect him from the landing and from Nust, as the renegade weapon was circling to come back after its first attack.

Managing to land on his feet, he strengthened the shield and watched as Nust sped in. Even with the shield, Banain felt the terrible power behind the impact. Reaching out with his mind, he tried to take control of Nust as he had before. On contact, a very strange event occurred. Nust froze in mid-air, and then one half started to glow until it was an iridescent white, the other going cobalt black. As it changed colour, it also started to change shape, the arms curling towards each other until they joined. Then Nust split into two, each part curling into a spiral shape, one to the left, the other to the right. The left white part shot towards Banain, passing straight through his shield and hitting him in the centre of his forehead, the right black part, doing the same to Isbjorn. On contact, they both collapsed to the floor.

Chapter Fifty-Six

When Banain's eyes opened, he was standing facing the three stones set in front of the entrance to the building. He did not know how he got there. He tried to turn his head to look behind him, but he had been immobilised somehow. He could just see that to the right of him was Isbjorn, who also appeared to be unable to move. After a few moments, the two outer stones started to emit a low hum. Then the one directly in front of him started to glow, as if a bright white light was shining from within. On the other side, the stone opposite Isbjorn was also glowing, but with a strange dark light. Then a bolt of swirling white and black flecked light came out of the sky and connected to a fourth stone, set a little apart from the other three. As it hit two bolts, one white and one black emanated from runes set into the stone and connected with the two glowing stones.

Slowly the stones started to change shape, the one in front of Banain turning into the figure of a white deer; the other into a creature so strange, Banain could not comprehend how it functioned. It looked like a large undulating blob of blubber, with thousands of tiny teeth filled mouths. There were no eyes or ears, nor arms or legs. In fact, the closest thing he could equate it to, was the worm he had killed in his brain.

Then Banain heard a soft feminine voice, dripping with disdain.

"The recruitment laws, which you are flaunting as usual monskilk, state that you must present yourself in a form that the native species of a planet can relate to."

"Oh, do they not have grundle bugs here? How remiss of me for not doing my homework. I don't think your trainee is going to light much darkness Shranska."

A deeper male voice replied, dripping with sarcasm.

"That will be for the Lord of Light and Dark to decide, not you or me. Our job is to instruct and inform, as you well know." I do not understand why we have two subjects here at the same time though. It is very unusual," the deer said.

"One or two makes no matter, except that I have to endure your presence. When dark claims its rightful place as the Lord and Master, things will change," the male said, his voice rising with pent up anger.

"If that happens, none of us will be around for very long to argue about it. However, we do not have time for an argument about the expansionist theory. It will be Solstice here soon and we have a job to do... Banain, you are the chosen trainee for the Spirit of Light. You will go to train on Splendor and then to assist with the fight against the army of darkness. Is this your final form?"

Banain did not know what to say, every word he was hearing made no sense. It was as if he was supposed to know why he was here and what to do.

"I am sorry, but I don't know what you are talking about or what The Army of Light is. I know none of these things. I am Banain, Leader of the Protectorate and of the Freedom Army." He sent, trying unsuccessfully to read the mind of the deer that stood gazing at him quizzically.

For some time nothing happened, Banain thought he felt a presence slipping through his mind, but if it was, it was so subtle that he did not have the skills to detect it. Then another pure white light shot down to the fourth stone and deflected into the centre one. This stone immediately transformed into the figure of a large reptilian creature, which was similar in appearance to a snake, but with stubby arms just below its head. In one of its hands, it carried something that looked similar to Nust.

"Banain, my name is Solissolar and I am an arbitrator for the forces of the Spirit of Light. Shranska has called me to decide your fate. It seems that you have found your way to this place without the proper training or instruction. In normal circumstances, the artefact that you know as Nust would only lead those ready for final training to a portal and give them the mark of Solice. However, it has done both with you. Shranska has reviewed your logs and it appears that the Immortals did not finish your training, which is why they called me... Solis law is a little vague regarding what to do in this situation. As your present form now carries the mark of the Solis, this is what Nust implanted on your forehead, it is impossible just to send you back to your people. The only options open to you are, rebirth, or training. The problem we have is that you can only journey to Splendor, the training planet, via the portal of Newgrangoris, which is where you are now. It can only happen once an earth year, at a time you call the winter solstice. That will be in thirty three minutes Banain, so in that time you must decide."

A thousand thoughts collided around each other in Banain's mind as Solissolar spoke, but before he had time to say anything, the arbitrator continued.

"I am sorry Banain but we do not have time to observe the normal niceties. I have monitored your thoughts and think it best if I explain the complicated nature of things as simply as possible and answer some of the questions that burn within you.

The world you live in is just a tiny part of a universe that is either expanding or shrinking, depending on the balance between light and dark. We believed that darkness once ruled all and that lights purpose is to combat its hold on the universe. Darkness feeds on negativity, such as suffering, enslavement and death; and light on positivity, such as happiness, freedom, and love. The power of light is contained within trillions of suns that provide life throughout the universe. The power of dark resides within black vortexes, which can consume entire solar systems. Suns have voracious appetites, they need the energy provided by the countless species that inhabit the worlds they have created, to continue to exist and grow. Only strong suns can hold black vortexes at bay and if we do not keep the existing suns strong and create new ones, the vortexes will return the universe to darkness.

Every single living species that has developed to a certain stage, your nearest word for this would be sentience, is host to a fragment of its nearest sun. You have had three hundred and twenty three hosts and this is your fifth human. You have also been many other species including twelve ants, three wolves and a tiger. Once a sentient being dies, its fragment returns to the nearest sun, imparts the energy it has collected and then returns to inhabit a new host. If during that life cycle the number of positive acts outweighs the negative ones, the suns power is replenished. If however, the negative acts outweigh the positive, the suns power is diminished.

When a fragment leaves its host, it takes those memories gained whilst it lived that life with it; but when it returns, although they are saved, it does not have access to them. Therefore, each life with a new host is unique and unrelated to the previous one. Whether a fragment acts in a good or bad way, is dependent on the type of species, environment, and the dominance of other beings. However, in rare instances, such as yours and Isbjorn's, the fragment will live a predominantly positive or negative existence. In Isbjorn's case, he only contributed to the light thirty times out of five hundred and seventy two. In your case, you never contributed to darkness once! They called me because your record is unique Banain. Although you have not reached the normal assessment period of five hundred lives and you should not have found you way to this place, here you are."

As the voice in Banain's head paused for a moment, he physically shook his head, as if to try to shake all this information into some type of meaningful order. The whole of life as he knew it was being ripped apart with every word that this being was uttering inside his head, and it hadn't finished.

"From the trillions of shards that possess life, only a few ever progress far enough to join the forces of The Spirits of Light, or the Forces of Darkness. These forces exist to encourage, cajole, influence, or otherwise effect the populations of planets towards either the light, or darkness. Ambassadors of light and dark should never be in conflict, but in reality it does occur and soldiers need to be able to defend themselves, should they need to. You and Isbjorn will be the first to originate from this planet in the last five thousand years. It used to provide hundreds of trainees for the forces of light every year; which is why we believe the Forces of Darkness manipulated the humans on the planet to self-destruct.

Therefore, Banain, you have two choices. Either you can accept your fate and agree to go to Splendor, where you will receive the training necessary to take up your place amongst the defenders of light, or you can be reborn here. But understand this, if you are reborn, you will not remember any of this, or your previous lives."

When Solissolar finally finished talking, Banain tried to take on-board all he had heard. There were only a few more moments before he had to decide between life as some type of light warrior, or re-birth! In either scenario, it seemed he would never see his friends or family again. He would also never see Teague again. The arbitrator confirmed each of his thoughts. It was impossible and so unfair. Tears of sadness welled in Banain's eyes as he realised the finality of his situation, then another very familiar voice spoke in his mind, but as if from a vast distance.

"All is not lost Banain, you are very special, more so then anyone could ever imagine. Follow the light and what once was, could be again. Follow the light." It was the voice of Krask. Banain wanted to call out to him, but something deep inside stopped him from doing so.

"What is happening? Your thoughts were closed to me for a second, which cannot be!" The Arbitrator said, alarm in its thus far serene voice.

"I do not know why that would be, but I have made my decision, I will go to Splendour," he sent. This time before the Arbitrator could read his thoughts."

"That is good Banain, given what just happened, along with all the other exceptional circumstances regarding your existence thus far; I do not believe the option of rebirth would still have been available. Now walk to the entrance, place your palm against the left hand side of the entrance stone on the middle left circling rune, and wait.

Whatever force had been holding Banain, released its grip on his body and he took a few seconds to regain his balance and calm his mind. Then he followed the instructions, which brought him to the side of Isbjorn.

"We will meet again, child of the light, and when we do I will take great pleasure in snuffing your sickly glow from the heavens."

Before Banain could reply, a shaft of light hit the stone and the runes on either side lit up. The one under his hand shone so brightly, that he could see every bone, muscle, and tendon, along with his lifeblood in its translucent state.

Looking across, he could see the same thing happening to Isbjorn, except that his paw just seemed to disappear in the blackness emanating from the rune. Then the bear took his hand from the stone and moved towards the entrance of the structure, which was now blacker then the darkest starless night. As Isbjorn entered the tunnel, he disappeared into the blackness accompanied by an anguished howl that left Banain feeling almost sorry for the creature... Almost.

Then a hole appeared in the cloud-filled sky and a beam of winter sun streamed through piercing the very centre of the blackness. For a moment, it seemed as if a battle raged between the two, but the sun's rays won, illuminating the passage.

"Now walk into the light and join its defenders Banain," Solissolar said.

Taking his hand from the stone, Banain followed Isbjorn's route and entered the tunnel. As he walked through its entrance, the rune etched into his head by Nust burst into light, and tendrils from it danced across the walls of the passageway. As they touched certain runes carved into the walls, they also illuminated, adding to the incandescent white light now filling the small space. As Banain continued deeper into the tunnel, the tendrils of light danced around his body, swirling like a small sparkling tornado. As the light swirled, his whole body started to glow so brightly, that it became indistinguishable from the maelstrom of light around it.

Then with an iridescent flare, a comet of light leapt from the entrance and into the night sky. For a few seconds if hovered there, dispelling all clouds for miles around. In those seconds, a fiery image of Banain could be seen, and as always, his eyes burned more intensely then all else. Then with a glowing trail of bright light following him into the early morning sky, he was gone.

A few miles away, every head turned upwards to watch the spectacle of Banain's passing overhead. Many hearts filled with both great joy and sadness. None more so then Teague, who looked up with tear filled eyes at his passing.

Those who witnessed the event spoke of it in hushed voices, their stories repeated and embellished with the passing of time. There were those who said they heard a whisper of a song on that morning, sung by Krask, the great golden eagle.

In red tinged night and golden dawn,
Our love, our life, our spirit born.

Above the clouds… Above the clouds…

Thanks for reading NORTHLINGS.

I hope you enjoyed it.

Paul Svendsen

29999395R00170

Printed in Poland
by Amazon Fulfillment
Poland Sp. z o.o., Wrocław